THE MERCY:

ANGEL OF DEATH

Have mercy!
Sara Ennis

THE MERCY:
ANGEL OF DEATH

A Psychological Thriller

BY SARA ENNIS

Dedicated to:
Tony Burson, Alicia Rideout and Mariëtte Whitcomb

CHAPTER ONE

ANGEL

You have three new messages.
My mouse hovers over the Komorebi inbox and previews the new emails. *Kait, Jimmy, Dr. Lisa.* They can wait.

Right now, I'm curious about the new kid.

Ugh. I'm trying to do a better job articulating my thoughts, and that was a big hairy fail.

Curious is a deceptively morbid word. There's the seemingly harmless standard definition: *interested in knowing something.* That's legit for the youthful crowd when they wonder about stars or butterflies or the inner workings of NASA. For everyone else, you could change it to "interested in knowing something that's none of your business," and it would be accurate most of the time. There's also the old-timey definition: *strange, unusual.* String the two together, and you get "interested in knowing (about) something strange or unusual (that's none of your business)."

See? Morbid. In my experience, nearly all 'curiosity' is the *noneya* (business) kind, as my friend CB says. I'm well aware the color of my glasses is closer to blood-red than rose. *Whatever.*

I know his basic story, of course. When a kid who's been missing for years is found alive and physically well, it's big news. Chuck Carson, aged ten, was taken while riding his bike. He was kept inside a small house in a residential neighborhood in Madison, Wisconsin, for six years. Not once was he allowed to go outside. The man, who instructed Chuck to call him B-Doh, told the kid if he tried to leave, he would go to Chuck's house and kill his sister Dawn. Chuck believed him.

The days became weeks, became months, became years.

B-Doh loved to bring Chuck books. He delighted in Chuck's thirst for knowledge. He seemed proud of him. Novels, textbooks, comics, anything he discovered at garage sales and used book stores came home. It was all good by Chuck. Reading kept him sane.

One day, B-Doh didn't come home after work. Chuck didn't know why he didn't come, but he was afraid to open the door and risk his little sister's life. He did not know B-Doh—known to his coworkers as Brad Stevens—had suffered a widow-maker heart attack at work. His coworkers thought Brad lived alone, with no room-mates, not even any pets. Chuck might have been in the house forever if the landlord hadn't come by to clean the place for a new tenant.

Investigators learned Brad Stevens younger brother Paul was abducted twenty years earlier while Brad and Paul were riding their bikes. Brad didn't do anything to stop the man from taking Paul, and Paul was found dead a few weeks later. Brad suffered extreme guilt and saw Chuck as his opportunity to make things right. Paul called his big brother B-Doh.

That's the publicly available information.

According to the biography submitted by the survivor himself, the boy that was Chuck Carson became emancipated and changed his name to Charlie Car. He lives on his own in Indianapolis. He's in the Forensic and Investigative Sciences Program at the University of Indiana. He wants to become a forensics scientist—Dexter without a dark passenger. His words, not mine. I'm pretty sure I'm going to like him.

Charlie's profile and bio are in the Welcome section. The photo he provided for his biography did not appear every night on the news for months and months after he was found. In the media photo, his brown hair was long and stringy, like a 1980s rock star wannabe. Acne spotted his pale skin, and his eyes were hollow and haunted. A Madison Police Department t-shirt hung from bony shoulders.

In the bio photo, he's a totally different person. It's been two years since he was found. Charlie is eighteen or close to it. His sandy blond hair is shot through with streaks of white, shaggy in an intentional way. He paid money for that style. His lake-blue eyes are open, clear, and without shadow. He has sharp cheekbones and a strong jaw. His t-shirt no longer hangs on him; muscles push at the short sleeves, a promise and a warning. Chuck Carson is no more. Chuck Carson is gone. Long live Charlie Car.

He's very nice to look at, but it's not his looks that have my interest. How is Charlie functioning two years post-recovery? How deep are the scars, and how does he show them?

In about ten minutes, he'll join his first Komorebi video chat. Coming to Komo, as we call it, is one of the most important decisions he's ever made. There are very few places where we survivors can talk about the darkest things in our lives with people who genuinely understand. Of course, we've each experienced our own version of hell, but we share foundational elements.

When my guardian Peter Baden first told us the Foundation was creating Komorebi, I wasn't sure what to think. But that was ten years ago. I'm a believer now. Hell, I'm practically a cheerleader.

There are two sides of Komorebi: Promise, for the friends and family of abducted people, and Hope, for survivors. The Promise side is much larger. People are encouraged to stay, whatever the status of their loved ones. Still missing, found alive, or deceased, they will continue to have unique needs that can be hard to manage without support.

Komorebi is a private cloud-based platform, similar to something the earliest Internet users knew as AOL and CompuServe. Promise and Hope share the same technical features. There are forums where we can post questions, silly cat pictures, or share stories. There are scheduled chats on various topics. We can start a one-on-one or small group text or video chat. There are files with resources and information. It's a clubhouse for a club no one would ever want to be invited to join.

Because of Peter and the Foundation, the services of Komo and its team of experts are 100% free. The family of an abducted person might need financial support, mental health counseling, legal advice, or guidance on how to work with the media.

A survivor needs those things, plus a place to talk with others who 'get it,' not from an anecdotal perspective, but from lived experience. That's us.

There are currently thirty-four Hope members. The oldest is Kait, in her fifties. The youngest is a thirteen-year-old named Alicia.

All three Dollhouse survivors are here. Grace doesn't participate in public sessions much, although I think she and Alicia chat regularly.

Olivia shows up primarily for Peter, her dad. I see her name in group chats, but she never turns her camera on and never takes herself off mute. Many people don't share their cameras, but very few attend and never say anything. When I'm cranky, I wonder why she bothers coming since she doesn't participate. I try not to be cynical or paranoid. She can't talk about Komorebi outside of Komorebi—thanks, Tyler Durden!—so she's not using it as a flex for her career. Olivia has published two best-selling books and hosts her own talk show. She's become a cross between Brené Brown and Kelly Clarkson. She's won Daytime Emmy awards and met First Ladies. Olivia Baden does not need to look for things to bring her to the world's attention.

I've fallen into being a guide to some of the new folks, and surprisingly, I enjoy it. My brother would laugh at the idea of his shy twin sister willingly connecting with strangers, but it's true. I make sure they know they have someone they can come to with questions or gripes, or fears. Every once in a while, when someone's story is too close to my own, I bump into issues with the events of my past and retreat into a hole, but that hasn't happened much lately. Most of the time, I like to believe I'm doing good—or at least I don't do harm.

That's why I'm here today. I was supposed to run over to New Mexico to look at a couple of dogs, but I changed my schedule when Marnie told me about Charlie and asked if I'd be his guide. Sadly, there are always reservation puppies.

I'm interested—there, that's a better word than *curious*—to see how Charlie is doing. Sometimes what people say and what's reality are two very different things. I hope he's as healthy in real life as on paper.

CHAPTER TWO

ANGEL

There are three ways to communicate in Komo: internal emails, message boards, and text or video chats. Today we're doing a chat.

Charlie and I are the only ones who have both our cameras and our microphones on. Jimmy, Kait, Hannah, and a few others have their mics on but have left their cameras off. Everyone else has turned off both their cameras and videos. They're quiet except for encouraging notes of welcome that appear in the chatbox.

We simply share our name and age when we introduce ourselves in Komo. Anything else is provided by participants in their bios or at their discretion in conversations, which happen all the time. If you need to chat at 3 am, you'll likely find someone hanging out in the 'community center' which is the Komo name for the Hope forum.

This first meeting is just to let Charlie meet the rest of us and become familiar with the system. He may have read through some of our bios, and he's likely heard about many of us on the news. Like him, we have each had our own 15 minutes of infamy at some point in the past.

Kait Conradt is in the role of den mother, as usual. Her camera is off, her avatar a still photo of a woman in silhouette. No one in Komo has seen her, as far as I know. She never leaves her home in Connecticut. Her perpetrator got great pleasure from causing physical and emotional pain. She has more than 430 burn marks. He burned the word "BITCH" with cigarettes into her skin. Every year on the anniversary of the day he took her, he would amputate one of her fingers with heavy-duty shop scissors. She was with him for nine years. She jokes she's always ready for tea with the Queen because her one remaining finger, the left pinky, is always pointing. The Komo team got her full-hand prosthetics which gives her freedom. She can type and cook and do all of the everyday things we have to do. She's amazingly resilient.

The meet and greet is going fine, and then things take a turn.

Kait asks Charlie what his plans are after college. Simple enough question, right?

"I'm studying forensics. I haven't decided exactly which path I'll take when I graduate, but it will give me some semblance of control in a chaotic world." Charlie says, smiling in a way that puts a dimple on his left cheek.

Tiffany types rapid-fire into the chatbox, words appearing in bursts. She's been non-verbal since her rescue, but she could break speed records with those fingers of hers. Unfortunately, she has not handled freedom as well. She doesn't trust anyone, and I can't say I blame her. Who's trustworthy after you're abducted and tortured by a respected man of God? That is why the words on the computer screen don't surprise me. "It's great to have a plan. But you need to accept that life can never be the same. It will NOT be the same."

I try to control my facial expression since I'm on video. She must be in one of her funks. I say, "Life may not be what you dreamed of when you were a little kid, but it can still be satisfying."

Jimmy, Mr. Know-It-All, snorts audibly. His photo shows a man in his mid-20s with thick, curly dark hair puffing out around his head, a goatee, and wire-framed glasses. His smile is forced and somehow angry. Sometimes, I imagine the still photo coming to life like one of those animated cartoon villains when he's got an especially cranky attitude. "Don't sugarcoat it. Tiff's right. The best we can hope for is 'manageable.' That we can *manage* to paddle along to survive. The concept of 'thriving' is bullshit. We need to accept what's normal for others isn't normal for us, and try to embrace and honor our uniqueness through the way we live our lives."

I try not to sound condescending while throwing silent apologies to Emily and Olivia for using them as examples. "I'd argue some of us are living extraordinary lives. Emily is building an impressive music career. And Olivia, well, she's clearly taken lemons and made them into lemonade with a side of lemon meringue pie."

Jimmy snorts. "They can answer for themselves, but I put this question to you, Angel: Is your life everything you dreamed of before?"

I think about it, then shrug. "I was fourteen and definitely not an achiever by any means. I wasn't plotting a big career or preparing to go to college. I had vague ideas of what I wanted to do or be–a circus performer was one of those things, so my ideas may not have been the most realistic. The point is, my life plan wasn't derailed by what happened in the Dollhouse. I changed as a human, of course. This may be controversial, but I'd dare say I grew in positive ways from the experience. I had to learn to be brave, to focus."

We promise to be totally honest here. That includes admitting something others might find shocking or secretly agree with. So I add, "I didn't choose what happened to me, and I wouldn't wish it on anyone else. But it happened, and I went through it, and in the process, I learned a lot about myself. What I'm capable of. What my talents are. What really matters to me. As to the rest, I have a circle of people I love, who love me. I'm not missing out on anything."

Charlie is silent during this back and forth, his face neutral.

Jimmy 'feels' angry. I'm not sure why I think that. His intensity does not match the situation. His tone proves me correct when he asks, "Are a husband and kids part of the family you're building?"

Maybe Jimmy and Olivia have been talking. Her name is on the participant list, but as usual, she's not contributing. If she was present, I don't think she could keep herself from jumping in. She's always going on about how I need a relationship, a husband, kids. Basically, I need to be like her. I laugh and hope it comes off as legit as I try to change the subject. "Charlie, you're getting a firsthand look at our honest conversations. We argue and fight and disagree, but we're always here for each other. We're happy you're here with us."

Jimmy mutters, "You're a deluded child." His window closes. The screen announces he's left the discussion.

I'm embarrassed, and that makes me angry. I've known Jimmy has had a little crush on me for a while. He's tried to hang out one-on-one a couple of times, but I politely disengage when he swerves toward romantic. I'm not interested. My heart is off the market. I'm not going to tell him or anyone else that. It is none of his business, but it's also complicated.

"I'm sorry! I didn't mean to cause trouble!" Tiffany keys into the chatbox.

Kait jumps to reassure her. I'm glad. Despite the smile plastered on my face, I'm annoyed. Jimmy can be kind of creepy. Although none of the administrators lurk in our conversations, everything in Komo is recorded if something happens and they need to see it.

Dr. Lisa is the psychologist Peter added to the team before Komorebi was built. He wanted her input on how best to structure the platform to benefit both sides of the house. She's smart, she's kind, she's honest, and she's tough when she needs to be. She's also the first psychologist I've ever been able to be my authentic self with.

If Dr. Lisa were to watch this session, Jimmy and I would both be scheduled for anger management sessions. She knows our tells.

CHAPTER THREE

ANGEL

We chat for a few minutes after Jimmy's exit. Kait gives Charlie a list of the scheduled group meetings he can join if he wants to. I say he's welcome to open a chat with anyone in the group anytime or send an internal message. "We're here for you as much or as little as you want us to be. By 'here for you' I mean we can offer support, or we can talk about the latest viral cat video."

After the group ends, Emily opens a private chat with me, as does Kait. I reply to Em first. Ten years ago, Emily Bright and I nearly died trying to save her best friend from a madman. We failed, but we're tight. She's one of my very best friends.

"Hey, you," she types. "What's with Jimmy? Jesus."

I send a smile emoji. "His inner caveman is acting up. Honestly, if we were Norms, and I met him in a bar, I'd ask someone to walk me to my car." 'Norms' is the Komo version of muggles, I guess. People who have not been through what we've been through.

"Be careful with him," Emily types. "He seems to have a hard-on for you."

"I will. How's my man, White?" White is seventy pounds of love in the form of a blue-nosed pit bull mix. He has the big build and muscles of a guard dog but is trained as a psychiatric service dog, ready to attack with kisses and cuddles at the slightest indication Em is feeling down. His size and appearance make him an excellent companion. A person with ill intent would see him and reconsider whatever bad ideas they started with. They don't need to know that he has his own closet for his sweaters, shirts, and hoodies, and he sleeps with a stuffed bear.

A photo slides into the chatbox. The canine himself, in a USC T-shirt. He's grinning at the camera. Such a good boi.

"So handsome!" I type. "Wait, isn't your landlord a UCLA guy?" I know he is because there's a building named after him on the UCLA campus. Em sent me the *LA Times* announcement.

Em lives in the guest house of one of the most prolific music producers in LA. They work together often, so it's a win-win. More than once, I've wondered if there's more to the story (*cough, wink*), but I'm not going to pry. She'll tell me if she wants to. The only thing I care about is that she's happy and safe.

"White supports all education institutions. Gotta go. Singing backup on a new album, and the music just arrived. Watch out for Jimmy." Em's box disappears.

I suppose I should talk to Kait. She's a sweet, kind woman, but she's a bit of a busy body. I take a long swig of tea. "What's up, Kaity-Kait?" I type.

Kait responds with a smile emoji but gets right to business. "I'm worried about Jimmy. His temper seems close to the surface lately."

"Have you mentioned it to Dr. Lisa?" Half-listening, I glance at my little family, piled on top of each other on the old couch in my guest room-slash-office. I've never actually had a guest. The dogs, Asa and Nope–Penelope if you're feeling fancy–are snuggled together, and Cat–yes, that's her name–has stretched herself Superman-style across their backs. My three loves.

"I'm hoping he'll pull out of it," Kait says, and it takes me a second to come back to what we're talking about. Oh, yeah, Jimmy. Dots flash on the screen as she types, pauses, and flashes again. Finally, words appear. "Jimmy needs a friend. Someone special."

I don't know what to say. Jimmy is the only person in Komo who makes me uncomfortable. He's hot-headed, he's arrogant, he's misogynistic, and he's a narcissist. I'm not going to share those feelings with Kait. They're friends, and she thinks the best of everyone.

Then she adds, "I think you could be that friend."

I nearly swear. While I'm considering more appropriate words, she floods the screen again. "I'm going to be blunt. He has a crush on you. Have you–would you–have you thought about that kind of life, a real relationship?"

Before she can get too deep into her pitch, I type, "Kait, I appreciate your intentions, but I like my life the way it is. I don't have any interest in dating, and if I did, I would never be with someone from Hope. It would be such a bad idea." A stupid, dangerous idea.

More flashing dots. I type fast to cut off whatever she's going to say. "Maybe we can encourage him to find a wonderful Norm. I'm sure Dr. Lisa has suggestions about how to go about dating in a way that would be healthy and safe."

Kait is silent. No flashing dots. Sometimes she takes the mother hen role too seriously. Jimmy isn't her kid. And even if he was, he's a grown-ass man. She doesn't need to involve herself in his love life.

"I understand. Charlie is going to do well. You have a good day, Angel." And poof, Kait's gone.

Whatever. My menagerie will start demanding dinner soon.

Still, I make a mental note to tell Dr. Lisa about this during our next chat.

CHAPTER FOUR

OLIVIA

Beautiful, sweet, smiling child. I look at you, and I see myself. I see Christopher. I see your namesake, your grandma Susie. She would have adored you. Worshipped you. Your grandfather thinks you hung the moon. Your Daddy... he can't get enough of your perfect little fingers and toes. He willingly changes your diaper. That's devotion.

The good news is, you have so many people who love you. The bad news is, you were born to the wrong mother. You deserve someone who looks at you like you're magic. I suppose I try—less now than when you were born. But I feel no connection to you. The only thing I feel is resentment. You were supposed to fix me. You were supposed to make me a better person. You were supposed to help me feel again.

I feel nothing. At least nothing good. Irritation? Check. Frustration? Oh yeah. Anger? All too often.

Dad and Christopher and the doctors think it's postpartum depression. I wish it were true because that would mean there is some kind of hope for me. But I felt this way before you were born. Before we even talked about conceiving you. You were supposed to be my cure, but the medicine didn't take.

"Can I have her, O?" LouLou, the nanny, interrupts my thoughts. She's leaning against the door frame. She doesn't look or act like other nannies I've met in LA. When I hired her, I invited her to call me Olivia. She immediately shortened it to O. I told her to wear whatever makes her comfortable. She lives in tights and tutus and tank tops. She's got pink and blue stripes in her curly blond hair. Her nose is pierced. She's my god damned hero.

Absolutely, you can have her. She's all yours. I smile and wave a hand toward the crib. "You two have fun!"

Today I'm working from my home office. We're done in the studio for a while. The next three months will be busy with travel—book signings, guest appearances on other people's shows, keynote speeches, and a million conversations with publishers, producers, agents, and staff. My work is the one thing that brings me joy. It's the place where I feel the most okay. *Alive. Real. Useful. Unsoiled.*

I'm on edge. Maybe it was the Komo session this morning. I don't know, but I don't like it. I don't like feelings I can't source. I just know something is wrong, and it's got me off balance.

Being in my office relaxes me. It's perfect. The large wall behind my desk is a mural of blown-up images from my talk show and book covers. The desk itself is an expensively simple single piece of glass formed into a swoop. The only things allowed on it are my computer and monitors, an old-school red telephone, and a leather Baden Foundation coaster to keep condensation from spoiling the sparkling glass. My desk chair is oversized and royal blue. It makes a stunning backdrop when I'm on Zoom calls.

Opposite my desk, there's a sofa the same color as the desk chair, a Knoll Platner table, and six original Jens Nielsen Laminex chairs. A floor-to-ceiling edge-to-edge bookcase holds books, sculptures, and memorabilia. My husband is the only person in the world who would identify the pieces that actually mean something to me: A tennis trophy. A dog's collar. One photo. The symbolism of the wall isn't lost on me; the real me is buried in a giant display of pretend.

To my right, an unbroken expanse of glass shows off all of Los Angeles, from Hollywood toward the far west. My city. My home.

I open my email and scan the list of unread messages, but the one I hope for is not there. I click the shortcut to open Komo. No messages there, either. I learned long ago not to expect much in the way of communication from Angel. For years, I've managed to live with her distance. Lately, it's rubbing my nerves raw. After spending months locked together in a basement, I think of her as a sister, but she constantly makes it clear she doesn't feel the same.

I click the New Message icon, type AN into the box, and watch it auto-fill Angel Evanston. "Hey! I need to talk with you. I know you're busy being a hermit and all, but please? Find five minutes and give me a call?"

I'm about to add something else, but Christopher bounds into the room, all male energy and smiles. I can't help smiling back. My husband is a beautiful human, inside and out. "Hey, gorgeous."

"Hey, yourself."

Whatever I was going to add to the note can wait. I hit 'send.'

CHAPTER FIVE

PETER

Hey, next time you're out here, let's sneak over to Canter's for a pastrami on rye. Just don't tell Marnie. I tack this to the end of a status email, click send, and the system makes a w*oosh*. My email flies from a suburb in Los Angeles toward Virginia. However, Nick Winston, FBI Special Agent in Charge, could be anywhere. He's not home very often. I imagine his townhouse still has unpacked boxes from when he moved in fifteen years ago.

Outside the window, the sky is blue, nary a cloud. The rocky, overgrown landscape of the western edge of our property drops off. It is replaced by a breathtaking view of the Pacific in all her wild glory. The sky is so clear I even catch a glimpse of Catalina Island. It's a perfect day.

For *me*, it's a perfect day. For the five families who have come to our attention in the last two weeks, it's as far from a perfect day as you can get.

It would be great if the need stopped or slowed, but it never does. I've been doing this work since 2005. Back then, I was simply trying to find my daughter Olivia. In the years since, it has become so much more. We counsel the loved ones of missing people. We provide resources. We do our best to help them navigate an experience no one should have to go through, but they shouldn't have to go it alone if they find themselves there.

Now it's not just me. Nick, Marnie Hartling, Dr. Lisa Clarke, and a whole team of experts are the best of the best at what they do.

This building is only a structure. The hearts and souls within are the "it" of the Baden Foundation and Komorebi.

There's a mural on the wall in the entry of the Foundation office which sums up our purpose:

Komorebi: Light through the trees | Komo: Advise, encourage, offer

When someone is abducted by a stranger, the Foundation can help in several ways. For example, we send a team immediately to provide information and comfort. If the victim is found quickly, we offer assistance with whatever they and their family might need while they recover that won't be provided by other resources–missed paychecks, paying medical bills, arranging security.

If the victim is gone longer, that's when Komo really comes into play. Komo is a locked-down, invitation-only website broken into two parts.

The *Promise* side of Komo is for friends and family of a missing person. We coach, we counsel, we comfort, we provide. Promise members are welcomed as part of the Komo family forever because the trauma of having a loved one abducted lasts a lifetime, even after their case concludes. Some need our help for a while and choose to move on. Others are here years after their loved one was returned... or found dead.

The yin to Promise's yang is *Hope*. Hope is where the survivors themselves go. No one understands what they've been through like another survivor, although each story is unique. They are there for each other in a way no one else can be. As with Promise, people come and go as they desire. We're always here.

Other than my children, it's the thing I'm proudest of.

I don't know how Nick will respond to my offer. He's passionate about his career with the FBI. He's proud of the cases he's worked and the people he's saved, and the loved ones he's comforted. He's not even forty yet. That's young to retire from any job, especially the one you dreamed of as a child. I don't want to push him to change if it's not what he wants in his heart.

I won't push him, but he will have to choose. The FBI doesn't necessarily look at our relationship as a positive thing. They see it as a conflict of interest. Of course, I disagree, but they are the government; I am not.

Nick and I have worked together for years, and I trust the man with my life. He earned that trust when he helped save my daughter, and our relationship has strengthened with each addition to the flock of people I have come to think of as my family. Where would we all be if it weren't for Nick? I don't want to think about it.

The Foundation needs a full-time leader to run the investigative arm. We need someone whose primary focus is building relationships with law enforcement, working with them, rather than running alongside from a distance. We have no interest in replacing law enforcement officers (we call them LEOs) or the FBI. Still, it will empower us to do more good. Nick is the dream candidate. He has experience investigating, managing teams, partnering with federal and local law enforcement. He's got a big picture view and an eye for detail. People like and trust him. They believe in him, not because they have no choice, but because his mannerisms say he will do everything to help.

But if Nick's not ready, if it's just not the right time for him, he'll help us find the second-best person for the job. I need to be careful about the conversation. I don't want to push him into something that is not the best choice.

Through the glass wall of my office, I see Marnie and Dr. Lisa enter the conference room, which is the center of our office cluster. The girls, big and small, refer to it as the Donut Hole. Today we have a full agenda. We'll discuss the new cases Nick reported and talk about the new families joining Komo. There's the new Hope member, Charlie. Some of our current Promise folks seem to be struggling. We never want to neglect the living because we're focused on ghosts.

Marnie gives me a look that makes me feel like a kid when I enter the room. Some people have resting bitch face. She has a constant happy face. Ask her what she's smiling about, and she'll say, "We're alive."

How the hell did I get so lucky twice?

I take a seat at the large round conference table, arranging my feet so as not to disturb Gustopher, Dr. Lisa's beagle and the Komo mascot, who is sprawled out on the cool stone tile. All the walls are glass, which lets us see through them to the outside and comes in handy for putting up sticky notes and writing in dry-erase marker. I pass copies of the information we need for the meeting.

"Before we get started, has anyone heard from Kait? She missed our one-on-one today, so I checked the logs, and she hasn't been online in a couple of days. It's highly unusual." Dr. Lisa Clarke frowns. She directs the entire health team and is the lead psychologist. Even though it's just the three of us working in the office most days, she always dresses as if she's going to a Fortune 500 company.

Probably a Fortune 500 apparel company because, according to the girls, she's 'fashion-forward.'

Marnie nods. "If I had to guess, I'd say she's never been off-line more than 24 hours since Komo began. Would it be inappropriate for one of us to call her? Old school, like, on the telephone?"

I look to Lisa. "Better safe than sorry, unless you disagree."

She makes a 'no objection' face, and I pull the conference phone toward me. I have a file that contains every member of Komo's contact information, whether they're in Promise or Hope or one of our staff or consultants. I tap Kait's number into the phone and pick up the handset. It rings, and rings, and rings. Six rings before it goes to voicemail. Kait's perky voice is always positive. "Hi! It's me. Sorry I missed your call. Maybe I dropped one of my bionic hands in the tub. Leave a message, and as soon as I find it, I'll call ya back!"

"Hey, Kait, it's Peter. Haven't seen you around in a couple of days and wanted to check-in. Give me a buzz or shoot me a note when you find your bionic hand, would you?"

Marnie nods. "I'm sure she's good. Maybe she has family visiting or something."

"That'd be nice. I think she gets lonely sometimes," Lisa agrees. "Who shall we start with?" And the work begins.

CHAPTER SIX

OLIVIA

"Why do you have to go today? Your first meeting isn't until next week." Christopher is confused and a little bit annoyed. He knows my schedule as well as I do because while he's my husband, he's also my attorney and business manager. He negotiates the contracts and the deals and approves the speaking engagements and book signings.

Christopher is not upset I'm leaving to work. He sees this as yet another time I'm choosing to be away from him and our daughter. Many wives would worry their husbands would sleep with the nanny in this kind of situation. I wish he and LouLou *would* get together. He's a great dad and a great husband. LouLou loves my baby, and she's the kind of exciting, carefree person he deserves to be with. Plus her groovy vibe is more aligned with his smart surfer dude self than I am.

I don't know why he thinks he loves me. Maybe he's mistaking 'protection' for 'love.' It wasn't always like this.

We met in one of the early conversations about me hosting a talk show, even though I was so young. Christopher was recommended by one of Dad's industry friends from back in the day–the 'day' before I was taken. My dad was one of the most famous names on television, delivering the evening news all across America until he gave up his career to find me.

Before Alfred turned my father into a full-time monster hunter.

When Christopher and I met, I clearly remember the look on his face when he connected me to the woman he'd seen on the news.

It wasn't the look I was used to. Of course, he knew who he was meeting with and what had happened, but instead of feeling sorry for me or showing that icky kind of invasive curiosity people feel entitled to, he looked at me as though I was real. A person. I felt as though he saw all of me, the whole me, the me I was before Alfred, and the me I am now. He saw not the trauma of Olivia or the story of Olivia, but the flesh-and-blood human that is Olivia.

That's why I said yes when he asked me to dinner. That's why I said yes when he asked me to go to San Francisco for the weekend with the promise of separate hotel rooms. That's why I said yes when he asked me to meet his parents even though we hadn't yet slept together. That's why I was the one who made the first move. He cried when he saw the scars. There was no pity, just love and respect. He honored the marks on my body. He touched them so gently and with such kindness, and then he stopped being gentle and kind and made me feel wonderful, freeing, mind-bending things I had never imagined I would feel.

Now, eight years into our marriage, sex is the only time he doesn't treat me as if I need to be protected. When we're making love, I am free. There's nobody watching, no cameras, no tabloids, no well-meaning friends and family. I can be as wild as I want, as bad as I want, and there's no shame or baggage, just my man and me. That's what I want from him, all I want from him.

I wish I could feel something for our daughter, but I don't. Not Susie and not Rosie. Christopher knows Rosie came out of my body. I won't say I'm her mother. To me, she is a gift for others. I knew she was going to be important to Angel and to Dad. I'm glad I was able to bring her into this world. But I was simply a surrogate. A carrier. An incubator. Not her mother.

Susie is a perfect doll—happy, funny, mild-mannered, sweet. Rosie is a fantastic kid, I'm sure. It's nothing about them. Something is broken in me. I don't enjoy the company of children, especially my own.

Christopher is right about the trip. I am going early because I want—no, need—to get away from my husband and my child. There is work, I'm not lying, but I'm going to take a couple of days for myself and do some processing and try to get out of this funk I've been in.

Christopher doesn't know, and I'll never tell him, there was almost another baby. A month ago, I was worried that I felt the way I did when pregnant with Susie. But before I was even sure, my body failed, confirming yet again I am unable to live up to expectations. I'm angry at myself. I'm frustrated by the failure of birth control. I'm hurt because I've proven that I am not who I claim to be once again.

Maybe I'll see a friend or two. I don't know. I just know I need to change, and I need some air, and this is the way I am going to get it.

CHAPTER SEVEN

Connecticut

Thanks for seeing me. I've wanted to meet you in person for such a long time. It means so much that you trust me enough to let me in. I know you protect yourself. I understand why. But I think you're magnificent.

I understand you don't want to talk about it. I rarely want to talk about what happened to me. I didn't go through what you did; but we share the afteraffects from the outside world. I understand how you feel. At first, you're hounded, everyone wants to know what you need, what it was like, what what what. . . and then they get bored with it, and move on, and don't understand why you can't move on as easily as they have. Why can't you just forget it and pretend everything's all right? It was terrible, but it's over; it's done. That's life, right? God never gives us more than we can handle.

But there are so many questions. Why me? Did I deserve it? What did I do to make him choose me, make him keep me? What about me said it was okay?

And then, later, when you try to have a normal life. How do you believe? How do you let yourself trust? How do you show your soft, vulnerable underside to someone who claims to care? How do you look in the mirror every day, see the physical reminders of what he did, and ignore it? How do you deal with the pain of trying to build a life when you can't escape the scars that have marked you both inside and out? How?

They can preach all they want, but we know it's impossible—a real life, a normal life, a happy life–after what we've been through. Trying to pretend otherwise just causes more pain, right? Always pain. So. Much. Pain. To make them feel better, you have to continue to suffer. I understand. I've been there. I am there.

What I've learned is . . . it never goes away. It controls everything you do, every thought you have, every word you utter. At some level. People think I'm strong. Because they don't see me yelling and pulling out my hair, because I put one foot in front of the other each day–as you do–they believe–because they want to believe–I'm fine and healthy and all better. I've built a hard coating around me, a shell, to pretend, so everyone can feel better for me and let go of the guilt and not feel bad when they've moved on.

But inside, at night, when I'm alone with my thoughts, when I'm just me for a little while. . . I hurt so bad, I want to scream. I want to hurt others the way I've been hurt. I want to share the pain because putting it on someone else might make it hurt less. Mostly, though, I just want it all to end. The pain, the wishing, the hating, the guilt, the voices.

You know what I'm talking about. I see it in your eyes.

Have you ever... do you think about it?

Me too. I believe, and you believe, once we leave this place, this earth, we are freed, our souls are cleansed, we move onto something pure where all that happened in the past is no longer.

Why should we fight to stay in this life because others expect us to? It's wrong of them to keep draining us by making unfair demands. We've already given so much to our abusers and those who claim to love us by helping them survive their guilt and move on from their pain.

You, of all people, have earned the right to make your own decisions. You have earned the right to choose between living a life that is really no life at all or going on to something beautiful and wonderful and free. Free of this endless, tormenting pain.

You have a plan? You're so much braver than me.

I'll help. Of course, I will! Let's have some warm and comforting tea while we talk a bit more. This blend is so relaxing, so soothing. Where are your cups? And your kettle? No kettle? No worries, the microwave will do.

Who loves you? Who will miss you? What would you say to them if you were going to be free?

The tea is lovely and calming, isn't it?

I'll help you write to them. You can tell them you love them, how much they mean to you. It's good to write it while you're thinking about it. Share what you're feeling, tell them you're sure you'll see them in the next life.

I'm envious. I'm counting the moments until I can be as brave as you and move on to the next part of the plan for us all. It will be my time soon. I have to help the others first, then I can go.

Those pills worked fast! You look sleepy. Here, stretch out on the bed, take a nice nap. Do you need help? You've got it. Okay.

I'll watch over you, so you're safe, so you can sleep. Oh, no, no need to worry. Don't fight it. Just close your eyes. Here, let's tuck the blanket around you and make sure you're warm. Are you still with me? Are you here, sweet one? Sleep tight. Forget the pain. There you go. . . there you go.

CHAPTER EIGHT

PRIVILEGED & CONFIDENTIAL

Komorebi File #107

Conradt, Kait

[Two photos: A stylish, put together woman in her late 30s/early 40s with highlighted shoulder length brown hair, warm brown eyes, and a great smile. She's slightly plump, very attractive. Second photo of a woman in her early 50s. Graying waist length hair, hooded brown eyes, very thin.]

Location: Greenwich, CT

DOB: 11/12/1962   **Abduction:** 10/23/2002

Recovery: 2/17/2011   **Current Age:** 59

Offender Status: Killed during recovery

Notes: Taken hostage during a bank robbery. Physically tortured by the abductor. Missing 9 fingers. Hundreds of burn marks on the body. Multiple broken bones. Recluse, but very social in online activities.

Tell me about the day you were taken. What do you remember about that time?

That was such a bad day. Really awful. Of course, it was. I'm stating the obvious there. I still break out in a cold sweat when I think about it.

But I try not to dwell.

It was a Friday in the fall, starting to get a little chilly. I was running late. George, my calico kitty, coughed up a hairball, and I stepped in it in my stockings. That's a disgusting feeling if it's never happened to you. I had to change my stockings, and that got me a little—well, anxious. Promptness has always been so very important to me. It's a sign of respect for others. Hairballs aside, it took me seventeen minutes to get to the bank, and I always got there a few minutes early. I liked to be the first one to welcome the staff, and set the mood for the day.

I got myself together, took a deep breath, and said my morning affirmations. I'm a big believer in those, even now. When your head's on straight, you can do anything.

At the time, my home had an attached garage. I hit the opener while I was still in the kitchen, and headed out the back door, the same way I did every morning. I remember being grateful it was sunny out since it was cold. And then...

[24 seconds of silence]

He came out of nowhere. I must have left the side door to the garage unlocked. I didn't see him until it was too late. I was just feet from him. He was a tall, slim man, dressed all in black, with one of those ski masks on. A balaclava is what they're called. I didn't know the name at the time. I started to scream, and he grabbed me, covered my mouth with his hand. That's when I saw the "plumbing" van that had pulled into my driveway.

It was blocking my car. I could see two men in the front seats, also wearing masks. My captor dragged me to the van and shoved me into the back. Of course, I fought, kicking and screaming, but… and I'm ashamed to admit this… I'd been raised not to make a scene. My conditioning to be ladylike fought my instincts to survive.

They took me to a forested area. There are hundreds of those in Connecticut, so I had no idea where we were. They dragged me out of the van, and the tall, thin one who had grabbed me began to carefully undress me. Understandably, I was panicking. Were they going to gang-rape me? My whole body began to shake. I was shaking so hard the thin man yelled at me that they were not going to rape me and to stop 'freaking out.' When I was standing there in my bra, slip, and stockings, another of the men brought over a black harness sort of thing. It fit over my shoulders and strapped around my chest. I still didn't understand what was happening. And then—and then they began to add sticks of dynamite. At least that's what it looked like—later, I learned it was fake. Of course, I didn't know that. I had to believe, or their plan would not work. Once the harness was on, the thin man put my skirt and blouse on, then my blazer. He took care to smooth my skirt, tuck in my blouse, straighten my blazer. I was loaded back into the van and driven to the bank. I was shaking so hard I was afraid the dynamite would somehow go off.

Normally I'm in the bank no later than 7:30.

When they parked out front, it was almost 9:00.
Everyone was worried, wondering where I was. I
would never just not show up. They used to tease
me that even if I were hit by a bus, I'd make the
bus driver call work before calling 911. The thin
man told me to go inside and collect all the money
from all the tellers. If I took more than 10 minutes, he would trigger the dynamite and blow me
and everyone in the bank to smithereens. Obviously,
they didn't blow anyone up, or I wouldn't be here.
But that's the last thing I remember about all of
that.

[32 seconds of silence]

I'm sorry. The next thing I do remember is being
at a cabin-like house in the woods. Again, as I
said, Connecticut is full of trees, so there's no
way to know exactly where I was. Only the thin man
was there. He was furious. Terrifying. I didn't
understand what was happening. The harness was no
longer on my body. I was wearing my skirt and my
bra. I wasn't the only one exposed, however. The
thin man had removed his mask. That was very bad.
I've watched enough television to know once you
see their faces, they have no intention of letting
you live! I didn't dare ask where the others were
or why he was so upset. As it happens, he told me.

His 'pals' double-crossed him. As soon as he got
me out of the van, they took off with the money.
This was his house, his home. I was sure I would
be killed any moment. In a way, I wish I had been.

**Would you like to talk about your time in cap-
tivity? It can benefit short-term and long-term**

recovery, but it is totally understandable if you choose not to talk about it today. I will follow your lead!

I'm not ashamed. I'll tell you. It will be useful to you to understand why I am the way I am.

Frank—that was his name, I learned eventually—kept me for nine years. Nine long, angry, horrible years. I learned Frank drove a forklift at work, and he hated his job and hated his boss. The bank robbery was supposed to be his path to freedom. He couldn't risk trying again. After they betrayed him, he didn't trust anyone. Especially me. Somehow I became a stand-in for those who had cheated him, and he would get "his" one way or another.

At first, I was his daily rape victim. Thank God that ended after the fifth year. I was also his housekeeper, his cook, and his punching bag. I was kept in a casket while Frank was at work and while he slept. As many as sixteen hours each day. Do you know the difference between a casket and a coffin? A casket has four sides. Coffins are fancier, with six sides and a taper that conforms to the shape of a human body—wider at the top than the feet. Coffins are lined. Caskets like mine are not. Please make a note in my file that I would like to be cremated.

If Frank had a bad day at work, I had a bad day at home. Frank loved whiskey and Marlboro Light 100s in a box. The cabin stunk like a dirty ashtray. Nothing I could do about it, but I don't think he cared. If his day at work was bad but not terrible, he'd have a drink or two, be mean, maybe throw a plate at my head or kick me in the gut. After I came home, one of my doctors told me I had more than two dozen fractures or breaks.

If he had a terrible day... if he had a terrible day, he'd strip me out of the boxer shorts and T-shirt that were my uniform. He'd force me to stand naked in front of him and turn slowly while he smoked a cigarette and studied me. The first few times, I was humiliated and didn't understand terror was a more appropriate emotion. It didn't take long to catch on, though. Once the cigarette was down to about an inch, he'd tell me to stop turning. The first couple of times, he'd stop me while I was facing away so I couldn't look at his face. Later, he enjoyed watching my expression as I anticipated what was coming.

He would take the cigarette and press it into my flesh. Firmly but not too hard. He didn't want to put the cigarette out. He wanted it to leave a mark. For a while, the spots he chose were random. Eventually, though, he decided it would be fun to tattoo me. He burned the word 'bitch' into my left side, starting at my waist and running up under my arm. Do you understand what that means? I had to stand still and raise my arm to give him access. I was forced to participate in my own destruction.

I'm sure you've heard about—the burns weren't the worst thing Frank did. Each year, Frank would sit me down on the anniversary of the bank robbery. He'd strap my forearm across the kitchen table on a thick wooden cutting block. He'd make a big show of bringing out his heavy-duty shop scissors.

[79 seconds of silence]

Each year... [whispered]

Frank would use those shop scissors to amputate one of my fingers each year. I was with him for nine years. Only my left pinky remains. The pain was—there are no words for that kind of pain. I never got used to it; in fact, it seemed worse each time. Perhaps that's because the anticipation of the event would begin earlier and earlier in my mind. I became obsessed with the anniversary date nearly immediately after that year's amputation had started to heal. For a few years, I tried to convince myself he would find some other way to torture me. Or I'd be rescued. But no. It was the same. Year after year after year. My dread would build in tandem with his excitement.

I don't want to talk about this anymore. I'm sure you have enough information.

What do you remember about being recovered?

The detective I first spoke to told me one of the other idiots in the robbery snitched! He was arrested for something else, something big, I guess. In exchange for a lesser sentence, he confessed to the bank robbery and told the legal folks where I was. Foolish Frank somehow let the other two know that I was still around. Idiot. He deserved what he got. I'm not proud of myself when I say I enjoyed watching him be mowed down by bullets. I enjoyed it, I cheered it, I wish it had taken longer for him to die. The coward got off lucky.

What's your day like now?

My days are very satisfying. I don't leave the house. I'm afraid I'd frighten children. But there's still a wonderful life to be had thanks to modern technology. I have these excellent prosthetic hands, thanks to you and the kindness of Komorebi. They allow me to do most things—keyboarding, cooking, holding a book, dressing. I'm not an invalid. I'd despise that. I'm not yet old, and I'm certainly not ready to be a hermit, so I volunteer as often as possible.

As you know, I try to help with the new people at Komo. My library book club is very active and engaged. There's a lost pets Facebook group I facilitate.

Thank you for sharing your memories and experiences; I can imagine it is difficult to talk about.

It makes sense that recovering after something so traumatic can be emotionally messy sometimes. Would you consider yourself happy since your recovery?

Happy. Well. That's a tricky word. I'm not unhappy. Can we go with that? Most days, I'm content. I'm a bit lonely, but I'm fortunate to have many friends, some of whom you know. There's kindness and affection there, and really, that's the point of life, right? To have people you care about who also care about you?

Notes were taken during her initial Komo session. LC

CHAPTER NINE

OLIVIA

This is my first time in New Jersey. It's not what I was expecting. The area I'm visiting is bucolic, with rolling hills and woods, historic sites, and beautiful old homes. I'm struggling to envision Jimmy Zamora as part of this environment. It's much easier to imagine him in rough-and-tumble Jersey from 1980s movies and more recent reality TV.

I'm trying to remember what I know about him, beyond his 'incident.' He was abducted by a man whose wife desperately wanted, but couldn't have, children. Jimmy was young, six or seven, when he was taken. If I remember correctly, he was with the couple for two years. Not as long as some. But not a short while by any means. I have no idea how he came to be rescued. Maybe I'll ask. Probably I won't.

The helpful Google voice tells me to make a right in a mile. *As you wish, happy British lady.*

Jimmy and I are the same age. Kidnapped kids weren't something I was aware of when he was abducted. My thoughts were probably on my role in the 2nd-grade school play. But we talk about our experiences in group, sometimes. Well, the others do; I eavesdrop.

Bits of his story are coming back now. Before Jimmy was taken, his parents were on the verge of divorce. His abduction pushed everyone over the edge. The break-up was messy, angry, and loud, with accusations on both sides implying the other parent was responsible for their son's disappearance, either directly or through neglectfulness. Their divorce added kindling to the media fire. After Jimmy was recovered, his presence fueled the fire rather than calming it. Nine-year-old Jimmy was tossed back and forth between his parents and their new families. By the time he was in middle school, he was self-medicating with alcohol and when he should have been starting high school, he was using drugs daily. He dropped out and became a full-fledged heroin addict. In group, he shared the information that he spent multiple nights in New Jersey and New York City jail cells after being busted for theft, dealing, and in one case, breaking and entering. Young Jimmy was not okay. It's a miracle he survived as long as he did.

I don't know how he came to the Foundation and Komorebi. Dad and the team don't talk about us, which I appreciate. What I do know is Jimmy was one of the first Hope participants. He went through recovery, perhaps with Foundation support, and has been sober for the time I've known him. I may be wrong, but I want to say he cooks for a nursing home or some other institutional facility.

Posh Google lady announces my destination is on the right. I pull up in front of a cute little Cape Cod-style house with bright blue siding and white trim. There's an older green Prius in the driveway. The property is well cared for. When I cyber-stalked him, I didn't notice whether it was his or a rental. Dad and team make sure none of us Komo people are easily discoverable, but my job gives me access to additional skills and resources.

I don't get out of the car immediately. I didn't tell him I was coming. I didn't ask if he wanted to meet. Should I call now? Or just walk up to the door and knock?

The decision is taken out of my hands. The front door swings open, and a man I assume is Jimmy stands there, looking at me. I see him take a deep breath, then make a "Come on" gesture. Without waiting for my response, he turns his back and goes inside.

This could be a big mistake. Jimmy has one hell of a temper. But

I'm the idiot who drove herself here and didn't even bother to hide the car. I guess I'm going to have to have faith.

I'm not great at that.

CHAPTER TEN

OLIVIA

"Are you surprised to see me?" I step into the foyer.

"Yes." Jimmy motions toward the sofa. When you've only ever seen someone's photo, it's strange to finally meet them in person. Jimmy is taller than I would have guessed–maybe 6'1". He's dressed in baggy Army green pants and an old Princeton sweatshirt with tears at the edges of the sleeves. He's wearing a Mets cap over his dark hair, and there are crumbs in his goatee, which has a reddish tint. He's wearing glasses like those in his photo. I'm sure he's changed the frames out in the last eight years, but he seems to have a style when it comes to eyeglasses.

I'm very aware I'm inappropriately dressed. I'm wearing jeans, but they're wide-legged and cost more than his monthly rent or mortgage payment. My oversized graphic sweatshirt is vintage and highly collectible. Even my sneakers are ridiculous. If I decide to sneak up on someone else in the future, I will put a little more thought into my outfit.

The inside of the house is nowhere near as charming as the outside. There are piles of books, magazines, comics, and videos on every flat surface. A large screen TV takes up most of one wall, with a home store sofa opposite it. The couch is relatively clean. The coffee table is piled with video controllers, empty soda cans and bottles, discarded fast-food wrappers, and cigarette packs. I don't notice that old cigarette smell. He must smoke outside. Two desk lamps provide dim light for the whole room. The drapes are drawn except at the front window, which is how he must have spotted me.

I take a seat, trying not to jump when an empty potato chip bag crunches under me. On the floor beneath the coffee table, there's a single pink sock with lipstick kisses. Interesting. I smile at him. "Sorry to just barge in. I'm on the East Coast for business, and I had an extra day, so I decided to drive around. Then I thought about who I know who lives out this way..."

Jimmy sits at the other end of the couch, twenty-four inches of tan microfiber between us. The monitor is on, a game is paused. A war game. I don't know which one. Not my thing. He reaches for the remote and blacks the monitor when he notices me looking. Before it goes off, I see a small K in the bottom right-hand corner. The Komorebi icon. Maybe he was chatting with someone from group.

"I'm sure you know lots of people out here if 'here' means Manhattan. But Morristown, New Jersey, isn't exactly down the road from the City, which is where your business is." He's deadpan as he shines a light on my bullshit. He doesn't seem upset or angry, but he also doesn't seem happy to see me. In a way, I'm surprised. Jimmy is the type who would be flattered by a celebrity seeking them out. I am a much-loved celebrity to millions of people in the US and Canada.

"You're right." I agree and decide to be somewhat truthful. "The day Charlie joined group, you said some things, and I hoped we could talk about them."

His dark eyes narrow defensively behind the lenses of his glasses. "Yeah?"

"I agree with you."

His eyes widen, and his bushy eyebrows rise in surprise. "You agree? Isn't your brand 'be positive, we shall overcome, it's all part of the journey'?"

Pretty much. "That doesn't mean I can't have personal thoughts and feelings or change my mind."

"Hypocritical much?"

It is. But my 'brand' has become a train I can't slow, much less redirect. "Aren't we all different people—our outer selves and our inner selves?" I sit at an angle to look at him more directly. He continues to sit facing forward.

"How can I help you? What exactly is it you want?" He's rubbing his hands on the legs of his pants like he's drying them. He's nervous. I wonder if he ever has people over. I wonder if he's ever had a woman here. Then I remember the pink sock. So the question is, did the sock come with a woman, or did he steal it? I don't know that I want to know.

I decide to get to the point. "Do you really think there's no hope for us? That the most we can have is 'manageable'?"

"Don't you feel like a creeper, sitting in on the sessions and listening to everyone's thoughts but never sharing your own? Do you do it for your show?" His reaction is swift and brutal. I've always sensed the anger in Jimmy, but in person, it's a tangible thing. He radiates it.

The suggestion gets my hackles up, but I suck in a breath to calm myself. "I never, ever use anything about Komo on the show. Ever. I would not. This conversation is about me, for me. Not for the world."

He nods once but says nothing more.

Usually, I'm great at waiting people out, letting the silence pressure them to talk. But, I feel out of my element here. With each moment, I feel less Olivia Baden, professional interviewer, and more Olivia Baden, girl kept in a basement. That must be why I blurt, "You asked Angel if she ever thought about a family. Husband, kids. I have those things. They don't solve everything." They don't solve anything.

Jimmy half-laughs, that weird sound we make when something

catches us off guard. Acid rises in my throat.

"I'm not saying I don't love my husband," I say, and add hurriedly, "and my daughter." I wipe at a non-existent spot on the knee of my jeans. The wrongness of my clothes is making me very uncomfortable. "I'm just saying there's no magic cure. The way you put it, saying we manage at best, is accurate. We don't really get to choose. Everything feels like settling, like being grateful for what we're offered, whatever survives the toxic past we carry like an aura."

Finally, Jimmy is relaxing. He's nodding at my words. "That's exactly right. And people are surprised when we don't jump up and down in gratitude. Or, just as fun," his tone is bitter on the word, "they're shocked we cope at all. Like they're secretly disappointed we're okay."

Something has loosened in me, and it feels so good to share this with someone who gets it. My voice notches up an octave as I mock, "'I could never be as strong as you!' If I hear it one more time, I may snap. It takes everything in me not to say, 'You're right, you never could!' but of course, I don't."

For the first time, Jimmy smiles. I've never seen him grin before because all we see in Komo is his old photo. His smile reaches his eyes and makes them brighter. "There are so few people who could survive what I went through, what you went through and come out intact. We're superheroes. They have no idea." He pauses. "Well, not all of us. Some of our peers don't seem ready to join the superhero league."

This time I manage to control myself. I wait for him to elaborate.

"I worry about Kait. And Tiffany, good God, the woman can't even speak! Karmen. She tries to be tough, but she seems ready to crack into a million pieces if someone blows on her." He waits a beat, then says, "And Angel."

My back straightens protectively. "What about her?"

"She acts so tough, so independent, so 'fine', but I don't buy it. If it were up to her, she'd live in an off-grid cabin in the woods and never interact with another human."

Exactly! "She practically does now. People act like it's normal for her to live in the middle of nowhere by herself. It's not the woods, but a town in the desert is just as bad. It's where you go to climb rocks and ride mountain bikes and take Instagram photos of rock formations. You don't live there. It's not normal or healthy. She's completely alone, all the time, except her pets. She's hiding from the world, and it breaks my heart."

Angel would argue her dogs are far more than pets. She talks to CB and Nick often. She's active in Komo. She gets to do what she wants, which is all she needs to be content. That's what she says.

Like Jimmy, I call bullshit. "I worry about her. I try to check in," I don't add, *but she doesn't return my calls or texts,* "but she has made herself as inaccessible as possible." I realize I'm ranting and focus on calming myself. "The point is, I agree, Angel should be living a fuller life, a more satisfying life."

Jimmy lights up. "Absolutely! She needs to get out of her own head. She needs something outside of herself to get her living again."

Something about the way he says it makes me think, *and I bet you're ready to offer yourself as tribute.* Except Jimmy is not her type. I wonder if she even knows her type. I do, but he won't make her life any better.

We chat for hours. Eventually, Jimmy suggests we order food. We keep talking.

As I drive back toward Manhattan in the wee hours of the morning, I feel better than I have in quite some time. I'm more than a little surprised Jimmy Zamora is the one who helped me get there.

CHAPTER ELEVEN

NICK

"Isn't Kait Conradt part of your little side project?" The voice arrives before the body. Wayne Jameson, part of the Special Operations Group, drapes himself over the half-wall of my cubicle, the very half-wall that is supposed to shield me from passersby.

"Yep, she is. Why?" I pause with chopsticks halfway to my mouth, a cascade of glorious noodles dangling above the ceramic bowl I brought from home. I've been looking forward to pho all day, and I resent Wayne for interrupting my meal. I resent him for other things, too: his aftershave, poor driving skills, and a terrible sense of humor. But keeping me from my pho is my main complaint at the present time.

He picks up Batman, one of my Lego figures, and fiddles with it. I want to tell him to put it down, but that will prolong his time in my personal space. "What is that?" Wayne comes around the half-wall and leans over my desk, uncomfortably close to the bowl of fragrant broth, perfectly cooked beef, and vegetables. "Pho?"

He pronounces it 'foh,' and I cringe. Heathen. I don't point out it's pronounced 'fuh.' I just want him to be on his way. I do, however, move the bowl away from his mouth-breathing. His eyes follow it. I remind him, "What about Kait?"

"Hate to tell you this, but she committed suicide. She was found yesterday morning."

Shit. I only met her once in an online chat. Still, from what I've been told, she was an intelligent, kind woman who'd suffered unspeakable torture and come out the other side. I admired the way she took back control. I remember she was lightning with her hand prosthetics. "How did you hear about it?"

"Lori and I were in Manhattan for our anniversary. It was on the news. She's from—was from—Connecticut. I guess they consider that local." Wayne shrugs. "Enjoy your pho." He says it wrong again and wanders away to bother someone else.

I wonder if the Foundation is aware of this. How would they know? Who would tell them? Kait has no family, if I recall correctly. I push the bowl to the side, appetite dampened, and open a file on my phone. She lives in Greenwich. I find the Greenwich Police Department number and dial. I identify myself and ask to speak to someone about Kait Conradt. A couple of minutes on hold, and a woman takes the call. We introduce ourselves. "I'm calling about Kait Conradt. I understand she was found deceased."

"Yes, very sad. She's a bit of a fan favorite around here. She was discovered yesterday morning after a neighbor reported her grocery delivery was never brought inside. Apparently, she had groceries delivered every Sunday morning. We sent officers, and they found her." I hear the sound of moving paper. "It appears she used a suffocation bag."

That would have taken some work, even with her prosthesis. She must have been determined. "Any idea how long she'd been gone?"

"We're waiting for the report, but based on the body's condition, a couple of days."

"Any chance it wasn't suicide?"

"There was a note." She offers to email it to me, along with case notes.

"Thanks." *Shit.* I disconnect the call and stare blankly at the ceramic bowl, its contents now cold.

I am not looking forward to having a conversation with the Komo team. I could wait until the autopsy is done—that will be in the next day or so. The toxicology report will take longer. I'm not sure about Connecticut's backlog, but it's anywhere from four to eight weeks in most states if you're lucky.

Somewhat surprisingly, this is the first suicide of the Komo folks. To the best of my knowledge, no one has decided to end it. Not even the Promise people whose loved ones are found deceased. Protecting the mental health of all the participants is one of the critical missions of Komo. So far, they've been highly successful. I suppose the odds had to come up against them sooner or later.

I'll do a little more digging around on timing and then contact Peter.

CHAPTER TWELVE

PETER

"Hi," Marnie runs a hand across my shoulder before sliding into the chair next to mine on the patio. Rosie and Grace are inside, doing the dishes. On the days we cook, they clean up, and on the days they cook, we clean up. It was taco night. I'll admit, part of what determined the menu was a thirst for revenge. Last night Rosie and Grace made sushi bowls. It took over an hour to get the kitchen looking decent afterward. Wasabi is hard to get out of grout lines.

It's a gorgeous night, a steady 70 degrees. I loved the house Susie and I made our home in Westwood, but the Nest is otherworldly. We have a 180-degree view of the Pacific Ocean. I recognize how privileged we are to live in this perfect place, overlooking one of the most beautiful cities in the world. I'm not the one who got us here. My financial circumstances are mainly my father's doing. He was a brilliant investor, supporting young companies that became behemoths after his death. Apple, Microsoft, Amazon. The money I made as a successful journalist, although significant, was pocket change compared to what I inherited.

If I do things the way I intend, I'll spend the majority of my inheritance doing good, helping people, changing the world. Yep, I'm one of 'those' people.

Fortunately for me, so is Marnie. We're not married, but we might as well be, and we will be someday if I have my way. She's the roadblock. She is the most confident, self-assured woman I know–well, maybe second, next to Olivia–but the age difference, and the way we met, make her jittery. I'm forty-nine; she's thirty-seven. I say that's nothing. She responds by calling me her DOM = Dirty old man.

She could care less that my net worth ends in ten zeros. She knows she'll inherit the Nest and enough money to care for herself and the kids and any future humans who come into our orbit. Olivia, Ben, Grace, and Rosie have trust funds that are reasonable but not ridiculous, and none of them care. Ben and Olivia love their careers, which support them just fine. The Foundation is permanently endowed. Funding will never be a concern.

"Yo, pops," Grace says, doing a fancy dance shuffle-walk onto the patio. "Operation kitchen clean-up is complete." She takes a deep bow.

Rosie is always hot on her heels, Tank the one-eyed Chihuahua in her arms. "Daddy-O! Marnie, loves of my life!" She swoops down to kiss us both on our cheeks, loud smacking kisses because everything she does is loud.

Grace is a classical beauty. To us older folks, she'd be considered a Hitchcock blonde. Her hair is nearly white, her skin creamy and flawless, her features delicate, and her build slim but feminine.

Rosie is the opposite except in coloring. Her hair is a dark blonde, streaked yellow from being outdoors so much. Olivia, Angel, and Bud all had blue eyes, which made them appealing to their abductor. Olivia's are a clear watery blue. Angel's eyes are a darker blue. Rosie has eyes like Bud's, dark blue flecked with green and grey.

Whereas Grace is tall and graceful, Rosie is petite and weirdly flexible. Grace loves riding her horse and swimming. Rosie is all about action: skateboarding, snowboarding, dirt biking, surfing. Grace is quiet, Rosie is loud. Grace is thoughtful, Rosie is impulsive. Grace loves school, Rosie loves life. They're opposites, and they're absolutely perfect together.

"Did we decide we're doing movie night? Or going down to

Abalone Cove?" Marnie asks, catching Rosie around the waist for a snuggle.

"Cove, please!" Rosie yells. Seriously, the girl has one volume.

"Cove it is!" I rub my hands on my khaki shorts and shove my feet back into my sandals. "Before we head out, let's discuss birthdays. I believe someone will be—what is it, eight years old?"

Rosie makes an outraged sound, hands Tank to Marnie, and slams her fists into her hips. "I am about to be twelve, and you know it, old man!"

"Old man?" I gasp, clutching at my gut. "I'm mortally wounded."

"Whatever. Don't die until after we go to the Cove, okay," Rosie grins. "So back to this birthday chat."

Marnie laughs. "What is it to be: birthday party or adventure?"

They always get to choose. Grace usually chooses a party; Rosie always chooses adventure. The question is merely a formality. At least that's what we thought.

"Birthday party!" Rosie announces.

Marnie and I look at each other, not bothering to hide our surprise. "Really?"

"Yes! I want a cirque party."

I have no idea what a cirque party is, and I say so.

"Acrobatics, on poles and silk banners and hula hoop things hanging from the rafters. I would like to have a stripper pole—well, not an actual *stripper* pole, but you know what I mean," I do, but how does she? "permanently installed in the gym. And for the party, I would very much like someone to come and teach us how to do the things."

"The things?" Marnie repeats, her voice a bit squeaky.

"Like Pink. I want to be able to do the cool stuff Pink does," Rosie explains, clearly trying to be patient as we old fogies catch up.

I see Grace sucking her lips in, trying hard not to laugh. She knew. She let us walk into this trap with no warning.

Marnie says "Okay," in a drawn-out way, which means she and

I will discuss this surprising turn of events later. "We will see what we can do."

"Cove time!" Rosie declares enthusiastically with a shimmy of her narrow hips. She and Grace disappear into the house to collect things or change clothes or do whatever young girls do. They've been best friends always, despite their three-year age difference.

"This will be very interesting," Marnie grins.

"If she's asking for a stripper pole for her 12th birthday, what do you think she's going to want for her 18th?" I make a horrified face, and she laughs at me. My phone pings, and I pull it from my pocket because it's Nick's unique sound, and he only texts when it's essential.

The words are shocking. "Kait Conradt is dead. They say she died by suicide."

CHAPTER THIRTEEN

OLIVIA

Since I'm in first class, I'm alone with my thoughts on the flight back to LAX. One question returns, no matter how hard I push it away. Should I tell Dad I was with Kait when she ended it? He's going to find out she's gone soon enough. The Foundation doesn't keep tabs on us, but it won't go unnoticed when someone as engaged as Kait is suddenly absent.

This has never happened before. None of us have ever... taken the exit. The families will freak out, worrying about copycats. The Foundation team will go into protection mode. It's going to be a bit of a shit show, I'm afraid.

Something's holding me back from telling Dad, or even Dr. Lisa, who would have to keep it in confidence. I didn't kill Kait, but I certainly helped. A gossipy fly on the wall might say I encouraged it. I certainly didn't try to stop her. If anything, I made things easier. I suppose if she had a last-minute change of heart, my presence might have prevented her from taking time to think about it.

She left a suicide note for the authorities on the nightstand. But then there's the matter of the envelope. It's so flowery against the pale beige plastic tray. There was just one person Kait cared to say goodbye to directly. I promised to get the envelope to them, but I've been having second thoughts.

If I had delivered it, there'd be no hiding the fact I was there. What I should have done was mailed it while in New York. Too late now. I'll keep it in my carry-on and leave it with a hotel concierge for posting sometime while I'm traveling. It's not like quickly getting the note to its addressee would have changed anything.

That's it, then. I've made up my mind. There isn't any reason for anyone to know. No good would come from telling Dad or the police. Kait is dead. Someone will worry and send help.

CHAPTER FOURTEEN

The shrieking is horrific. I tuck my head down and practice my breathing. In through the nose, count to five, out through the mouth. *Stay calm. You'll be okay.*

But with each step, the scream grows louder, angrier. I close my eyes until they're nearly slits and press on. If I can't see them, they can't see me.

For just a moment, I wish I was in a big city with 24-hour grocery stores and carts with wheels that don't sound like they're tearing small children limb from limb. But I live outside Moab, Utah, and the City Mart is only open 'til 9 pm, 8 on Sundays. On the weekend, you're lucky to get any cart at all, which is why I wait till later to do my shopping. The trade-off is getting stuck with a broken cart from hell.

The horrible, terrible, very loud cart holds everything on my list except items from the meat counter, which is at the back of the store. The shriek is getting louder, *grindier*, if that's a thing. There aren't many people in the store this late, but those who are, are definitely staring. My face is burning. I debate abandoning the cart and running for the door. But no. My commitment to myself is not to be a coward, and being chased out of a store by a loud grocery cart would be very cowardly, indeed.

The man behind the meat counter is new. City Mart isn't large, and if you're here even a few times, you start to recognize the employees. His name tag says "Donovan." He gives me a mildly aggressive look as the cart throws up yet another ungodly sound as if I'm personally responsible. "What can I get you?"

I open my phone, glad for the temporary silence, and navigate to the notes app on my iPhone, where I store my list. "Two pounds of ground sirloin, in two packages, please. A roasting chicken. And a pound of salmon."

He sets about weighing and wrapping. I enjoy the moment of blissful quiet. Learning to cook was supposed to be relaxing. It's my one and only resolution this year, and I intend to succeed. I'm getting old enough that I can't live on cereal and PB&J sandwiches without consequences.

He slaps the package of salmon on the counter and glances at me before starting the next item. "Do I know you?"

I shrug. "I shop here. You've probably seen me." I hope that ends it. It doesn't.

"Nope, that's not it." He studies me while he wraps the chicken.

I don't respond. I turn my attention to my phone. I'm excited to learn to roast a chicken. It's been at the top of my recipe wish list for a while now. I'm going to go in two directions with the salmon: one with a dill sauce, the other with a sticky ponzu and mirin glaze. I had to order the mirin from Amazon. The Mart doesn't carry anything more ethnic than tortillas and refried beans. A pound of beef is for burgers for the dogs. The other is for chili for me.

He slides the paper-wrapped chicken toward me and pulls out a tray of ground beef. "Two packages, you said."

I nod once. His hair is tucked into a paper cap covering a hair net. Thick, dark curls try to escape. He's got an interesting face, narrow with sharp features. He's tall, his body lean but muscular under the white T-shirt and apron that is the City Mart uniform. A few hundred years ago, he might have been an Aztec warrior painted on a temple wall. There's something off, though. Something creepy about the way he's watching me. I may need to start shopping at one of the smaller markets.

He slides the first package of beef onto the counter, and I quickly retrieve it and put it in my cart. He puts the second pound up, and I move my hand to grab it... and he lays his hand on top of mine, pressing hard, holding me captive. "I know you."

"Let go," I say, as calmly as I can.

He is staring at me, staring *into* me. My gut gurgles in a familiar unwelcome response.

"Let. Me. Go," I say, more loudly. "I will scream."

His mouth opens just a bit and curves into a small smile. His hand slides off mine and behind the counter. The smile grows bigger and bigger. His tone is seductive. "Well, hello."

I'm definitely not coming back.

CHAPTER FIFTEEN

ANGEL

My trip was delayed by a couple of weeks, but I'm finally here. There are dozens of puppies at the reservation rescue at any given time. There are shepherd mixes, lab mixes, husky mixes. One or two have a suspiciously wolfish air to them. I love that look, but it's not the look I'm after.

Nadine took over leadership of the rescue when her mom was forced to retire because of arthritis and early-onset Alzheimer's. This rescue is vital to the Navajo Nation, sprawling across New Mexico, Arizona, and Utah. The Navajo Nation is similar in size to the state of West Virginia. It is a difficult place for both humans and animals. More than one-quarter of the homes do not have electricity, and one-third do not have running water. Dogs on the reservation are working animals kept outside, fending for themselves for food and water. They are not spayed or neutered. Puppies often don't survive. The average lifespan of a reservation dog is just two years. Two veterinarians serve the entire Navajo Nation, and there are just four shelters. Only seven percent of the animals in those shelters "make it out alive," and that's because of the hard work of rescue groups dedicated to these animals.

Nadine knows my type. She leads me around a corner to a run of kennels, and I spot him immediately, a forty-pound brick of canine. He's the size of an adult Cocker Spaniel. He's solid glossy black, with a blockhead and stocky body. He's kind of terrifying looking but in the most fantastic way. He drops into a bow position and yawns, then lowers his back half and rests his head on giant paws, eyes closed. No barking. No whining. No cowering. He's confident and self-assured.

"I call him Chonk for obvious reasons. Can you believe he's only four months old? You might need a bigger vehicle if you decide to take him," Nadine jokes.

"He sure has the look." I watch him. If his temperament works out, he could be the perfect companion for Hannah. I don't approach the kennel. I am curious—Aha! An appropriate use of that word—to see how he reacts to a stranger standing nearby, ignoring him. Does he bark for attention? Growl in warning? Or simply wait and see? At the moment, he doesn't seem to care at all. I need a dog that's aware of the world around him but not excited by it. "Tell me about our chonky friend."

She laughs. "He's built like the Rock, but his soul is Robin Williams. He's the most kindhearted, sensitive dog I've ever seen. He gets his feelings hurt. If you're nice to another dog, he's supportive as all get out. He's just so delighted a friend is getting attention. But if you get done with the other dog and don't stop to give him a little love too, I swear it breaks his heart. He looks like he's gonna cry." She pauses and looks directly at him. His eyes are open, watching us. He blinks at her.

"Does he know his name?" I ask, and when she nods, I whisper, "Chonk."

He raises his head, and I gasp in surprise. I've never seen a dog whose eyes look so human. They're pools of gold in the middle of a sea of black velvet. He's stunning. He really is smiling, one of those beautiful pittie smiles. He knows we're talking about him, and he's just waiting for us to step up and acknowledge his wonderfulness with a petting session.

Who am I not to oblige? I step to the cage and lower my hand slowly, letting him take in my scent at his own pace through the chain link. He sits with perfect posture. It's hard to believe he's a baby. He's so calm. He pushes his muzzle toward my hand, and I slip my forefinger through the fence to stroke his soft nose. Silk.

"Have you done any work with him? How is he as far as training goes? Is he confident or shy?" As if I can't already tell. "Do you know anything about his heritage? Any issues I need to know about?"

Nadine is unfazed by the volley of questions. "No issues other than he's terrifying to look at if you don't like the blocky breeds. His dad is Cane Corso, mom a street pittie. He's got 'sit' and 'shake' down. He walks nicely on a leash. He can be a little hyper if you get out the flirt stick, but he also responds well to correction. He learns quickly. So far, the only flaw is that sensitive side." Nadine laughs and makes kissy sounds at him.

She holds up a hand in my direction. "Don't make up your mind yet, though. I have another candidate." Nadine leads me onward through the maze of kennels, some makeshift, some store-bought. She has so many dogs here.

We stop in front of what looks like an empty kennel, and I wait to see what magic creature will present itself. Nadine taps her fingers against the fence. Nothing happens. She taps again. Eventually, the strangest dog I've ever seen strolls out. She's half the size of Chonk. She moves like a party girl strutting her stuff. She's got long, nearly hairless legs, but her torso is covered with fluffy gray and white fur. The black and gray tufts on her regal head suggest she put her paw in a light socket. She has a long delicate snout and a short curly tail with a knob of fur at the end. She might be the Martian version of a dog. I've never seen anything like her.

"What—is she?" I ask finally. My brain isn't succeeding at working it out.

"One of our sponsors was intrigued, so she paid for a DNA test." Nadine giggles. "Ready? Chinese Crested, Affenpinscher, with a splash of greyhound to give her some loft."

My mouth is hanging open, I know. I try to close it, but it just drops open again.

I feel my forehead wrinkle. "Okay, I give. Why her?"

Nadine laughs again. "Winnie is incredibly smart. I'm convinced she's fluent in human. She understands everything we're saying, and I'm pretty sure she's judging us."

As if to prove Nadine correct, Winnie sits and offers a paw.

I approach the kennel, and at Nadine's nod of approval, open the gate and accept the offered paw. "Nice to meet you, Winnie."

She retracts her paw, yawns, and stretches. I almost hear, "It's nice to meet you too, serf."

Dilemma. I can see this dog and Hannah together. But I also really like Chonk. Peter talked about possibly giving Charlie a dog. I've never tried to train two dogs simultaneously, but what the heck. "Let's take them to the playroom."

If Chonk and Charlie don't work out, or Hannah prefers Chonk to Winnie, I'm certainly not against having three canines. Cat might protest, but she'll eventually get over it. Am I nuts? I give a mental shrug. Probably. "Let's see what Asa and Nope say. If they approve, we'll take both."

And that's how Chonk and Winnie ended up in the Bronco headed back to Moab.

CHAPTER SIXTEEN

ANGEL

It's only two and a half hours from the rescue back to my place. The new kids are secured in steel-sided kennels in the back. Asa is curled up next to me, and Nope is stretched out across the back seat.

Asa was my first dog, the dog that introduced me to all the ways dogs and humans can work together. CB and I found him at a truck stop in Tennessee about six months after the drama at the Oklahoma ranch. For CB, it was love at first sight. She said it would be a good idea to have a bit of canine protection to back up her infamous pink pistol.

I'll admit I'm a bit of a pessimist sometimes. I imagine all the things that can go wrong. A dog in a semi traveling the country seemed rife with possible disasters.

"The fact we found this poor dog before we pulled out of the parking lot, possibly smashing him under Casita2's wheels, proves he's a lucky dog. The fact he found you and me, of all people, proves he's an extraordinarily lucky dog. I'm not about to turn away that kind of luck." CB said, squatting next to the trailer. Poor little Asa had tucked himself, wet and shivering, under a mud flap. When CB offered her hand, he pressed his cheek into it. I'm pretty sure my soul joined his at that moment.

His name is Asa Lucian Evanston. I call him Asa, and CB calls him Lucifur. Asa is half pit bull, half blue heeler. His flat coat is brown with black and gold speckles like someone splattered him with paint. He's got the requisite pit blockhead, but his ears are two black triangles that stand straight up. I sometimes grunt, "I am Batman!" when I look at him. He must have some Aussie in him because his left eye is blue. He's an adorable mess of dog parts, oh-so-smart, and utterly devoted to me.

Nope's full name is Penelope–I didn't name her, by the way–and she's a three-legged black lab corgi mix I bought from a homeless man named JR for $200. She was born with three legs, which is how he ended up with her in the first place. She was a throwaway to someone, but she was JR's reason to live.

Penelope and JR were sitting outside a homeless shelter in Chicago one frigid night when I stopped by to help CB serve meals. I asked why he wasn't inside. He said they wouldn't let Penelope in, so he wasn't going in. I offered to sit with Penelope while he ate and did what he needed, and for some reason, he trusted me and agreed. When he came out and saw her stretched across my lap, he asked if I would take her. Tears coursed the deep crevices of his weathered face, and Penelope licked them away. He didn't want to give her up, but he was pretty sure he had "the cancer" and needed to know she was in a good place before he could let the doctors try to fix him. I told him I'd get them a motel room, and he and Penelope would have a warm night. I'd come by in the morning, and if he still wanted me to take her, I would. If not, no harm, no foul. I'd buy them breakfast and slip a few bucks into his pocket.

When I arrived in the morning, he had packed a little 'suitcase' for her in the form of a plastic grocery bag. Kibble, food and water bowls, a battered squeaky toy, one of his sweaters.

He didn't ask for money, but I gave him cash and a prepaid cell phone I would keep replenished. I wanted him to check in with me. Penelope and I would send him notes and photos. When he was all fixed up, I'd bring her back.

We never saw him again. A nurse sent a single text for him, saying, "Tell my girl I love her." I did, and I swear Nope was quiet for the next few days.

Five years ago, when CB decided to move up to Chicago to be closer to family, my first act on my own was to buy a patch of land in southwest Utah and call it home. The land came with an old single-wide trailer with no water and no heat. The pups and I slept there while we built a 40 by 60-foot post frame building on the highest hill. Our living quarters make up an L shape chunk of the building, with the remainder used for training, vehicle storage, and equipment maintenance. It's not huge, but it works well for my life.

Cat just showed up one day after we moved onto my property. I didn't name her because I didn't know she was staying. By the time she made that clear, I'd been calling her Cat, and the name stuck.

This will be a new adventure for Winnie and Chonk. They've never been in a house. They were born in dirt, their kennel sat on dirt, and dirt is all they know. Their first lesson is how to be good house companions. From there, we'll move on to the more complex things.

It's still light when we reach the road that passes the gate to my place. There's a small sign with the word *Stargazer* above the mail slot. If you didn't know what you were looking for, you might think this is a Bureau of Land Management asset. But it's mine.

I turn left into the short driveway and hit the remote to open the gate. The pups are rustling in the back, and Asa and Nope are antsy. They know we're home.

Something across the road catches my eye, and I turn my head. A rusty green Ford Ranger pickup is parked fifty feet ahead, engine off. Broken down? Then I see a ponytail of dark curly hair and a sharply drawn nose. Before I can pull my phone out to take a photo, Donovan from the City Mart meat department drives away.

Well, shit.

CHAPTER SEVENTEEN

ANGEL

Long ago and far away, I met a woman named CB. She claimed her name was Chickee Boom. Turned out it was really Concetta Bonaventura. Either way, CB is one of the most authentic humans I've had the good fortune to meet. She's Dolly Parton, and Salma Hayek rolled into one: five foot nothing of deep thoughts, fiery temper, and boundless love. I was her copilot for three years as we drove back and forth across the US, delivering car parts and computer chips and, once in a while, offering a good ass-kicking to someone who needed it. We're settled down now, living the good life in our preferred locations. I'm in the middle of nowhere, Utah. She's reveling in the joy that is Chicago's Lincoln Park.

But once a month, CB and I have a dinner and a movie date. We set up our laptops in our kitchens and chat while cooking the same recipe. After we eat, often with CB's fiancée TJ, we watch a movie together; usually, a horror flick, because those are my favorite and CB likes to spoil me.

Tonight we're making pork Milanese and coconut rice. I had to go to one of the smaller grocery stores in Moab to find all the ingredients, and they didn't have plantains, which we were going to use to make patacones.

"Didn't we make something with plantains once before? I thought they were available there." CB says as she pounds the pork in her kitchen in Chicago. It's a bright, colorful space filled with art, flowers, and sound. There's music in the background, and I hear TJ singing along to the blues.

"They are." I wasn't going to mention the weird grocery store guy, but I change my mind. "I didn't go to the larger store this time. They have a new employee, and I'm pretty sure he recognized me. He got really weird. Then I saw him across from my gate when I got back from the reservation."

"And you called Nick immediately, yes?" CB says, raising her eyes to stare at me through the digital portal, still pounding on the pork with her rolling pin.

I chew my lip and reach for my beer. "Not yet. I don't want to become the girl who is always in trouble. Maybe this time, I freaked myself out."

"And maybe this time you didn't," CB growls. She holds up a flattened pork cutlet. "Mix the Parmesan into the panko. Dip the cutlets into the egg, then the breading. Got it?"

I nod and run my cutlets through the process, then set them to rest on a cookie sheet.

"Slice the lemon into quarters. How's your rice?" CB asks. TJ pops into the frame to hand her a cocktail, gives her a deep kiss, then winks at me before dancing his way back out of the frame. It's funny to watch him dip his 6'2" self down to reach her 5'3" mouth.

"My coconut is a paste," I say. This has been one heck of a process. Nearly an hour ago, I opened a can of coconut milk into a pan and have monitored it as it reduces and turns into the necessary golden-brown paste. I tip the pan to inspect the color, and she nods approvingly.

"Add the rice, sugar, and salt now," CB instructs.

I do. We wait a few minutes and then add water. Once it boils, I know we will cover it, reduce the heat and let it simmer for 15 minutes. "The oil for the pork is ready."

"Okay. All pups and Cat are out of the way, yes?" CB says.

"They're on the couches." I nod.

"Okay. Start frying. Only three or four minutes on each side. You don't want them to brown too much, and you definitely don't want them to burn. Don't crowd the pan." Her instructions come fast and furious. She's doing the same steps in her kitchen, and I hear clicking and clacking and watch her petite frame moving fluidly as she glides around the kitchen. She's probably wearing five-inch heels.

I follow along, carefully monitoring temperatures, bubbling, and steps. It smells incredible. My mouth is watering. I take another drink of beer, a local offering. "How's TJ's project going?"

"Good!" He yells from off-screen. "We start construction next week!" TJ is an architect by education, but he recently veered into entrepreneurship. He and CB are building an art gallery/distillery in one of Chicago's up-and-coming neighborhoods.

"You'll be up here for the opening this fall," CB tells me. Of course, I will.

The food is ready. We're both quiet while turning burners off, moving pans back, and plating up. I carry my plate to the small table between the open kitchen and the living room. All four dogs are alert on the couch but behaving, for the most part. Chonk is fighting the hardest against temptation.

"Don't think I forgot what we were talking about," CB says as she slips into a chair in her dining room. We've both moved our computers, and now I can see TJ. He lifts his wine glass in salute to the chefs and the three of us 'clink' glasses.

"Ha! As if you ever forget anything," I laugh and take a bite. I want to close my eyes. It's incredible. And I'm the one who made it! I'm giddy with pride.

"Jesus, woman, will you please marry me already? I can't risk losing access to your insane cooking," TJ grunts around a mouthful of food.

"What we have is perfect. And my cooking isn't the only thing you're afraid of losing access to. Now be quiet. Angel and I need to have one of our come to Jesus discussions."

"You have a lot of those."

"That's because someone is stubborn and thinks she knows every-thing," I say before CB can pipe up. Her face makes me glad we're hundreds of miles apart. I grin. "Kidding. Mostly."

"Angel, please, don't make light of this. You've had enough trouble in your short life. When you see the light bearing down on you through the tunnel, assume it's a train and get out of the way for once!" CB laughs, but her eyes aren't laughing.

I sigh. Chonk tumbles off the couch and comes to sit on my foot, his fat butt on the edge of my slipper. "Okay. I'll tell Nick. I'm not going to call him just for this, but I'll tell him when we have our regular check-in this week, okay?"

CB makes a face and sighs dramatically. I know she's making fun of me. "Okay." Then she smiles for real. "Thank you. I can't get down there fast enough to save your ass if you get into trouble again. Now, what horrible gorefest are we watching tonight?"

"I'm thinking *The Invisible Man*. It's got great special effects, and the heroine kicks the bad guy's ass."

CHAPTER EIGHTEEN

I have one of those ubiquitous email addresses I use mainly for ordering stuff online. The Baden clan and CB and Nick use it too, but it's not something I hand out to people willy nilly. So when I click on the "new message" icon and see the sender name JDomme244 and subject line "Stars," my gut clutches. Who is JDomme244? How did they get my email address? What the actual hell?

> *"My dearest Angel,*
> *Forgive me for emailing you outside the Komo system, but I felt this was too personal and private to share with judgmental people who think they know what's right for everybody else. After recent events, everyone appears to be on high alert, and I feel it is important to avoid prying eyes. I'm sure you'll understand once you've had time to absorb and digest my thoughts.*
>
> *We have known each other for several years now. I have been entirely upfront about who I am and what I believe, and I like to think you have, too. I've been patient. Now it's time for us to have an honest conversation about our lives, dreams, and future. Notice 'future' is singular.*
>
> *I firmly believe the events in our lives happened for a reason. You and I are meant to be together.*
>
> *I want to meet in person. I want to discuss what our*

future would be like. You say you don't want to be married. If you're honest, you don't think anyone decent would have you. You're right about most men, but I'm not most men. I would have you. I would accept you as you are, with your flaws, baggage, scars, and insecurities.

You're damaged. That's just a fact. You've been badly broken. You're a flawed individual who can never be as good as you might have been before bad things happened to you. You need to be with someone who can see past all that and recognize the value, and ignore the bad parts. Someone who will love you despite your problems. So few men can do that. They're blinded by their egos and only want what is whole and perfect. They only care about their needs and what others will think. I'm not like that. I'm the most perfect man you could be with because I understand you, and I can see past your broken parts and ignore the baggage you haul around. We'll have a fantastic life together.

I don't care that your body is scarred. You can be attractive when you want to be, and with me, I know you'd work hard to be appealing to me. You'd want to keep my attention. That's your focus as a wife. The husband's job is to provide. Since you have the trust fund that would care for our financial needs. I would take care of the yard and the cars and make the decisions for our family, and you would be a great mom and wife. I understand you value your privacy and want to stay away from the public. We will buy property in the country and create our own version of homesteading. We can homeschool our children. Live off the land. Because it will only be us on our compound, you'll feel safe to be attractive and sexual. You will have nothing to fear. There will be no other men to see you, to want you. You will be mine, alone, and I will keep you safe from all the others.

Once we're together, you will no longer need your animals. Animals don't like me, and I don't want to be around them. You'll also need to tell Peter you don't need him or Komo anymore. You'll have me. I'll be your family. We'll be family to each other. Just us. We don't need anyone else.

You might be overwhelmed by my proposal. I understand. You no doubt thought love would never happen for you, so you didn't dare to dream of it. But it can happen; it will happen. You'll see. Please, let's not tell anyone else about this just yet. Not until we've had a chance to talk and work out the details. I don't want them getting into our business and trying to control everything. They have so many opinions. Dr. Lisa... I don't even know where she earned her supposed degree. Maybe in some third-world country. She's a quack. So no telling tales, my Angel. I sometimes lose my temper, but I'm working on it. Their interference would make me sad and angry, and I don't want to be sad or angry. Help me be the best version of myself. Help me by keeping this our secret.

I will contact you soon to make arrangements to meet in person. Until then, think about how wonderful our life could be—will be—when we're together.

All my love, Jimmy."

I barely make it through the whole email before I have to grab the trash can near my desk and empty the contents of my stomach. Asa whines and jumps down from the couch. "It's okay, bud. I'm fine." I pat him reassuringly, and he curls up on top of my bare feet.

But I'm not fine. Not fine at all. I'm disgusted. I'm horrified. I feel violated. Worse, I'm a bit scared, and that makes me angry. Jimmy is unhinged. He can't really believe any of this! It has to be a joke. But I know it's not a joke. He's serious. I flashback to my conversation with Kait. Clearly, she had more knowledge of what was happening in his head than she let on. I remember his outbursts in group. This is more of the same.

I need to tell Dr. Lisa that Jimmy has gone around the bend. I need to tell Peter he violated the Komo agreement by contacting me outside the system without invitation. Except if I do those things, he'll be kicked out of the group. What will he do then, without the support he draws from but doesn't seem to want to acknowledge? He'll become a monster. I know it in my gut.

Shit.

I get myself under control and am about to push away from the desk when another email from JDomme244 appears on the screen. I really don't want to open it. I really, really don't. I hope against hope this email will say, "Gotcha! JUST KIDDING!"

I know it won't. Which is why I can't leave it unopened. I click the icon. At least it's short.

"Angel: Do not tell anyone about our communication. I am deadly serious. I don't want to start our relationship off on a negative foot, but if I must, I will teach you how important it is to do as I tell you. All my love, Jimmy."

CHAPTER NINETEEN

WICHITA

You caught me. I'm not really with a real estate company. I know it isn't fair to sneak up on you like this. Don't get upset. It's OK, I promise.

Relax, please. Let's just talk. I know you don't like to talk. I can talk, and you can listen? Make signs? Nod? I'm sure we'll figure it all out.

I have a theory, and I'd love to know your thoughts about it. I believe you don't speak because the man who took you was a minister, right? Wasn't he a man of God? I think he said you were stupid, had no value, were unimportant, and nobody cared about you or what you might have to say. And hearing that, over and over, became so ingrained in your core beliefs about yourself it silenced your voice permanently. I can see I'm right by the look on your face. I'm so sorry that happened to you.

They mean well, your friends and family, especially the Komorebi people. Of course, they do. But there are some things they can't fix. Some things they can't undo. Some words they can't take back. Right? I get it. I really do.

Are you happy? Really happy? I don't mean this particular minute. I mean, in general. If I were to guess, I would say no, I don't think you are. Your words in the group feel angry and hurt. Don't frown. I don't mean that harshly. I just mean you don't seem to feel hopeful about the future.

You don't have a family you're close to, is that right? Don't you live here with a couple of roommates? Are they people you knew before? No? It must be very hard to live with strangers. That would scare me if I were you. They must be okay, though. I'm sure they were thoroughly checked out. Are they nice? Do they include you?

That's too bad. I'm sorry. You could ask the Komo team to find you somewhere else. No? See, that's why I worry about you. You're just accepting this life the way it's been given to you.

Is there anything that excites you? That you look forward to? You're young. Are you satisfied talking to strangers on your computer all day long? That's what you do for work, isn't it? Customer support really just means subjecting yourself to angry people. Sometimes that must feel like you're right back in the trailer with the preacher. What a terrible way to live.

You don't have to work, you know. The Komo people will pay for you to go to school or learn a different job. Nah? Not interested? I get it. I really do.

Hey, I'm thirsty. Could we make some tea or something? You sit, just tell me where to find everything.

CHAPTER TWENTY

PRIVILEGED & CONFIDENTIAL

Komorebi file #134

Gifford, Tiffany

[Two photos: Photo of a teenage girl wearing short-shorts and a halter top. Very curvy and confident. Box-dyed blonde hair, heavy eye makeup bordering on goth, and a number of pearcings in her ears. Second photo hair and makeup are similar, but she's wearing jeans and a leather jacket. She's just 19 but looks closer to 30.]

Location: Wichita, KS

DOB: 6/23/1993   **Abduction:** 5/6/2010

Recovery: 7/31/2012   **Current Age:** 27

Offender Status: Life sentence in Kansas prison system. Has significant fan following.

Notes: Sent by mother to clean minister's house. He locked her in a trailer on his property. Made & distributed pornographic films. Found when the property was hit by a tornado. Remains of other victims were discovered on the property. Non-verbal since recovery. All conversations are text-based. _NOTED HERE with Tiffany's original spelling and grammar._

Tell me about the day you were taken. What do you remember about that time?

Mama was pissed I was hanging out with Brandon instead of going to school. She was always saying I wasn't going to live in her house whether I graduated or not, so I best get me enough education to pay rent. We fought a lot, but that's just how we were. I wasn't tryin to be a rebel. I just thought she was too strict. Sometimes I would try and make peace though and that's what happened that day.

She was big on church. Me, not so much. Minister McCauley seemed okay, I guess. I mean, you'd never look at him and know he's the devil wearing a minister suit. I sure didn't. I don't think Mama did or she would not have sent me there. One Sunday, she comes home after church and she says the Minister needs someone to clean his house and I might as well get started learning how because that's the only future I got. And honestly, I like cleaning, so if I was gonna end up with that kind of job, might as well get a start, right?

I took the bus out as close as it would go—Minister McCauley lives kind of near McConnell Air Force Base. The bus goes there, but not much past it, so I had to walk some, prolly a mile or two. Of course, I'd never been there before, and I only ever met the Minister once or twice when Mama would drag me to the church. I wasn't a hundred percent I was even at the right place until I saw the sign at the driveway that said "God's Country" in like ten-foot letters.

God must pay well 'cuz Minister McCauley had

three or four expensive cars in the driveway, and the house was ginormous. I was a little afraid about trying to clean all that but I wasn't about to go home without at least getting a drink of water. It was quite the walk and I was tired! I knocked on the door. The Minister invited me in, said his wife and sons were in town at a basketball game or something. I don't remember. Anyway, he walked me through the whole house, showing off, I kind of think. He's a big guy, at least six-foot-four and prolly three hundred pounds. He's got that red face thing going on. Mama once said it means the person drinks too much, but she would never say anything bad about the Minister so… When we were done, he asked what did I think. I told him I could do it, would take me most of the day. I asked stuff like would he provide the supplies because I couldn't figure out how I'd haul everything out on the bus and walk. He said that wasn't a problem.

And then he said, all casual, "Oh, yeah, let's go look at the office. I'd like you to clean that too." He said it was away from the house so we had to take a golf cart. That was kind of fun. I'd never been in a golf cart before. His 'office' was an old—I mean, really OLD—camper out in the middle of nowhere on the back of his property. Couldn't even see the house from there, or any of the other outbuildings. Seemed a weird place to have an office, since people might want to come talk to him. But I didn't say anything. Stupid me, wanting to please Mama, and maybe even a little bit to please

God, hopped out of the dumb golf cart and followed Minister McCauley right on in the door.

I never saw the punch coming. He hit me in the face so hard I blacked out. When I woke up I was naked, with a metal collar clamped around my neck, and a chain attached to that. He was grunting on top of me. The noises he made, he sounded like a damn pig. He was swearing at me. "Bitch! Whore! Slut!" and once he saw I was awake he said even worse. I was crying, and asking him to stop, but he didn't, just kept rutting. It hurt. Mama would not have believed it, but I was a virgin until that day, and Minister McCauley wasn't just tall and big, if ya know what I mean.

When he left he strapped me down to the nasty old mattress so my body made a cross. I couldn't change position much at all. He pointed to a camera in the corner of the ceiling and told me he'd be able to watch me and hear if I yelled or anything so to keep my mouth shut or he'd come and make sure I never said another sound. That was the start.

He came every day. Sometimes he came with other people but on those days he put a thick black hood over my head so I couldn't see who they were. They did whatever they wanted to me. None of them were nice. I felt like an exhibit in an interactive museum. They'd say "Hey, stick your gun in her butthole and see how far it'll go!" and someone would do it.

Later I found out they were recording it! All of it. One of the people—a lady, which shocked the shit out of me let me tell you!—was talking to Minister McCauley about how much money he could make if he sold the videos. I knew right then I was never getting out.

Can you tell me why you choose not to speak? The notes from your doctor say it's not a physical issue.

It's stupid and it makes me mad because it's not like I don't WANNA talk. I have a lot to say and it's hard to get people to listen when you type everything. The best I can figure is that my voice got scared out of me. If I said anything, made even a noise, whatever, the Minister would tell me he was gonna cut my tongue out and make me lick my own pussy with it. Sorry. I know that's gross. But that's what he said. Minister liked to yell "Proverbs 21:23!" the few times I tried to say something. Once I was out, I looked it up. "Those who guard their mouths and their tongues keep themselves from calamity." True enough I guess.

What do you remember about being recovered?

If you live anywhere there's tornados, you're used to hearing the sirens and you don't always pay much attention when they go off. That day the sirens were going, but I couldn't see out the windows, they were covered up, and so I didn't know if something was happening right there, or miles away, ya know? I didn't worry too much about it. Not like I could go hide anyway. By that time the Minister had set a up a little portable radio he'd leave on when he was gone. It was a religious station, so a lot of God talk and singing and stuff, but it was the only real company I had so I didn't mind.

The day I was saved, there were tornados all over around Wichita, some bad ones. I didn't know it at the time, but the Minister's fancy house got taken out, and him and his wife were hurt. Him worse than her. I think she had a broken arm or something but he was pretty beat up, in the hospital.

Me, I was in that camper one minute, and outside it the next. When I came to, I was laying on a trampoline. I couldn't even see where the camper was, I don't know how far away I was, because I only ever saw the camper from outside that one time. Not enough to have landmarks, ya know. The collar was still around my neck and the chain was wrapped around the trampoline frame. But my hands and feet were free because the mattress was gone.

I didn't know that there were volunteers on the property looking for various stuff to help. That's normal. When someone gets hit, the whole town comes out to help them find their wedding album and granny's cookbook and all. Anyway, yeah, a couple of guys found me. Boy let me tell you they were shocked as all get out to find a dirty naked girl chained to a trampoline…

What's your family situation now?

Minister told her I never showed for the cleaning job so she figured I'd run off. When the truth came out—well, she didn't really believe it. She said I was making up lies about the Minister, he would never do something like that. Even after they found bodies of two other women on the property, and after his trial, and all the things that came out, she still took up for him more than me, although she let me live with her for a little bit, before Komo helped me.

What's your day like now?

Thanks to you all, I live in a house I really like. I have my own room—a suite, my roommates call it, with a bedroom and a sitting area and my own bathroom. I only have to share the living room and kitchen with them. I don't like them that much. They don't talk to me. They only live here because it's cheap rent I think. But it's all right for now. Maybe next year I'll look at getting a different place. Komo also helped me get a customer service job, which I like. It's all typing and I do it from home so I don't have to worry about talking.

Everything I tell you is confidential, right? You can't tell anyone else? I like to mess with some of Minister McCauley's friends. He has a whole Reddit board all his own where they talk about how he's innocent and even if he's not he was trying to save me. You could say hanging out there's my hobby. They don't know who I am. They like to show their butts and prove what monsters they are.

I don't wanna tell you exactly what I do, but I found something that makes me feel kinda good.

Thank you for sharing your memories and experiences, I can imagine it is difficult to talk about.

It makes sense that recovering after something so traumatic can be emotionally messy sometimes.

Would you consider yourself happy since your recovery?

Before all of this, I figured I'd waitress or maybe if I was lucky I could work at a daycare. I really like kids, wanted a whole bunch. I didn't need a rich guy, just a good guy who would be a good husband and a great dad. That was my Big Plan. None of that happened, obv. It's never gonna. Am I happy? Nah. But I'm okay.

Notes were taken during her initial Komo session. LC

CHAPTER TWENTY-ONE

ANGEL

I've never trained two dogs simultaneously, but I'm looking forward to it. The fact they are so smart will probably make it a greater challenge, but I'm up for it.

In the few days they've been here, we've focused on learning to dog. They need to understand what a house is, what a bed is, what a couch is, what an alarm clock is, what a cat is. Having spent their entire lives outside, in a dirt-floored kennel, everything is new. Even having the autonomy to wander around and investigate is new to them.

Asa and Nope have been excellent canine ambassadors, teaching the youngsters positive skills and correcting them when they get out of line. This isn't their first puppy rodeo. We've trained a half dozen dogs in the last couple of years. They know the drill.

Today is the day Hannah and Charlie will 'meet' their potential buddies via Zoom. We'll decide which pup will be the best companion for which human, although I'm pretty sure I know how it will sort out, based on the humans and canines in question.

I've got my laptop set up in the training area of the barn. The dogs played while I did barn chores, and then we went for a pack walk to burn off energy. Asa and Nope are back in the residence, and the puppies are crashed on an old recliner next to the sofa I've claimed for myself.

Charlie logs on first. We've had a couple of one-on-ones before today, and I've got a good feel for who he is and what he needs. He reminds me so much of Bud. I feel like I'll be training a dog for my brother. I have to stop thinking that way. It's creepy.

"How're classes? Learn anything criminal today?" I'm stretched out on the couch, laptop on a rolling table so I can move around as needed. In the chat window, the puppies are visible over my shoulder.

"Experimental chemistry is not particularly criminal, sadly," Charlie explains. "But it's all foundational, and I'm lucky it comes easily to me."

"I'm always amazed by people who 'get' science. I am not science-minded." I admit. A ping notifies us Hannah has joined, and her beautiful, unsmiling face claims half the screen. "Hi, Hannah."

She nods and smiles self-consciously. She's one of the younger members of Hope, recently turned eighteen. She was rescued a year ago after being kept in a locked closet for six months. She was taken from her home in the middle of the night by a friend of her cousin's. Her mother and little brother were killed during the abduction, and she carries a lot of guilt about that. Now she lives with her Mom's best friend and her family. She's finishing high school online and has been talking to Em about a career as a graphic designer. Em and Hannah chat regularly about creative endeavors. Em recently offered Hannah the chance to design the cover for her first album.

For the most part, Hannah is doing well. According to her guardian, she still has night terrors, which is understandable. I do, too, and I'm ten-plus years past my trauma. She's not confident enough to leave her house alone yet. Dr. Lisa and Hannah's guardian think having a dog will be good for her. Dogs can release endorphins and lower stress, provide friendship, reduce anxiety and increase feelings of security. Their care builds a consistent pattern which is very helpful during times of emotional distress. They are specifically trained to alert to and interrupt certain dangerous behaviors. Although they have basic training demonstrating protective behaviors when a threat is detected, they are not, by any means, security dogs.

"You two have met, yes?" I ask, smiling and waving a hand between their screens.

Charlie laughs. "Yes. But what if we hadn't? We really need to work on your social skills."

Hannah smiles too but doesn't say anything. It's a genuine smile, though, and that's what matters.

"You're not the first to point it out, but I'm not worried as I have no plans to compete in Miss USA or meet the Queen any time soon." I grin. "Before we get started, I want to talk about what these dogs can do for you and what they can't, okay? There are three different types of 'working' dogs: therapy dogs, emotional support dogs, and service dogs. Therapy dogs and service dogs are both certified after completing training. Emotional support dogs are not. All three are useful and provide valuable and important support for humans. There's a fourth type of canine partner–security dogs. They, too, provide valuable and important support, but your dogs will not be trained for those duties."

Both Charlie and Hannah are tracking so far.

"Therapy dogs are trained to be comfortable with human behavior like repeated touching from many different people, for example, or having a child hang on their neck. They are canine volunteers who go into specific settings like senior centers or schools, or courtrooms and provide comfort to folks. Then, they go home with their human handler." I pause and take a sip of coffee.

"Emotional support dogs–and ducks, and ferrets–are not specifically trained, but they still provide an invaluable service by comforting their person and providing companionship. Security dogs are often used in the military or law enforcement, and they have very specific, very intense training. They can be good family members, too, but their primary job is safety. But that's not what we're after. Questions so far?"

Two heads shake negative.

"Which brings us to our pups, who will be trained to provide specific service to help us when we are in physical or psychological need. I've chatted with each of you privately. We've discussed your triggers, manifestations, and mental and physical health issues that might require the aid and intervention of your canine bestie. Once we get the basics down, I'll be working with each dog so they are fully equipped to support each of you. Then, after they're ready, we'll train you, as well."

Charlie laughs. "I've got 'stay' down."

"I give a mean high-five," Hannah offers. She's so far out of her normal shell I hardly recognize her. Winnie is going to be life-changing. Getting ahead of myself. Assuming she chooses Winnie.

"Let's get to the good part. You see this pile of snoring fur behind me?" I tilt the laptop to give a better view. Chonk is on the bottom, his blackness nearly absorbed into the dark brown leather recliner. Winnie is sprawled across him, her almost hairless pink belly up, legs spread in a very unladylike manner. "The hussy is Winnie, and her support fellow is Chonk."

Hannah laughs. "Chonk? So mean."

I hold up a finger in a "wait a minute" sign. Next, I move the rolling table to a safe position across the room and adjust the laptop to face into the room. Then I wake the sleeping beasts by calling their names. Winnie yawns and stretches, wiggling this way and that, still laying belly-up across her friend. Chonk pushes out from under her and slides down to the polished concrete floor. Winnie follows, doing an elaborate series of yoga-like stretches as if she knows she has an audience.

Once she's done with her warm-up, I ask them to sit, and they comply instantly. I feel a warm glow of pride. "Chonk and Winnie are both about five months old. He's Cane Corso and pit; she's a wholly unique blend all her own. I'm going to ask them to do a few things so you can get a feel for their physicality."

I run them through a series of down, stay, wait. I demonstrate "up" to get them on the couch and "off" to get them down. They take turns staying while the other heels, which is typically hard for puppies, but they're both brilliant at it. For the finale, I demonstrate Winnie's unique skill. "Winnie, sing!"

She begins to howl like it's her job, so proud of herself I can't help grinning. There's no rhyme nor reason to her *a-wooing*, but it's very entertaining and only a little bit hard on the ears. The most impressive part is when I say, "Winnie, stop!" and she does.

As I'd hoped, Hannah falls into giggles.

"Damn." Charlie grunts. "Chonk, my man, you better have some amazing talent to compete with that."

"Winnie is pretty cool." I smile. "She enjoys being the center of attention. But she's also very smart, and very kind. She understands when it's okay to be a diva and when she needs to pay attention and cooperate."

I release the pups from their sits and let them know they're free to play. Winnie immediately begins to play bow to Chonk, who is more interested in the collection of toys in a wooden box by the door to the residence. He ignores her as she chews on his ear.

"Chonk does have an amazing talent. He is an empath. I didn't realize dogs can be empathetic, but it makes sense. It's hard to tell on the screen, but his eyes have to be seen to be believed. I'll get a photo and send it." I pull the laptop back and sit in the recliner, pointing the camera so Charlie and Hannah can watch the pups. "What do you think?"

"I would love to have Winnie," Hannah says quickly as if she's afraid if she doesn't speak up, she'll lose her.

"Excellent! Chonk is exactly the kind of wingman I need." Charlie grins. "I might change his name, though. Something a bit more dignified. Spencer."

I'm sad that Chonk won't stay Chonk, but he's not my dog. "Spencer, it is."

Hannah makes a sound that's remarkably like a delighted squeal. "Good, I'm glad these kiddos will work out." *Work out?* Hannah is beaming. I've never seen her look happy before, and it makes *me* happy. "Next steps: I'll train them in the more advanced basics, and then–" and the words come out of my mouth before my brain realizes the thought was even there, "I'd like you both to come to my place, and we'll spend a week working together to get you comfortable with them."

It's a great idea, and I'm not upset I said it, just surprised. I've never invited anyone to Stargazer. It's time. This is the perfect reason to bring people to my home.

"If you're willing, of course," I say for Hannah's benefit because she's not comfortable going out in the world just yet. Maybe Winnie will change that.

"I'm willing!" She grins and claps her hands. "Thank you, Angel. Thank you!"

For the hundredth time, I think dogs are miracles in fursuits.

CHAPTER TWENTY-TWO

NICK

When Peter's son, Ben, accepted a position at a DC nonprofit after college, I promised Peter I'd look after him. I also promised Ben I wouldn't be in his business all the time. Our agreement is that Ben and I get together for pick up basketball and greasy food once a month.

He's lived here for years and has never once required my assistance. He's a grown man, and he doesn't need anyone watching over him. But our friendship is solid, so we've kept the tradition going.

Ben's three-bedroom row house is in Logan Circle. It's a spendy neighborhood full of properties listed on the National Register of Historic Places, surrounded by art and great food and drinks. It's a twenty-minute car or train ride to his office.

As a lowly FBI agent, my budget doesn't allow me to live in such swank. Ben likes to remind me his salary doesn't either. Baden family money allows him to live so close to his office. He pays it forward by providing two of his coworkers with affordable housing in an area they could never touch otherwise. Ben is a good kid. Strike that. A good man.

My FBI salary affords me a two-bedroom rented townhouse in Georgetown. I really don't need the second bedroom, but it was the only place I liked. And it gives me somewhere to store my stash of superhero collectibles. Maybe someday, I'll actually unpack them and create a display. Someday. The townhouse is just a couple of blocks from the Potomac, and I have a nice little deck where I can watch the sunsets when I'm home, which isn't often.

On mate nights, as we call them, Ben and I join a pickup game at a community center and then grab dinner at one of the many excellent restaurants in his neighborhood.

I really look forward to these get-togethers.

We pop into his place to change from grimy, sweaty athletes into gentlemen of the District.

"Have you talked to Ang lately?" Ben tugs an artisan cabled sweater over his dark head. He's not the gangly teenager I met twelve years ago. He's a guy who works out and dresses well. He's a Baden, after all.

I slide my arms into the sleeves of my leather jacket. It's May, and it's still a little chilly. Summer hasn't sunk her teeth into us yet. "She called on her way back from New Mexico. She'd just picked up a couple of pups."

Ben zips up his workout bag. "I'm thinking about asking her to help me find a dog."

"I'm sure she'd love to. She lives for it. I'm convinced she likes canines better than she likes us humans." I laugh. We head out to the street. "Where are we going for dinner?"

He smiles shyly. "I was thinking Le Diplomate."

I stop in my tracks. "Are we celebrating something? Not our usual burger and fries kinda dive."

"Just shut up, and let's go," he's blushing. Something's happening. This is going to be good.

It's not a long walk, but I can tell he's nervous. I wonder if I'm going to finally meet the person he's been seeing. I don't want him to get more anxious, so I distract him. "Have you talked to O? How's she doing? I hardly see her, even when I'm at the Nest."

"We don't talk much," Ben mutters, and instead of looking nervous, he seems uncomfortable.

"Did you have a fight?"

"Nah, nothing like that. We're just... she's not... we just don't have much to talk about, I guess."

Olivia and Ben are normal siblings to my outsider view. They may not be in each other's business like my sister Dru and I, but Dru wasn't kidnapped. They didn't spend most of their formative years in foster homes like we did, which is probably why we're so close.

"Sorry, man. Sisters are a pain in the ass, but they're also kind of cool to have."

We arrive at Le Diplomate, and Ben pauses on the sidewalk. He smiles nervously. "Don't be an asshole."

I jokingly rub my hands together with maniacal glee. He glares. I sigh. "Fine. I'll try to behave."

He leads the way onto the plant-laden outdoor patio. I see a coworker, a newer agent I've found to be intelligent and ambitious, and tip my head in hello. "Hey, Alex."

Alex looks surprised. "Hey, Nick. What are -"

Ben is staring at us, and he doesn't look happy. "How do you two know each other?"

"We work together," I say.

Alex pales.

Ben turns an angry red.

I'm confused. "What did I say?"

"You liar. You goddamn liar." Ben's hands are clenched at his sides.

Alex has gone from pale to gray.

"Please, someone catch me up. What's happening?" I've figured out Alex is the guy Ben wanted me to meet. But why is Ben so pissed off? Aha. Alex didn't tell Ben he works for the FBI. I can't think of a good reason to keep it a secret, and now I'm tense on Ben's behalf. "Alex, what's the deal, man?"

Ben shakes his head and holds up a hand. "I don't want to hear it. I don't want to know. For fuck's sake. You know... we've talked...

I've told you... and you lied. I'm going home. I'll pack your stuff up and put a box on the steps."

He's gone.

I'm left staring at my coworker. "Seriously, Alex, what the fuck."

CHAPTER TWENTY-THREE

ANGEL

Spencer has morphed from a chunky chonk of black coal into a sleek panther. He's already taller, slimmer, and more muscular; his rolls of puppy pudge melted away. While his body develops, so has his brain. He is highly attuned to everything going on around him. I can't wait to watch him live up to his potential.

When I went through my own training, I watched a dog recognize his owner was about to have a seizure. The dog alerted her by nosing her hand multiple times, and when she ignored him, he jumped up and encouraged her to sit on the ground. Then he laid across her lap. The seizure had begun by the time she was down, and he was across her. He stayed on top of her until the seizures ended, then went to get help.

Dogs are amazing. As the saying goes, we really don't deserve them.

I worked with Spence–I can't seem to call him by his full name–on deep pressure therapy this morning, known as DPT. Service dogs can be taught to recognize the onset of certain mental and physical conditions in their humans, even before they are actively happening. Once they sense the condition coming on–for example, a seizure, low blood sugar, or a change in heart rhythm–they can apply pressure to specific parts of their person's body. Pressure has been proved to relieve emotional and physical distress. Charlie confessed he has occasional episodes where he disassociates, so DPT will be an essential component in keeping him safe.

Winnie and I are working on distraction. It's a three-step process. First, I teach her the action I want from her. For example, I want her to poke my leg or hand with her nose. Second, I want to name the behavior of poking her nose—in this case, I'll call it "Calm." And third, I want to connect the prescribed action on her part with a behavior on my part.

Hannah says she scratches herself when she's upset, often until she bleeds. This is a common PTSD behavior. When Winnie has learned the Calm routine, she'll recognize when Hannah is scratching, and she'll interrupt the behavior. She'll use her nose to poke, or if Hannah does not stop, she'll insert her snout between Hannah's hands and the part of her body she's scratching. Winnie can't ask politely and give up if Hannah ignores her. I want her to continue to interrupt the negative behavior until it stops.

Fortunately for all of us, not all training happens in the barn. Some of our work is to learn how to be part of a pack, whether it's me and four other dogs or just one human and one dog. This kind of training is relationship building, and it's best done in various environments. Since we're on my property, completely fenced, we don't need leashes. Expectations will be modeled by Nope and Asa. I tuck my phone in the back pocket of my jeans, throw on a light hoodie, and attach a plastic water bottle to the ugly fanny pack that goes everywhere I go on the property.

"Walk!" One minute they're napping, the next the pups are bouncing off Nope and Asa like popping kernels of corn.

I open the sliding door to the patio, and they all charge out. Nope and Asa are great with them, engaging in the rough and tumble, correcting when someone gets too nippy or doesn't maintain established boundaries. I don't have to worry about any of them running off. I chose Winnie and Chonk—er, Spence—in part because they passed a simple test to assess whether they wanted to be part of the pack, which they do. They do not yearn for independence, so I don't need to worry about them running off and not returning. Giving them space to explore will build their confidence. They'll return with a simple recall, happy to rejoin the rest of the pack and me.

It's a perfect day, with tiny white clouds dotting the bright blue sky. There will be lots of stars tonight. I can talk to Bud and tell him about the puppies.

I love my home. It's the place I'm happiest and feel most myself.

I remember the very first time I saw Stargazer. I'd been exploring Utah, deciding whether this was the place I wanted to settle in. Peter suggested Colorado or Northern California, but I wanted a little more breathing room. Colorado is surprisingly busy. Moab is, too, but in a different way.

When I first saw Stargazer, I was headed south on Highway 191 to take the pups for a hike. A cheap garage sale sign had been repurposed with the word "garage" crossed out and the word "for" on top of it.

There wasn't a gate, or a fence, at the time. Just a red dirt road. I decided that if I quickly found the sign on the way back to town after our hike, we'd swing in and take a look. I swear that sign increased 4x in size. Not really, of course, but it jumped right out at me. I made a left across the highway and put the Bronco in park.

"Whatcha think, kids? Should we look see what's up the hill?" Nope and Asa were both awake and interested, surveying the land around us. I took that as a yes, and we headed up the path. The drive was a bit of a snake, and I could see why. There were–and still are–spots that are obviously washed gulleys. The track was made to avoid as many of those as possible.

The incline was sufficient that we couldn't see what was around the next curve. Yucca, pinyon, and juniper shared space with boulders and more prominent rocky outcroppings. It was so damn peaceful. Birds love this land. I rolled down all the windows so we could enjoy the concert.

Roughly five hundred yards up the road, we arrived at a level spot. Someone must have started the work to put a building here. The rocks and boulders had been removed, and there was a blank slate of land big enough for a house and outbuildings. It was ringed with trees, but the trees were not so dense you couldn't see through them. That would have been a true crime. Because Mother Nature really showed her talents here.

At the time, I had never been to the Grand Canyon. Later I realized that Utah has much of the same geography, just in smaller batches. From the flat land of Stargazer, you have a nearly 360-degree view of one of the most glorious parts of Utah.

Eventually I learned the Colorado River is the property's western boundary. A public access road marks the southern end, and another private property the north. Highway 191 is the eastern marker. It is 140 acres of perfection.

I bought the land with Peter's help and Alfred's money. I found a company that offered pre-designed post and beam barn structures and, within a few months, had my dream building up and livable. Half of the space is my residence, and the other half is for vehicles and dog training. There's a loft that runs down the center of the second floor, and it's already plumbed. Someday I may convert that into official guest bedrooms if I decide I like company.

For me, it's perfect.

We head up the hill now, following red clay tracks through the pinyon trees and Utah juniper. As we near the crest, there are blue, green, and red hills and valleys as far as the eye can see. The red tones of my little barn home blend into the landscape. Tree skeletons mark the soil, reminding us this land has been here much longer than we humans.

Nope pauses to dig at some intriguing scent, her two front paws shoveling dirt out behind while she balances on her single back leg.

Spencer comes to investigate and offers an assist. I step out of the way to avoid being showered in red dust.

"Asa! What ya see?" I call to my eldest, who has clambered onto an outcropping of rock and is grinning down at us. Winnie is trying to follow him, but she hasn't quite got the height or the brawn yet to propel herself up the slick rock face. Asa comes down and playfully nips her as he passes. I imagine him teasing, "Shorty too short!"

I decide to check the fence line to ensure there are no gaps to provide entry to unwanted animals, four-legged or two. One hundred forty acres used to sound like a lot to me, but it's not as big as it sounds. Because the back of the property is bordered by a canyon and the Colorado River, that portion isn't fenced, but the other three sides are. The only other building on the property is a small hunter's hut, ten by ten, just big enough for a sleeping bag and supplies. I keep the door closed with a slip-lock so animals don't get inside and make a mess. As we pass, the pups explore the shallow porch, a single step off the ground. There's a heap of bones on the old wooden porch. Something small, a squirrel or a rabbit, died here. No blood, probably natural causes. Winnie grabs a piece of the skeleton and tosses it gleefully in the air. She looks so sweet, but she's a warrior.

Pausing for investigation, playtime, and navigating various terrains, walking the perimeter takes two hours. I find a couple of spots where the fence needs to be repaired, but nothing major.

Until we're near the front gate. An L of chain link is lifted up and pulled away from the bottom pipe nailed into the soil. Maybe an animal dug under and messed with the fence on the way through. But it's enough of a gap that a slender human could wiggle under if they wanted to.

An image of the guy at the grocery store comes to mind. I'll be getting that fixed ASAP.

While we're at the gate, I grab the mail. The mailbox is a metal bin like one of the blue boxes in front of post offices. There's a slot for regular mail on the public side of the fence, similar to where you'd drop your Christmas cards. Below, there's a larger area for packages that requires a key to unlock. UPS, FedEx, and the postal carrier have keys. On my side, I open the box with a numeric keypad. The door gives me access to all the contents at once. Today there are a handful of envelopes, two small packages that are probably books, and a couple of magazines. It's a surprisingly robust haul.

Back at the house, the canines claim favorite spots to nap. I start thinking about dinner. When I toss the mail on the breakfast bar, one of the envelopes catches my eye. My name and address are printed by hand, and the colorful envelope looks handmade. There's no return address. I know I shouldn't open it; of course, I shouldn't. Have I learned nothing in ten-plus years being a pinup girl for Alfred's fans? And yet my stupid misbehaving fingers pull the paper apart anyway.

There are three Polaroids. Each has a different Barbie doll body posed in a violent position, with lots of creatively placed blood and tiny weapons tearing apart her plastic self. Barbie's head is missing... and my face has been pasted where it ought to be.

What the fuck.

CHAPTER TWENTY-FOUR

NICK

As I pull into a parking spot, I think, I hate LA. The traffic and the sprawl are just too much. Of course, some might say DC is just as bad, and I can't argue, but at least when you're talking to a bartender in the District, there's minimal risk they'll slide you their script or headshots.

I'm savoring my first bite of pastrami ten minutes later, and I change my tune. "Please never move the Foundation from LA." We have good delis in DC, but not like this. Canter's is deservedly famous for its food and its atmosphere. There's even a bar–the Kibitz Room–in the back.

Peter laughs and wipes a dab of mustard from his chin with his thumb. "Won't happen, I promise. I assume we're going across the street to Du-Par for pie after, yeah?"

I make an "Um, yeah," face. I'm not going to stop chewing to use actual words.

We finish our sandwiches in silence, then lean back into the seats, full and happy. I'm nerdy enough to wonder if any of my favorite actors or musicians have warmed the seats of this particular booth. "More people should eat pastrami. They'd be happier. Happy people don't do asshole things." I sigh.

"Agree," Peter grins. He smiles his thanks at a server who whisks away the dirty dishes and napkins. Then he turns his laser sights on me. He adopts a terrible British accent. "You're probably wondering why I've asked you here..."

I tip back my cream soda, draining the glass. "Well, not really..."

"You're blowing my bit." He chides.

"Sorry." I grin. "Continue."

Peter sighs dramatically. "Fine. As you know, we've talked for a while about adding an investigative arm to the Komo team."

Oh. It's time for *the* talk. I nod.

"We're getting to the point where we need to take action, stop talking about it. We've got great connections in the various organizations, thanks to you. And we've got some solid private folks on the payroll. It feels to me, though, that we need something more organized. Right now, it's a bit of information here, a contact there. There's no coordination. No structure. No strategy."

I nod again. I'm good at waiting.

"And, there's another thing." Peter scratches his chin. "You know, Chuck McNamara, and I go back." Chuck is an Inspector's Aid, my boss's boss's boss. "He's given me a head's up that there's some discomfort with your relationship with the Foundation. There's concern it's a conflict of interest.

That doesn't surprise me. If I look at my situation with a clear lens, I can see how it might look like I'm serving two masters. "Okay. Is this concern career-threatening? Or just 'keep an eye on things'?"

"I don't know. But he believes we're nearing a time where you'll be told to make a choice," Peter says, looking me straight in the eye. He's not the prevaricating type. He also values our friendship and would never try to push me to do what's best for him.

"So..." I say, prompting him to say aloud what I know is on his mind.

"So... It won't be a secret that I believe you're the right man for the job. I can't think of anyone who would be a better fit, serve the needs of the organization, or get the same level of personal satisfaction from the work." He smiles at the server, who pauses to refill his iced tea. Always showing gratitude, my friend Peter. "I also know that being in the FBI was a dream from when you were a kid, and it wasn't easy to get where you are. You may well not be ready to give that up just yet."

"It was everything to me when I was a kid," I agree. "I don't think I'd have survived those first few years after our parents died if I wasn't already plotting how to join the FBI." I smile at the memory. "I was Billy Batson. Orphaned, living in a foster home. I knew superheroes aren't real, but the FBI is pretty darned close. That knowledge gave me something to fight for."

"SHAZAM!" Peter grins. "Maybe it's time for a superhero at the Foundation."

"The Baden Foundation already has more superheroes than the Justice League."

Peter smiles at the compliment, but I'm serious. He continues. "Of course, we can talk out the details, but you know you'd set your own terms—salary, benefits, whatever you need to be satisfied and secure your future. You'd be creating the job, so that's up to you. You'd decide your staffing needs and do the hiring with your own budget. You'd be part of the Foundation board and leadership, not just Komo. You can live in Virginia if that's where you're happy. Honestly, you can live anywhere you want. Although only LA has Canter's and Du-Par's."

I laugh at that. I'm not sure what I'm feeling. This isn't exactly a surprise. It's just come sooner than I had expected. Maybe sooner than I'd hoped. I'm not forty. I figured I'd be in the FBI at least until my fifties. I have my sights set on Headquarters Supervisor. Does a title matter? Or does the work matter? My paycheck would go up significantly at the Foundation, regardless of what Peter says about setting my own terms. Whatever I tell him, he'll double or triple. The idea of living "anywhere" is kind of exciting. Or, perhaps, living nowhere for a while, traveling, seeing the world. I don't know. It requires some thought. A lot of thought. Maybe a call with Dru, my sister, to get her bossy opinion. "What're you thinking about for timing?"

"I guess I'd like to have someone in place by the beginning of the year, but it's only May. So there's no rush," Peter responds. He signs the credit card slip and puts his wallet in his back pocket. "Pie?"

"Pie." I nod and squeeze out of the booth. "Can we walk over? I need to work off a little pastrami first."

CHAPTER TWENTY-FIVE

ANGEL

I've lived in Utah for five years and have never had reason to visit the Moab police department. I resent that I have to now. Stubborn I may be, but stupid I am not. Shrugging this off would definitely make me stupid.

The man at the front desk points to chairs against the opposite wall and tells me someone will be with me shortly.

While I wait, I contact the only fence company in town and set up an appointment to repair the fence. It will be a couple of weeks, but it will be done before Charlie and Hannah arrive.

A very young officer comes through a side door, his black uniform as neat and tidy as if he were preparing for inspection. He's probably one of the newer LEOs. He looks cautiously optimistic, probably hoping I'm here about something more interesting than to make a barking dog complaint. "Hello! How can I help?"

"My name is Angel Evanston." I stand and give him my address. "I have fenced acres where I live and train service dogs. I've never had any issues, but yesterday I found these in my mailbox. I'm sorry, I opened the envelope, not realizing what it was." I hand him the colorful envelope with its contents.

He steps over to the counter and nods at the officer behind the plexiglass. He slips on gloves and carefully removes the photos from the envelope. His eyes widen in surprise. Definitely not a barking dog complaint. "Do you have any idea who might have left these? Is there some meaning to the photos?"

I'm always uncomfortable when I have to tell my story. Thankfully it doesn't come up often. "When I was fourteen, a man abducted me and held me captive in a place he called the Dollhouse. While I was there, he forced me to recreate photos from his family's photo album. Polaroid photos, sometimes. I would guess this is probably related."

The officer looks unsure. He would've been my age when it happened, so he was probably not sitting around watching crime news. "You can look him up. Alfred—er, Edward Stanhope."

"That would have been a difficult experience. Was Stanhope caught? Is he alive?"

I nod. "He's in Florence, Colorado." The country's only federal supermax prison.

"Doubtful he escaped from there," the officer smiles half-heartedly.

"It's probably a fan. He has a whole club, as they all seem to."

The officer nods. "It's definitely a possibility. Have you had run-ins with his fans before?"

"Lots in LA, but not here. Recently an employee at the City Mart hinted he might be one." I describe the encounter. "Very few people know where I live, even generally. Most people seem to believe I live in LA with the man who was my guardian after everything happened. I'm fortunate. He has a team that protects me from all the crazies. They handle all media inquiries and filter the bad stuff. The fact this showed up in my home mailbox in Utah really caught me off guard."

"I'm sure it did more than catch you off guard," the officer says. "Since you didn't see him drop these off, I can't do much. We don't know that it's the City Mart guy since there's no evidence connecting him. I'll arrange to patrol out your way a little bit more often. You let us know if anything else happens—telephone hang-ups, drive-bys -"

"I did see him on the road across from my gate! I'd nearly

forgotten." I slap the counter in my excitement. "It was a few days before the photos came, so I didn't think about it until now. I was turning into my drive, coming back from New Mexico. He was parked across the road, staring at me."

"And you're sure it was the man from the grocery store?"

I nod. "He has very distinctive hair—curly, dark, thick—and a strong nose."

"Okay. I can at least talk to him. We can also see if there are prints on the photos or envelope. Do you mind leaving yours so we can eliminate them?"

"Sure, although they're already in the system from the Dollhouse." Oklahoma pops into my head, and I say wryly, "And maybe one other time." Not sure I want to share that story since there's a not-so-great officer involved.

He looks at me sideways. "Connected to this?"

"No, a separate incident. When you look me up, you'll find out about that, too." I'm embarrassed, and it makes me angry. I didn't do anything wrong. I stopped a crazy sheriff so he couldn't abduct, rape, torture, and hunt more innocent women. But it reminds me where I go, trouble follows.

CHAPTER TWENTY-SIX

OLIVIA

The Foundation offices are part of the Nest, a small compound Dad bought after the various Dollhouse trials were finally over. With all the new 'family members' we've acquired in recent years, the Westwood house wasn't large enough. More importantly, the Nest is in a gated part of the Palos Verdes Peninsula, at the southern end of Los Angeles. Twenty-four-hour security makes Dad feel better and keeps the damned paparazzi mostly at bay.

The house is a beautiful Italianate villa set back a quarter-mile from the road. It's perched on a sloping hill above the Portuguese Bend Reserve below. A series of covered patios provide views of the coastline from Long Beach north to Santa Monica Bay. Angel uses a pool house when she's here, further enabling her insistence on being alone. There's a full-sized, fully equipped gym on the backside of the barn that stables Grace's beloved horse.

Although we have a suite at the Nest, Christopher and I have our own home in Laurel Canyon, close to the studio where my show is recorded and closer to his offices in Century City. I pop down to see Dad often—well, not exactly 'pop.' It's an hour drive each way at 6 am on a Sunday and a two-hour drive the rest of the week. No complaints here; the time in my car is often the only time I'm alone with my thoughts.

I park my SUV between Marnie's Subaru hybrid and Dad's Jeep. Dr. Lisa's sexy pearly white Tesla is off to the side. Only Grace's Mazda is missing. She and Rosie should be in school.

And then there are the Komo offices.

Komorebi means "light through the trees." The meaning was significant when Dad hired the architect to build the Foundation space. The result is a circular building sited in a grove of jacaranda trees. The trees bloom with gorgeous lavender flowers from April to June, and they're right at their prime now.

Inside the building is basically a donut cut into five equal pieces. The first slice is the entry, with a kitchenette and doors to restrooms on one side. Dad commissioned a mural on the opposite wall.

The other four slices are offices. Marnie's is comfortable and inviting. Dr. Lisa is artsy and colorful and full of dog toys for her pup Gustopher, a beautiful lug of a beagle that keeps the Komo crew entertained with his antics. Dad's is full of books and TV monitors and is always a mess. The last office is empty but for a desk and chair. That's where Nick works when he's in town, and I often borrow it. A large conference room fills the hole in the donut's center, accessible from each of the rooms surrounding it. All of the interior walls are glass, an ode to transparency. The exterior walls are mostly glass, but steel beams hold the glass in place. This is earthquake-prone Southern California, after all. Reflective screening on the exterior windows ensures what's happening inside stays private.

Dad, Marnie, and Dr. Lisa are huddled in the conference room. Nick was in town yesterday–I don't know whether he's still using his desk, so I slip into Dad's office to wait. There's a pile of stuff on his guest chairs, so I drop into his seat. He spots me and winks. I smile and make a childish face at him. He grins and returns his attention to the work. Dr. Lisa is drawing on the glass with a dry erase marker.

Dad's monitor background is a photo of the whole family–Dad, Marnie, Christopher, me, Ben, Susie, Grace, Rosie, and Angel–standing on the patio with the Pacific behind us. I remember that day. It was around Christmas last year. Nick and CB and Emily were here too. I'm sure there's a similar photo with them included.

As far as Peter Baden is concerned, we are all his family.

I jiggle the mouse to move the screensaver and web browser, but his inbox opens instead. It was not my intention. He's in the midst of an email to Nick, so I guess he's gone. I tell myself Dad might lose the email if I close the window. But really...

They're talking about Angel. I skim quickly because I don't want to invade Dad's privacy, but I can't seem to stop myself. After I've got the gist, I minimize the screen without closing it and go to the search engine to complete my original task. Except I can't remember what I was going to look up.

My gaze pulls to the right. The view out the window is a sea of lavender jacaranda flowers against a perfect blue sky, the paler blue of the Pacific in the distance. Beautiful, but so dull. I feel like I'm meant for a wilder place, a rougher place. The coast of Ireland. Or Nova Scotia. Or some undiscovered island off the coast of South America.

My thoughts are pulled back to Dad's email to Nick.

They found something at Tiffany's death scene, and now they're going back to look for the same symbol at the site of Kait's suicide. The implication is they aren't, in fact, suicides. I'm not sure how to feel about this discovery.

In the second part of the message, Dad asks Nick for suggestions about getting Angel to come to the Nest since she's resisted so far. I very much want to see Nick's response.

Angel is really starting to anger me. I understand she enjoys being a rebel and takes pride in calling herself a hermit. But she's part of a family. You don't get to ignore your family. It's especially irksome because I know she talks to CB, talks to Nick, and I'm sure she chats to Ben. Ben is *my* brother. I've had to accept all the other people into my family, but he's the one who is really mine.

I seem to be the only one not worth Angel's time.

Angel can't stay in the damn desert training dogs forever. She's acting like a child yet again, even though we're in our late twenties, just a year apart. I've been an adult since I was 12. She's been a child forever. I don't think she'll change unless someone forces her.

Some of the things Jimmy and I talked about that night were directly relevant to Angel, and I don't mean his crush on her. What kind of a life is it to spend your days and nights alone on a patch of land in the middle of nowhere with animals as your only company? She can't be truly happy. She can't be satisfied. She's lying to herself. There has to be more to life to make it worth living.

Jimmy made it clear he believes he's the key to her happiness, although he didn't come right out and say the words. The only thing I'm absolutely sure of is he is not Angel's solution. I don't want to crush his dreams. He'll figure it out, eventually, one way or another.

CHAPTER TWENTY-SEVEN

PETER

I don't think I've ever been this exhausted in my entire life. I fall backward onto the bed, and Marnie groans when my weight shifts the mattress. "Sorry."

"Are we dead? If not, can we be, just for a few minutes? I'm so tired." She draws out the last word.

Twelve young girls. Ten parents. Six cirque professionals. Two days of setup. Dozens of pieces of equipment. Caterers. Enough sugar to fuel a jet.

So much 'squeeing.'

Tank performs his own version of acrobatics, jumping from a pouf to the bench at the foot of the bed onto the mattress, and the movement caused by his five pounds sets off a twinge in my left hip.

"I'm afraid we're alive. It couldn't possibly hurt so much otherwise." I try to roll onto my stomach, but I can't. "Whose idea was it for us to get involved? Weren't we just supposed to witness the awesomeness?"

"Not mine, doll," Marnie laughs and then groans again. "Parts of my body I'm unfamiliar with are complaining."

"Same." This time I make it onto my stomach. The back of my knees are sore, probably from hanging upside down from a trapeze.

"Did you put the girls away?" Marnie asks.

"I locked them in their suite," I confirm enthusiastically. They're in the suite, but there's no locking. Grace and two of her friends are in charge of the twelve younger girls. I expect chaos and more of that terrible squeeing. Please, no more squeeing.

"Pain aside, it was fun," Marnie says as if she's trying to convince herself.

"Fun. Uh-huh." I grimace.

"Rosie is good. Scary good. She was hanging from those silk ropes like she was born in the circus."

"Well, in a way..." I joke.

Marnie smacks me. I can't help noticing how fantastic her legs look in the hot pink leggings Rosie insisted they wear. Sadly, I'm too tired to do anything but admire. "She wasn't kidding when she asked for a permanent pole in the gym."

I try to shrug, but it hurts. "Like you said, she's good at it. I'm all about encouraging them to do the things that make them feel good. We need to put in one of those squishy floors, though, if she falls."

"You're a good man, Peter Baden," Marnie says, stroking my hair.

"Ouch," I grumble.

"Sorry." She pats my hand. "Hey, serious talk for a minute. Are you worried about copycats? This is two suicides in just a couple of weeks. We've never had even one before. What's changing? Do we need to do something? Say something beyond offering our condolences? I feel like we should have a plan. At the very least, a conversation."

I reach for her hand and give it a squeeze. "You're right. I asked Lisa about it this afternoon before the shenanigans began, and she agrees. We need to open dialog with both Promise and Hope. The idea that any of our people are feeling hopeless to the point of suicide is unacceptable. Whatever we need to do to let them know they're not alone, they have support, we can find solutions together. As worried as I am about copycats, I'm just as concerned for the families. They must be terrified. I am. I'll confess; I'm a little worried about our girls. I don't want to forget about the families in this."

"I'll work with Lisa to get something set up," Marnie says. "Now, wiggle your fine acrobatic ass over here. I don't have the energy to fool around but maybe in my dreams."

CHAPTER TWENTY-EIGHT

ANGEL

I've trained dogs in stress assessment before. This was a vital skill for Emily's dog, White, to learn. It's been a while, though, so I'm watching a few videos to see if there's anything new and refresh my memory. Winnie, in particular, will need this skill.

A small ping alerts me that someone from Komo has opened a chat window. I hover my mouse over the small icon and see Hannah's name. Perfect timing. She's such a good kid! It's been fun the last few weeks to watch her coming out of her shell.

"Hi! How's Idowa?" I tease, adding a laughing emoji to confirm that I realize Idaho and Iowa are two different states.

She responds with a raspberry emoji, then types, "It's good. I wish spring would stick the landing, though. We had snow again last night. How's Winnie?"

If Winnie could type, Hannah would've bypassed me altogether. I'm not offended. Well, not very. "She's good. Want to say hi?" I don't need to see her response. I call Winnie's name, and she yawns and hops down off the couch. She presses against my leg before I lift her onto my lap and face her toward the laptop. I click on the Video icon in our chatbox and suddenly see myself and Winnie the wonderful. Hannah's video opens onto the screen, and we're side by side.

"Winnie!" Hannah beams, and the pup grins back at her, her little butt wiggling. She already knows this is her human, and she's pleased to see her. "She's getting so big! I didn't realize dogs grow so quickly."

I hold up one of Winnie's paws for Hannah's viewing pleasure. Winnie allows this, which is an excellent sign. "I'm guessing, looking at her tootsies, she'll be in the 40 to the 50-pound range when she's done growing."

"Perfect!" Hannah says. "Thank you for letting me see her."

"Any time!" I grin and let Winnie scrabble back to the floor. She immediately goes to pester Nope. "I was going to email you and Charlie–I still will, but I'll give you the details while we're talking, in case you have any questions. It's nothing personal, but I don't tell people where I live. Big trust issues. Obviously, I'm moving past that because you both are coming... but we're going to take it slow. You already know the dates. Peter will arrange your flights and get you the specific information the day before. I hope you understand."

"I do. I really do." Hannah nods. "I'm so nervous about everything. I'm even nervous about coming to see you! I mean, I talk to you all the time. I know you're not dangerous. I know Charlie's not dangerous. But I'm still nervous. It's so stupid. I hate being this way."

"It's not stupid. It's smart to be cautious. We've been through things. We know what people can do. There's no shame in paying attention to the world around you." I believe those words. Maybe someday we'll both be able to move around and trust more freely. Time to change the subject. "How are things? You okay besides snow?"

Hannah pauses a moment, her long strawberry blond hair falling in a curtain across her face. "I'm a little bit scared, if I'm honest. About Kait and Tiffany. Why? Why are they doing this? They seem to be doing okay. Maybe not great, sure, but okay."

I've been thinking similar thoughts. "I don't know. I'm with you; it's scary and strange. I would never have guessed Kait would do something like this, even though she's got–she had–significant physical damage. Tiffany? Maybe. She always seemed a little bit dark. But it surprises me we didn't have any hints this was coming."

Neither of us says anything for a minute. Eventually, I ask, "Have you talked to Dr. Lisa? Have you told her you're scared?"

"She's nice, and I like her a lot, but I'm worried if I even admit I'm scared, they'll get all freaked out and put me under locked guard or something," she half-smiles at that, and so do I, because we both know she's not wrong. After you've been through something as we have, the people who love you can sometimes go on extra-cautious alert. I'd guess it's part of why Ben moved across the country, even though he was not abducted. Peter definitely has moments of being over-careful. Hannah gives me a look. "What about you? Have you talked to Dr. Lisa? Or... would you ever...?"

I realize what she's asking and shake my head emphatically. "No! No. After Bud died, I've felt like I owe it to him to live a good life for both of us. I'm pretty happy most of the time. No one is happy all the time. Except maybe Olivia because she controls everything happening around her." We both grin. "Truly, I promise I would not take my own life."

She nods, and I feel as though we've just made an agreement. But I want to confirm it. "If you ever start feeling like things are too much, you know you can talk to me, right? I won't judge; I won't freak out. We'll just talk about it, figure it out. Or not. You just have to accept and live with some things, and that's okay too. Deal?"

Hannah nods again. "Yep. I promise. Thanks. Once I have Winnie, I'll feel much better, much stronger. Having someone to care for and talk to will be so good. I'm even planning all the places we'll go once we're together. I don't want to stay in Idowa forever."

"Let's start a petition and change the name officially. Idowa East for corn and pigs and Idowa West for potatoes..."

We chat for another hour, being silly, talking about school, dogs, and favorite books and movies. When we finally disconnect, I'm even more excited for her and Charlie's upcoming visit.

CHAPTER TWENTY-NINE

OLIVIA

Christopher and LouLou are in the pool's shallow end, teaching Susie to swim. She's Buddha in a pink polka dot bikini, rolls of baby pudge gleefully spilling out. LouLou is wearing a yellow bikini that shows her own 'rolls'–hips, breasts, and a slight belly pouch she manages to make sexy. My darling husband, wearing board shorts as he usually does at home, seems clueless to the living, breathing woman in front of him. His focus is on his child. I should join them and read my book in a lounge chair in the shade. I don't move from the sofa.

He's been on my mind a lot lately. Well, not Christopher so much as our relationship. If anyone is going to make me happy in a relationship, it's Christopher. Recently, I've thought perhaps I'm not meant to be coupled. Would I be happier single? Could having no one else to worry about be the magic elixir I've been searching for these past few years? Perhaps instead of thinking a family was the answer, I should have done what Angel's done and stepped away.

I don't know why Christopher puts up with me at all. I'm sure he didn't marry me expecting to be a single father, which is what he's become. Perhaps it would be a kindness for me to leave him. Maybe he'd finally notice LouLou and choose happiness for him and Susie. There's no hope for me. I'm not going to change. This is who and what I am.

I have no delusions about myself. I'm self-centered, bordering on narcissistic. But I work for what I want. I've fought for every success I've had since preschool. I came out of the womb determined to win. I was training for the Olympic tennis team when Alfred stole me from the sidewalk in front of the club where I trained every single day. The damage he did to my body was too significant to resume that dream once we were freed, so I had to find a different outlet.

Initially, I grasped for control, and to me, that meant understanding the mental state that caused Alfred to do the things he's done. I wanted lenses to recognize a bad person coming toward me back then. In learning about mental health, I realized it's all too easy to hide your true self from others if you want. You can even hide from yourself. Some people do terrible things and honestly believe they are meant to do whatever bad thing they're doing.

Three years to earn my undergrad in psychology–although it often takes five–and then I was on track to earn my doctorate. Then Hollywood came calling. I didn't say "yes" to the books and the TV show for my own glory; I believe I can help others by telling my story and sharing the things I've learned. I'm an inspiration and role model to so many.

I have never bothered to finish the degree. There's no need. I've got a solid foundation of book learning and a lifetime of degrees from lived experience. There's nothing anyone can tell me that I haven't learned or understood on my own.

"Hey, beautiful!" Christopher grins as the threesome troop into the house, towels wrapped around wet bodies in various configurations. LouLou has Susie in her arms and is singing her a song. Susie is delighted, as always. She doesn't even notice me.

Christopher dips to kiss my cheek. "How about we get all fancied up and hit the town? Find some excellent sushi, maybe some dancing after?" He wiggles his eyebrows suggestively. "We could even get a suite..."

"Yes! That sounds perfect!" It does. When it's just Christopher and me, things are good enough, and until I decide what's next, good enough is plenty.

CHAPTER THIRTY

ANGEL

"What up, Buttacup?" Ben Baden, international man of doing-of-the-good, has deigned to call me on his telephone!

"Benjo! Banjo! Bingo! How's my favorite bleeding heart?" I hit the pause button on the TV remote, and actress Anna Taylor-Joy is frozen in place after turning to see James McAvoy slip into the driver's seat of her classmate's father's car. He is not the father. Things are about to get complicated.

Some people think it's weird that I love horror movies. They are particularly surprised to learn *Split* is one of my favorites. To me, it's not all that different than vets watching war films.

Two thousand miles away, there's a lot of background noise. Ben is probably walking home from some exciting DC happening. Maybe a newly opened embassy or a cocktail party at the United Nations. His life is much cooler than mine. *He* is much cooler than me. I adore him, so I don't get mad when he says, "Olivia's pissed at you for not responding to her messages."

I roll my eyes and make a rude sound. "Honestly, if she didn't leave so *many* messages, I would be more willing to call her back! Or at least text her. But when she's this intense, I'm sure I don't want to hear whatever she thinks she needs to yell at me about."

"I know. I tried telling her. But she's wound up about something. I'm sure these Hope suicides are freaking her out a little bit. They're freaking everyone out a bit. How're you doing with that?"

"It's bizarre. Neither Kait nor Tiffany seemed the type to kill themselves. Kait was so involved in everything. We called her our den mother. It's hard to accept she was secretly so unhappy she had to end her life that she wouldn't at least talk to someone and look for an alternative before making such a permanent choice." I run a hand over Asa's fur. He sighs in his sleep and pushes closer to me. "Tiffany never seemed to settle the whole time I've known her. I can see how it would get emotionally draining after a while. I don't know. Again, I wish she would have talked with someone first."

Ben makes agreement noises. "Dad and Marnie are worried there will be more."

"Really? I would never have guessed!" I tease. "They think they're being subtle, but they're about as subtle as a meteor crashing to earth." Winnie realizes I'm awake and comes to investigate my sock, which is still on my foot. Sorry, kiddo. No tugging on clothing or body parts. I redirect with an appropriate chew toy, and she settles down to gnaw.

He's quiet for a minute, then asks, "You never have thoughts like that, do you? You'd tell me? Or CB? Or Nick?"

I chuckle, even though it's a serious question deserving of a serious answer. "Heck no. I'm good. Promise." Time to change the subject. "What about you? Are those long, boring nonprofit meetings making you want to do harm to yourself or others?"

"I love my job, smart ass. I'm happy some of my ideas make other people's lives better. "He's trying to sound casual, but I know he means every word. One of the many things I love about Ben. He's richer than God and doesn't need to lift a finger to have anything his little heart desires, so he chooses to spend his time solving problems for people all over the globe.

"I know you do. I know. So, you finally going to tell me about your man meat?" I hoot as the words come out of my mouth because it is not what I meant to say. Well, not exactly. At least not out loud. "I mean, your man. Boyfriend. Love monkey. Whatever you choose to call him and his meat."

"Why the hell do I put up with you?" Ben asks.

"Because you love me?"

"Oh, yeah." Ben is grinning; I can hear it in his voice. He orders something from a street vendor then moves to a quieter spot. "He's good. Well, he was. Then I found out he lied to me."

"Uh oh. How big of a lie?"

"Pretty big. He works for the feds." Ben sounds as though he's learned the guy mows down butterflies for a living. I understand why it's not great he lied about being a federal agent, but it's not *that* bad.

"And? Does being a federal agent make him Romeo to your Juliet? I don't entirely get the problem. 'Splain, please." There's another pause as Ben retrieves his food. "What are we eating?"

"Yakitori. I was in the mood for Japanese but not sushi," Ben says, at the same time thanking someone. He's just like his dad, always showing gratitude.

"Is that the chicken skewers?"

"Yep. Yummo." He confirms around a mouthful. "Yakitori and a Japanese beer can make a tough day not so bad."

"I'll have to try it sometime. Back to—what's his name?"

"Alex." Munch, sip. *Rude.* "On our first date, I told him while I respect law enforcement, I could never be with someone in the job. He said he's a geologist -"

"Like in rocks? Soil?"

"Exactly like that. So I didn't think twice. We started hanging out more and more, and the night I was going to introduce him to Nick, I found out the hard way—they already know each other."

Oh, damn, I think, then say it out loud. "Oh, damn. Why did Alex say he's a geologist if he works for the FBI? I assume that's where he works if he knows Nick."

"Yeah. He's a *forensic* geologist. He analyzes rocks and dirt and pollen and construction materials to solve cases."

I try not to smile because he'll hear it. "Well. I get why you don't want to be involved with a LEO, but I also get why Alex might have fudged a bit. It's not like he's out in the field chasing bad guys. He's in a lab playing with dirt. No risk. No drama. Well, not much, anyway."

"I'm not an idiot. I know that. I'm not as mad–anymore–about him being a fed. I'm angry about him lying." Poor Ben sounds so morose. He must really like Alex. "I can't be with someone who lies. Trust is the most important thing to me–in a friendship, a working relationship, a partner."

"Have you talked with him about it?"

"I haven't seen or talked to Alex since that night."

"Ben!" I'm completely surprised. "That's not okay. I would guess he's tried to reach out? Maybe more than once?"

"Yes," He admits, and he sounds uncomfortable, as he should.

"And you haven't at least given him the courtesy of an in-person 'go to hell'?"

"No. Probably because I don't think I'll be able to say 'go to hell.' If I see him, I'm going to give in."

"Give in to what? Loving someone? You're an idiot." I cluck my tongue like an old woman.

"Shut up."

"It's true. Your pride is the only thing that'll be hurt, and it's going to heal quick enough if you're happy. And I know you. You'll never get over him if you run away without at least trying to talk it out."

Ben's silent. I hear the sound of a beer bottle tapping a wooden table. "You're right. Okay. You're right. I'll call him."

"Good. I expect a full report, one way or the other."

"Ang?" His tone is suddenly sugary sweet.

"Yes?" I ask, knowing I'm not going to like what he says.

"You could say the same about you and O."

I roll my eyes, and I swear he sees it across the miles; he knows me well.

He continues. "You could. I know she's bossy, and she's been obsessed with you lately, but I'm sure it's because she loves you and she wants what's best for you -"

"She doesn't know what's best for me -" I snap.

"The best way to tell her you've got everything under control is to talk to her. Like a grownup. Like the sister she is."

I start to protest then close my mouth. He's right. *Jerk.* "Fine. I'll talk to Olivia after you talk to Alex."

"Always negotiating."

I shrug and remember he can't really see me despite my imaginings. "It's part of my charm."

"Yeah," he draws it out playfully, "that's it. Okay, I'm going to call while I'm riled up. It'll help me stay strong. You, my darling, take care of yourself. If you ever do get to feeling a certain way... I'm right here. Always. Forever."

"Same." I hang up the phone and giggle. "Alex and Ben, sittin' in a tree..."

I hit the play button, and Anna Taylor-Joy's eyes get big as she realizes the man in the car's driver's seat is not her classmate's father...

CHAPTER THIRTY-ONE

ANGEL

A black box pops up in the middle of my monitor, covering the spreadsheet I use to manage expenses.

The box does not have an X to make it go away. Crap. Did I somehow get a virus? I'm usually smart about these things. I have malware installed. I do all the things. *Damn it.*

I click in the center to see if it closes that way, but instead, it seems to trigger an action. It's one of those audiogram images with the soundbar bouncing up and down under the audio.

I recognize Jimmy's voice immediately, but he sounds different. Sped up. Hyper. Ragey. Has he relapsed? Is he back on drugs? The fury in his tone makes my skin crawl.

"You're so special you didn't even feel the need to respond to my email? Stuck up much? You're pathetic! You tell everyone you're happy being single, but the truth is, you're scared shitless! You know you're damaged goods, and nobody decent will ever want you! No Norm could understand you, take care of you, and love you, so you don't even try. You're pathetic! You tell yourself you can be alone and be happy. No woman can be alone and truly be happy! You're just not created that way! It's bullshit, and you're deluding yourself. If there was a Norm who would have you, they would only have one use for you—you're a thrill! They get to fuck the bitch that was kept in the Dollhouse. They get to play with the toy without the consequences. Clearly, you think you're too *good* for *me*, *better* than *me*, but that's not true: we are the same. If there was ever a person in this world who could love you and care for you the way you need to be taken care of, it's me, and you're throwing it away, so have fun being alone for the rest of your life! One day you're gonna look back and realize you passed up your one true chance at love and a family and you're gonna wish you could go back and change everything, but it will be too late, it will be much too late. The truth is, you're not close to being good enough for *me*."

He's lost the minimal sense of control he started with. The words are flying out of him like angry bullets. "Doesn't matter. You're just a bitch. A pathetic little bitch. You deserve what happened to you. It never would have happened to a good girl, a worthwhile girl. Bitch. Bitch. BITCH."

That hits the target, but only because I've had that thought myself for years.

I think he's done, but then I hear, almost a whisper, "It's not fair. Why is it only the woman you don't want who wants you?"

The box goes to black, then fills with a demented-looking clown head.

I gape at the laptop. It takes a minute before my brain reboots and tells me to find a way to save the file. I don't see an option to do that. Can my screengrab software capture audio? I don't know! The fog lifts, and I find my phone. I thumb to the photo tool and click video, then hit record. Now I have to figure out how to get Jimmy's audio file to play again. No matter what I do, the clown in the black box stares at me, mocking me. Damn it!

The box suddenly swoops off my screen with a cackling laugh, leaving my spreadsheet file undisturbed.

I have nothing on my phone but a clown in a black box. The emails he sent before don't demonstrate this level of rage and crazy. At best, it will get Jimmy kicked out of Komo, but without a structured framework, will he spiral? I am so torn! If I tell Dr. Lisa, she'll have no choice but to kick him out of Komo. With no obligation and no resources, there's no telling what he'll do. If he's back on drugs, will it send him deeper? Will he do more than send messages? If I don't tell her, this may continue to escalate. I can't decide whether it's better to keep the enemy close.

Shit. Shit Shit.

CHAPTER THIRTY-TWO

ANGEL

My routine: I run five miles a day when I'm home. Asa is my running buddy. Nope stays home because that would be a lot for her round three-legged self. The puppies are young for that kind of workout, so I'll let Nope babysit today.

Four days a week, I spend 40 minutes in the gym in the barn doing weight work. I beat the crap out of my boxing gear the other three days. I've got a hell of a roundhouse kick.

I despise exercise. At my core, I am a lazy couch potato who would do nothing but read, listen to music and watch movies if left to my own devices. But after the whole Johnny Law thing in Oklahoma, I promised myself I would never be physically unprepared again. In addition to my physical training: I can load and shoot a pistol and a rifle. I can pitch a knife and hit the target 100% of the time. I can escape from duct tape, zip-ties, or handcuffs 80% of the time, depending on whether distractions occur concurrently. I'm working on improving that number. I can hotwire a car or motorcycle unless it's new enough to have a chip. I can navigate out of the woods without a phone or compass.

I never want to use any of these skills in real life. Ever.

The feature at Chez Stargazer this evening is salmon en croute with asparagus and chocolate mousse for dessert. Since I'm not about to go back to City Mart, I've been visiting different stores in Moab. The Square is my new favorite. It's busier, and the hours are shorter, so I can't sneak in and out as quickly, but I'm making do.

There's been no word about the person who left the photos. I'm not surprised, but I am disappointed. I wanted to report it and have the kind officer confront the bad man, which would be the end. No muss, no fuss.

One of my worst habits is to 'put my head in the sandbox,' as CB says, mixing up her English idioms as usual. I can't say she's wrong; I do it all the time, avoiding looking at things I don't want to see. Even worse, I know it doesn't serve me. Dealing with something, whether it's taking the trash out or being mindful of a potential creep hanging around, is best tackled head-on and in a timely fashion.

My trash bin is very full at the moment, emphasizing my bad habit. I add the broken ends of asparagus, the butcher wrap from the salmon, and the empty box of puff pastry. I have to flatten my hand on top of the pastry box and shove it down hard to close and tie the bag. Because I've waited too long. The bag is pudgy around the middle and doesn't want to come out of the metal cylinder, which was cute online and is a pain in the butt in the real world. I know it will fight me because it always does when it's overfull. Yet, every single time I get into the same predicament. Do I feel like an idiot standing over the bin, tug-tug-tugging until it gives a little bit? Yes. Will this keep me from doing this exact thing again? No.

Finally, the bag comes out with a pop, and I lift it up to keep from dragging it across the wood floor. Once it's over the metal rail of the slider, I let it touch the concrete. I'll hose off the patio after washing away the gross liquid muck that leaks from a tear in the bag. I turn the corner of the barn and nudge open the gate to the bin area with my foot. Have to keep them behind the gate or the desert critters will get into them and make a mess. I use my elbow to knock open the lid to the large green bin. I have to grab the bag with both hands to get it up and into the hungry mouth of the container. Only a little bit of disgusting trash juice gets on my hands.

Small blessings. Every week, I haul the bin down to the gate with my little Gator utility cart.

That's another thing the pups need to get used to. When Nope first joined the family, she wasn't too sure about vehicles–cars, bikes, motorcycles, golf carts–maybe because she spent so much time dodging them with her person while they were living on the streets. I don't want to make that mistake with Spence and Winnie. They need to be comfortable everywhere because who knows where Charlie and Hannah will want to go?

The dogs are investigating various spots in the yard. Nope and Spence are digging again. Maybe I'll plant something there if the hole gets big enough. Asa always heads up to the boulder, which gives him a prime view of his valley. Usually, Winnie follows him, but today she's more interested in what I'm doing with the weird-looking green snake.

When I turn the spigot and water gushes out the end of the hose, Winnie jumps a foot, then bows down to inspect the strange creature making everything wet. Eventually, she finds her courage and begins to bark at it as if that will stop the water flow. When it doesn't work, she attacks, trying to capture the water in her mouth. I can't help laughing. Her wiry hair plasters down around her face, and she looks like a very large and thin rat.

Over her noise, another sound gets my attention. I turn to see Asa launching himself off the boulder as if it's not ten feet in the air. He's tearing past the barn and down the drive toward the gate, as fast as if the devil himself is chasing him. What is he after? Asa doesn't usually go after wildlife. I drop the hose and dash after him carefully because I'm barefooted. There's a lot of rock and pine and cactus needles littering the ground. By the time I hit the driveway, which is gravel, my feet are already tender.

When I finally catch up, Asa is at the broken spot in the fence, barking and growling, hackles high. Someone was on our land.

Someone Asa didn't like.

I don't like them either. It will be a long couple of weeks until the fence company can do their thing. I'll take the Gator on a rock hunt in the morning and find some big ones to pile in front of the opening for now.

CHAPTER THIRTY-THREE

PETER

I'm in the middle of my workout when I get a Facetime call. Olivia's beautiful face pops onto the screen, and I wonder for the umpteenth time how she always looks so good online when the rest of us look washed out and kind of gray.

"Hey, you," I set down the barbells and drop onto the weight bench. Sweat is dripping into my eyes. I wipe it away. "Where are you?" She's clearly not in LA. We're in the midst of a pretty dramatic storm, complete with the occasional burst of thunder, which is somewhat unusual for SoCal. The sky behind Olivia is bright blue and cloudless.

"Heading to the studio." She smiles.

I run my arm across my brow to catch the drips. "The studio in LA?"

"Yes," she makes a silly face. "Of course, the studio in LA."

Something prevents me from calling her out on the lie. "Want to come for dinner?"

"I can't tonight. I have a lot of work. Maybe later this week."

I nod. "What's up?"

She catches the change in my voice, I can see it in her eyes, but she skips past it. "Nothing much. Mostly I just wanted to check in and see if you've heard from Angel lately."

"I haven't spoken with her, but we've emailed a bit and had a few chats on Komo. She's training dogs for Charlie and for Hannah."

Olivia smiles, but the smile doesn't reach her eyes. "That's great.

It gives her something to do, and the dogs will be good for the kids."

That's a bit patronizing. "You and Ang having troubles?"

"Nothing major. She seems to be avoiding me, and that's starting to annoy me, but I'll survive," Olivia laughs, but her eyes tell me it's not a laughing matter for her.

"You've spoken since Thanksgiving, right?"

Her eyes slide away from the camera. Looking at something? Or hiding something? "Sure."

I'd assumed all was well after what Marnie and I refer to as the Big Turkey Blowout. It never occurred to me to check on them. Honestly, we're lucky. There should be more squabbles with a family as large and complex as ours, but this is the only one I remember.

Angel was making cranberry chutney from a recipe she was excited to try. Simple enough. Olivia came into the kitchen and 'suggested,' in typical Olivia style, Angel tweak her recipe. Angel politely declined. Olivia pushed. Angel finally snapped, "You don't even think I can make cranberry sauce? You really do think I'm a baby, don't you?"

To which my beloved, educated, kind-hearted daughter responded, "Well, yes, most of the time!" As one might imagine, WW3 broke out. Other sisters have similar conversations. And mothers and daughters. Wives and mothers-in-law. But with these two, there's a dark and traumatic history. More than once, Olivia has suggested Angel is a baby, a coward, or weak, usually in a bossy attempt to 'help.' Angel is none of those things. Angel has proven she's intelligent, capable, resilient, and knows who she is and what she wants. Olivia simply disapproves of Angel's version of a contented life.

Now I realize it was a stupid thing to assume. "Olivia? Have you and Angel had a real conversation about what happened at Thanksgiving? Cleared the air? Hugged it out?"

Olivia still won't look at the screen. "No, we haven't spoken, other than a polite 'hello' in Group, and not many of those. She's still angry."

"Have you tried to reach out?"

"Of course! She avoids me like I'm carrying the plague. I can't get her to call, email, or even text." Olivia is the one who is angry now. I recognize the signs. She's not used to things not going her way.

"Angel has built a life she's proud of. A life she enjoys living. I'm proud of her. You should be too." I keep my tone soft. I don't want to flame the fire. Their history is complicated. As they've become adults, their relationship hasn't gotten easier, although I believe they love each other in my heart. "Anything I can do to help?"

Olivia pauses and nibbles her lower lip. "Do you think–I mean–I'm worried–after Kait and Tiffany, I worry. What if Angel isn't quite as good as she claims to be. You know more about her life than I do. Do you really believe her? She's not pretending?"

I think about that for a minute. "I do believe her when she says she's content. Of everyone in Komo, she's one of the few I am confident won't harm herself that way."

"Why?" Olivia's tone is confrontational.

"Because of Bud. She's made it very clear over the years that she feels as though she's living for both of them. She owes him a good life."

Olivia makes a snorting sound, and her face is twisted into a dark expression. "She's living for someone else. That's bullshit."

"It's only bullshit if she says it is, Olivia," my tone is firmer than I intend. Still, Olivia is wrong to think she gets to decide the value of someone else's life. "You know that. You write books and host a talk show that's literally about that. Are you questioning your faith, as it were? Should I be worried about *you*?"

I watch as her expression transforms back into the normal, smiling, relaxed face I'm used to seeing.

"Silly Daddy. I'm fine. Just overthinking, I suppose. Two suicides are worrisome."

"It is. We're going to call Hope and Promise together–separately–
and talk about what's happening. I hope you'll be there."

"When is it?"

"Thursday."

"I'll be traveling, but I'll make sure I log in." She smiles again.
"You're right, Dad; I'm worrying for nothing. Angel's fine. If you
talk to her, bug her to call me, would ya? That would make me feel
a lot better." She makes a smoochy face and waves, and the bright
blue background disappears.

Why is she lying?

CHAPTER THIRTY-FOUR

New Mexico

I shouldn't tell you, but I can see you're already feeling the effects. Don't panic. It's all right. People pay good money for the drug you're currently enjoying. Special K is a popular street drug with some. I've heard it makes you feel relaxed and happy. Is that how you're feeling? Oh, that's good! I should warn you, in a few more minutes, that will change a bit. You might start seeing things. If that happens, don't panic. Apparently, it's fun, like an intellectual amusement park ride.

Come on, let's get you comfortable. No, don't fight. I don't want to have to–damn it, I don't want to do this. Stop! No choice, no choice. Don't close your lips–drink this! Drink it! Now, damn it!

There. Okay. Just remember you brought this part on yourself. It could have been easy, a relaxed drift off. But since I had to give you more, there's a possibility you'll go into something called a K-hole. From what I've heard, that's a little bit scary. But you did this yourself. Remember that.

I don't understand the words you're saying. I can tell you're upset, but you're not making sense. I'm sorry. I'm sure it's the drugs. But it's all right. It'll be over soon. Oops! You're sliding off the chair. Good, that means it's time.

Don't worry, I've got you. I'm just going to carry you into the garage, and we'll get everything all set up.

CHAPTER THIRTY-FIVE

NICK

This time, Peter is the one with the bad news. The subject line of his email is "Another Hope person dead by suicide." *Shit.*

I'm in Chicago, so it'll be a bit until I contact him. Before I do, I'll connect with the local PD and see if I can get some information. I skip dinner with the team and head to my room. Before I call the locals, I want to refresh my memory about Karmen Villanueva. I have access to Dr. Lisa's file.

PRIVILEGED & CONFIDENTIAL

Komorebi file #139
Villanueva, Karmen (Erickson, while married)
[Two photos: First of a young Latina woman with
short, curly nearly black hair, pale skin, dark
eyes. Early twenties. Smiling, happy, holding
a baby in her arms, toddler next to her. Proud
husband at her side. Second photo, longer unkempt
hair, tired looking, very pregnant, alone.]
Location: NM
DOB: 3/5/1996   **Abduction:** 9/16/2017
Recovery: 4/6/2018   **Current Age:** 25
Offender Status: One in prison for 7 years, other
in prison working on an appeal
Notes: Abducted by two men while leaving a bar.

Kept as a sex slave. Pregnant when recovered, kept child. Her husband divorced her and trying to gain full custody of their two children together. She's fighting.

Tell me about the day you were taken. What do you remember about that time?
I'd just had my second baby a few months ago, on my birthday. Isn't that funny? Being a mom to a six-month-old and a three-year-old was exhausting, but I loved it. My husband Bob worked sixty hours a week. He was usually in a bad mood when he eventually decided to come home. That night was the first fun outing I'd had since having Zach. Bob was angry I was 'making him babysit' his children and did his best to bully me into staying home, but I wasn't going to give in this time. My friend Melissa was all about this trendy club with the young professionals in town.

I made it to midnight, but I was ready to head home. Melissa wanted to stay, so we said goodnight, and I called an Uber. When a well-cared for black SUV pulled up, I assumed it was my car and slid into the back. Of course, I realize now how stupid that was. I started texting Bob I was headed home, but then out of nowhere, another man shoved me down on the seat, and the driver sped away from the club. He'd been hiding in the cargo area.

Would you like to talk about your time in captivity? It can benefit short-term and long-term recovery, but it is totally understandable if you choose not to talk about it today. I will follow your lead!

Honestly? Mostly, it was boring. That sounds bad, but my story is dull compared to some of the other people in Komo. The two guys—I called them Red and Brown because of their hair—were wimps. Not brave at all. In fact, as soon as they were done raping me the first night, Red disappeared, and I never saw him again. Brown would come two or three times a week. Every time he'd bring a loaf of bread, a jar of peanut butter, a couple of gallons of water, and a box of powdered milk. I can't stand the smell of peanuts now.

He attached me to one of those dog-run cables. You know the kind people tie between two trees in their yards and then leash the dog? One of those. I could move back and forth across the room, but I couldn't get within ten feet of the one window. I could get to the bathroom, but it didn't actually work. I'd have to save up water from the jugs to flush. It smelled terrible.

Every time Brown came, he'd have sex with me—I can't really call it 'rape' because he wasn't violent even though I didn't want it. I know, that's messed up. It's rape; I'm not saying it isn't. But again, compared to some of the other people…

About six months in, I realized that the pouch on my gut wasn't baby weight from Zach. I was pregnant again. It took Brown a month longer to realize. When he did, man, was he freaked out. He'd told me a few times that if I had never seen their faces, he'd have let me go after the first night, but they hadn't thought things through. He said he felt terrible about what they did. He didn't want to hurt me. But he also didn't want the responsibility of a woman and a baby. He'd have to 'think about it,' he said. I knew, though. I knew he wasn't coming back. The next time he brought supplies, I made myself hoard them. I figured I could live without food, but I needed water. I wasn't going to let that baby suffer if I had any choice. She's what kept me going, her and the thought of my little boys.

What do you remember about being recovered?

For the longest time when I was there, I never heard a sound. Not under me or next to me. I didn't realize I was in an attic. But a few days after Brown left that last time, I started hearing noises on the other side of the wall. I think the angels were watching out for me. I couldn't quite reach the wall because of the cable, but I was able to stretch my legs and kick at it. Not hard. I barely swiped it with my toes. Somehow it was enough! A guy had bought the other half of the duplex, and he was turning the attic into a master suite. He heard my noises and thought there were critters. I went to sleep one night and woke up with an animal control officer staring down at me the next day. Best day of my life, except for having my kids.

What's your day like now?

Bob—we're divorced, and he's married to the woman he started seeing while I was gone—is fighting me for full custody of the boys. I'm going to beauty school. When I graduate, I won't be reliant on anyone. For now, it's Destiny and me except the weekends when Bob legally has to let me have the boys. The three kids are cute together, although Davis, the older one, has started being mean to Destiny. I think his father is turning him against his little sister. I worry about that.

Thank you for sharing your memories and experiences. I can imagine it is difficult to talk about.

It makes sense that recovering after something so traumatic can be emotionally messy sometimes. Would you consider yourself happy since your recovery?

Happy? Not yet. Hopeful? Absolutely.

Notes were taken during her initial Komo session. LC

The police report supplements the story. Karmen's husband thought she'd abandoned him and the children, the stress of being a mother too much. Neither Bob nor Karmen's mother Gretchen, who usually spoke with Karmen once a day, reported her missing for nearly three days. The detectives in charge of the case thought Karmen was probably dead, with Bob as their prime suspect because of the delayed report. They didn't have anything to charge him, but a report by the three-year-old that "Daddy shouted at Mommy and she cried!" was enough to put them on the path.

The two men, both recent grads from Arizona State, members of the same fraternity, worked together as customer service reps for a large bank. They were bored with their lives and one night, in a drunken stupor, decided it would be fun to have a sex slave. Unfortunately for Karmen, she was the first woman who presented herself after they made their plan. The men kept her in the attic of a duplex owned by one of their grandmothers. The grandmother was deaf and unable to climb stairs, so she never knew anyone was in the attic.

Bob, Karmen's ex-husband, is taking her to court to get sole custody of their boys, five and seven years old. Bob wants nothing to do with the "rape baby," a sweet little girl named Destiny. Gretchen, Karmen's mother, resents the inconvenience Karmen has brought into her life and constantly nags and complains.

This is a perfect example of why Komo exists. Even a solid relationship can be broken by the stress and trauma of abduction.

Karmen wants–wanted–to be a hairstylist, so Komo was paying her tuition to beauty school. They bought a three-bedroom house and gave her a minivan suitable for hauling kiddos. In court, Bob the ex used the fact that Komo provided these things as ammunition. "What if that place decides to stop supporting her? She is totally reliant on them."

The house and car were given to Karmen outright. The tuition is paid with no conditions. Komo has an excellent track record and a strong reputation, but not all judges believe in the mission. Personal experience and opinion can sway even those supposed to be impartial.

My call to the Phoenix PD confirms Karmen Villanueva is deceased, seemingly by her own hand. She was found by Bob, the ex, who came to check on her when she didn't pick up the three kids from daycare. Fortunately, he left the children, including Destiny, in the car with his girlfriend. Karmen was in the tub, six-inch gashes up each forearm.

There was no note.

CHAPTER THIRTY-SIX

ANGEL

I can't remember a time the Komo team called a meeting saying 'attendance is strongly encouraged,' yet that's what was in my inbox this morning. Peter and Dr. Lisa ask that we attend a group chat at 4 pm Pacific if we possibly can. I'm sure it has to do with Kait and Tiffany. Everyone is freaked out. I'm even a little freaked out.

Unfortunately, the press has caught wind, hounding anyone they can hunt down. Peter and crew expected it, I'm sure, and have put security on the Hope crew when they can. I refused to allow extra protection, but I agreed to respond to texts and emails and check in with Komo every day. I'm a jerk, but I'm not a total asshole.

I even promised Olivia I'd give her a call after the session. Really looking forward to that. *Not.*

I watch the names, and some faces fill the screen. It's weird seeing Olivia and Jimmy's names, but not Kait. Those three names are almost always on the screen. I've felt Kait's absence more than I would have expected. Aside from pushing Jimmy at me, I enjoyed talking with her. She had some great insights about people and loved to read. She suggested a couple of horror movies based on books–*Rebecca* and *Rosemary's Baby*–and they were spot on. It's not like she was domineering; she was just very present. Always. You could count on her.

As more names file in, I realize this is just the Hope side. I don't see any of the friends or family from Promise. Maybe they're doing another group with them. I'm sure there's a lot of fear on their side of the house. Two suicides in a month within such a small pool of folks is frightening.

Charlie pings me as soon as he enters, which is excellent timing because I was getting a little morose. He types, "How's my boy?"

"He's good," I tilt the laptop screen and turn my video on so he can see Spence stretched out on the blanket-covered sofa behind my desk. "Napping as usual. He's got two speeds: zoom and snore."

"Can't wait to get out there and meet him in person," Charlie sighs.

"Three more weeks! Hopefully, the stuff I ordered arrives by then." The residence part of the barn technically has two bedrooms, although I use one for my office. The couch Spence is currently snoozing on is a zillion-years-old, with rips in the faux leather from dog paws and old age. I ordered a sofa bed to replace it and a twin bed and mattress to put in the loft for Charlie. I'm not asking Charlie to sleep on hay bales. I'm getting nervous as we get closer to D day. I tell myself it's not because I'll be sharing my space.

"I can sleep anywhere. Don't worry about me." Charlie reads my mind. "No Hannah, huh?"

"Haven't seen her yet. She's probably online buying more stuff. Winnie is going to be one spoiled princess." Hearing her name, Winnie opens one eye to look at me from her fluffy bed. She stands, turns three times, and lays back down.

Peter and Dr. Lisa appear together at four on the dot from the Foundation conference room. Neither of them looks concerned or stressed. They're good at this. They ought to be. Peter spent twenty years as a highly-respected journalist before Olivia's abduction, and he's still in the press regularly. Dr. Lisa is equally poised. Before joining the Foundation, she spent a dozen years in private practice, consulting on high-visibility court cases. But she started her professional career as a social worker in LA's giant system and has a deep history of pro bono work with kids and teens who've been through unusually traumatic situations. There couldn't be a better person for the Foundation's lead therapist.

"Hey, gang!" Peter says, and there's a flurry of 'Hi!' posts in the chatbox and a few voices adding to it. There are thirty-four Hope members–oh, thirty-two. Damn it. The participants' list shows twenty-nine folks in the room, including Peter and Dr. Lisa. That's good.

"Hi, everyone!" Dr. Lisa says. I catch a glimpse of Marnie's reflection to the side. No secrets in rooms with glass walls. Not that she'd be hiding. Marnie is an essential part of the Foundation, too. She's the lead social worker, ensuring everyone has what they need to be healthy and okay.

Peter's got his trusted news broadcaster face on. "Thanks for joining us today. It's great to see so many of you here. I wish we were all together under happier circumstances. Marnie, Dr. Lisa, and I were talking, and we wanted to check in with everyone, see how you're doing, see how you're feeling. It's so difficult when a friend loses their fight, and we've had two. Two good people, two kind people, two valuable people have been lost to us, and I'm hurting, as I'm sure you are." Peter's eyes are wet, and I think for the millionth time what a big heart the man has. I haven't always made our relationship easy, especially when we first met. A dozen years later, I am very grateful for him and all he's done for me. For Rosie. He's a helper to all, but he's even more special for us.

Dr. Lisa nods. "It's hard to imagine Komo without Kait's helpful words cheering us all on in everything we do. And Tiffany was always ready with good advice and a willing ear. They'll both be missed so very much."

"I'll think of Kait every year when I make her stuffing recipe for Thanksgiving," Meg, one of the older members, says, although her video is off. A few "me too!" comments come through in chat.

"Tiffany was the best at music trivia," Christian, a younger twenty-something, volunteers. More agreement from the group.

"Do you have any questions we can answer?" Dr. Lisa asks.

"I saw on the news Tiffany died by carbon monoxide poisoning. Did Kait die that way too?" One of the younger members asked this question, and I wonder whether Dr. Lisa will answer. There's a general rule in the big world that you don't talk about methods because it might be considered instructional. Here, though, the overarching rule is honesty always. It's a conundrum.

Dr. Lisa tells the truth. "Kait died by suffocation."

"I saw on TV she did it with a bag over her head. That would be hard to do with those claw-hands of hers," one of the younger boys grunts.

Dr. Lisa shakes her head. "Where there's a will, there's a way. Let's be respectful in our wording, please."

"Are you afraid one of us will try to kill ourselves too? Is that why we're having this meeting?" The same teen boy asks, his tone confrontational, but I think he's scared.

Peter gives a gentle head shake. "We're not afraid, no. But we want to be sure everyone has the resources and support they need to feel safe and secure."

A young woman's teary voice projects from her still photo. "I feel sad for them. So bad for their families. It seems selfish to do this after everything they've already been through."

There are a couple of affirming comments.

Dr. Lisa takes this one. "You've got every right to be sad. Even mad. You get to feel however you feel about it. As to their families, it's not going to be easy for them, now or in the future. We will be there, however they need and want us to be. We're meeting with Promise to help them understand and give them the support they need. They're angry and confused and upset—and scared. It's scary when things like this happen inside a small, tight community."

She continues. "I'd like to ask that if you, or anyone in the group you're close to, seems to be struggling, please please talk to someone. We're a no-judgment zone. You know that. The whole purpose of Komo is to give each other support and friendship. I can think of no greater time to offer those two things than when someone is struggling, can you?" Grumbles and keyboard clicks of approval.

"What other questions do you have? Don't be shy. If you don't want to ask publicly, you can open a private chat to me," Dr. Lisa offers. Apparently, she receives a typed question, and it's not one she's thrilled by. Her perfectly composed expression slips just a tiny bit before she can recover. "Someone asked if they died because of what happened to them before. Were they unable to deal with the aftermath, and that's why they chose to die by suicide."

It sounds like something Jimmy would ask. The jerk.

I forgot I have the private window with Charlie open until I see words click in the small box. "I saw your face just then. Do you think that's why?"

"No! If I made a face, it was because of who I think asked the question, not the question itself. I very strongly believe the opposite," I type back.

"Good. Me, too." Charlie responds.

Dr. Lisa is mid-sentence when I return my attention to her. "Each of you had a very different experience, and each of you has a unique life, now. Some things are more difficult for you than they would be for someone else your age. Some things may be easier because you're more resilient. But absolutely nothing will prevent you from having a satisfying life you enjoy. You deserve everything good, and you can have it if you choose. It sounds simple, but the key to happiness is to be grateful for every good thing, big or small."

"Shouldn't *you* have seen this coming? I mean, you're a psychologist. You talk to each of us regularly." The timid voice with the big question is Kaley Beauchamp. I am floored. She's almost as quiet as Tiffany. *Oh.* She and Tiffany were friends. I'm sure she's hurting terribly right now. "I talked to Tiffany nearly every day. She never said anything to make me expect this. I don't get it. I just don't believe she'd–do this." She can't bring herself to say 'kill herself.' Can't blame her. Those are tough words to say.

"I don't disagree that Tiffany seemed to be doing relatively well." That is all Dr. Lisa says.

A movement over Dr. Lisa's shoulder gets my attention. In the reflection of the glass, I see Marnie jump to her feet, put a hand to her mouth, and practically run out of the donut hole.

What the hell...

CHAPTER THIRTY-SEVEN

PETER

As soon as the screen is clear of the Komorebi logo and I'm sure we're out of the group, I push away from the table and follow Marnie into her office. "Are you all right? What happened?" She's at her desk, head on folded arms. She's sobbing. The sound is pitiful and small and full of pain.

Lisa has joined us, but she's staring at her phone. "Nick messaged. There's been another death. Karmen."

I feel as though someone kicked me in the stomach. I can't form a complete sentence. Words trip out over my tongue. "What...how...I don't..."

Marnie's cries are wracking her body. I leave the doorway and wrap my arms around her.

"They found her in the tub this morning. She slashed her arms." Lisa reports. I hear something catch in her voice and look up. "Nick says there's evidence it may have been staged to look like a suicide."

"Staged?" I repeat. My head is spinning from grief and confusion. Marnie has stopped crying. She lifts her head, and there's a fire in her eyes. I squeeze her shoulder. "Meaning–not suicide? Meaning– someone purposefully harmed her?"

Lisa nods. "Nick says it appears that way. He wants to look into Tiffany and Kait as well."

Marnie cares about these people as if they're her children, even the older ones. "Did you really say–did you say someone may be murdering them? *Murdering* them? Fucking *murdering* them?" she screams. I've never heard her so angry. She hammers her fists on the desk, sending a plastic water bottle flying to the floor. "We will find them. We will hunt them down. We will make them pay!"

CHAPTER THIRTY-EIGHT

OLIVIA

Finally! I feel relief rushing through my veins. "About damn time."
I smile at the laptop screen.

Angel grins, and I feel another flood, this time of affection. She's
a pain in my ass, but I love her so very much. "Hey. Sorry I've been
incommunicado." In typical Angel fashion, she doesn't say why or
make excuses. I do admire that about her. She's not concerned about
what others think.

"I'm just glad we're finally getting a chance to catch up," I was
going to say 'talk' but that feels too serious. I need her to stop
working so hard to avoid me. "How are you? Sounds like you're
busy. Are things going well? How is the dog training business?" I
feel so awkward.

"It's good. I'm training a pup for Charlie and another for Hannah
right now. In fact," she pauses, as if she's debating telling me something, and then she does, and it's as painful as I'd anticipated.
"They're coming here to pick up their dogs in a few weeks."

I keep the smile plastered to my face through sheer will. If she
knows she's hurting me, she'll be uncomfortable, and then she'll
close down and hang up and keep avoiding me like I'm the plague.
"That's exciting! You've never had anyone visit before, have you?"

"It's time, I think," Angel says, and I agree, although I wish I were
the one coming to see her.

"Good for you! I'm proud of you." As if she cares. "Are you doing
all right with everything–" I wave a hand, hoping she understands

I mean the deaths. Behind the monitor, the sun is going down over LA, and a bright sunset crests the western edge of my city. It feels poetic.

"It's scary, confusing, and sad, but I'm fine," Angel says. "I'll keep on keepin' on until I can't keep on no mo'." Is she really as nonchalant as she's trying to seem? Her humor falls flat. She tips back a beer. "What's new with you? How's the show? How are book sales?"

I can't tell if she's seriously interested or mocking me. It's not a secret that she disapproves of me making myself, and her by extension, a public person. She doesn't understand how I can put the past on display. She doesn't realize that it's the ultimate form of protection for me. I decide who says what about me. I determine what they get to see. I control the narrative. It's power. "Book sales are strong. We're on hiatus with the show until September. I needed the break, so I'm glad. I've got plenty to keep me busy."

"How's Christopher? And Susie?" Angel is struggling to make small talk, I can see it on her face. She's putting the focus on me to keep it off of her. This is *my* skill. I recognize it when I'm on the receiving end. For a few minutes, I'll allow it.

"They're fine. Christopher is working on some exciting projects. Susie loves LouLou, her nanny." As always, when talking about my daughter, I feel uncomfortable. I reset my media face. Time to turn the tables back around. "Hey, I was thinking, what say you and I take advantage of my hiatus and run off on an adventure? Maybe we can find a private island somewhere. You and me and the monkeys."

Angel frowns. "Would you want to do that with Christopher and Susie? That seems like something you'd enjoy with your family." She takes another sip of beer. She's drinking a lot. I can see an empty can on the table near her elbow. "It would be hard for me to go for long. I have Cat and the dogs." She motions with her hand, indicating the animals on the couches behind her.

"I'm sure you could find someone to watch them." My tone is

snippy, and I change it quickly. "Sure, Christopher can come. We'll make it a family thing."

"With Marnie and Peter and the girls too?" Angel sounds interested now that it's not just the two of us. Does she really hate me that much? What did I do to earn such disdain? I've only ever tried to look after her, take care of her, be there for her. It hurts that she constantly pushes me away.

I control my expression. "Sure. Everyone." I pick up my iPad. "Tell me what doesn't work for you so I can get my assistant looking at dates."

"The only thing I need to work around is when Charlie and Hannah are here," she says, spinning a pen between her fingers. She gives me the dates.

"I'm surprised! As hard as you are to connect with, I figured your schedule was packed." Oh, that was snippy. Damn it. I smile, but it's forced.

"You asked about dates to work around, not if I had a lot of things to do here," Angel responds, with a false smile on her face. She's hardly trying to mask her annoyance.

"You're correct that I did," I sigh. "Are you happy, Ang?"

She's caught off guard. She looks like a fish out of water, mouth opening and closing. Finally, she laughs. "This question has come up a lot lately!" I'm sure she means at Komo, with all the talk about the suicides. "Yes, I am. There's always room for improvement, but I'm not unhappy. I enjoy my life. I get satisfaction from it. I am content. I have fun." Angel stops fidgeting and looks at me straight on. "Are you?"

"Happy? No. I'm not." There's no point in lying about it. "As you said, I'm not unhappy. But I'm also not happy. I'm under a lot of pressure, a lot of strain. It's exhausting being me." That sounds so arrogant and narcissistic. But it's true.

"You mean the books and TV?" she asks, and I can hear the

unspoken accusation that I am the one who created the monster machine that is my life.

"Being a wife, a mother, a public person. Yes. Of course, I realize the bed is of my own making." I fake a smile. "I'm not complaining." Oh, but I am. "I'm simply answering your question. I'm not happy. But I'm not unhappy." I'm just tired. And tired of you pushing me away. I'm tired of the one person in the world I should be able to turn to, to talk to, who might possibly understand everything I've been through and continue to go through, wanting to have absolutely nothing to do with me.

"I'm sorry, I really am. Can you make some small changes? Free yourself up a little from the craziness?" It's frustrating and amusing that she's trying to fix *me* when my intent for this conversation was me trying to help her.

"Perhaps. Christopher and I will talk about it soon and decide what changes need to be made." I need to get off the chat. It's not going as planned, and my emotions are bubbling too close to the surface. "Do you still talk to Bud?"

She smiles. "I do."

"Tell him I love him and miss him, would you?"

Angel looks completely surprised, but she nods. Of course, she's surprised. She knows how I feel about her having regular conversations with her dead brother. "Sure. Of course. Absolutely."

"Thanks. All right. I'm going to sign off. I'll get my assistant working on dates for our island trip. Thanks for taking my call. Please, let's talk more regularly? I miss you, too."

She nods, but I know it's a lie.

CHAPTER THIRTY-NINE

Southwest

I want to be the person I show to the world, but I have a different internal life. I recognize I'm not healthy, much less sane. I feel as though the two parts of me are tearing away my physical self.

I've known for a while I have borderline tendencies. I'm probably even a psychopath. Which came first? Was I always this way? Or did what happened to me make me this way? I don't know.

I do know I'm special. I've always been exceptional. That used to be enough to get me through the days and nights. But now... I'm just angry. Disappointed. Frustrated. I don't understand why people don't see what I have to offer.

Angel has to accept me. I'm her only hope. I really am. We could figure this out if she just opened her eyes and listened. I know what's best for her. I will take care of her. I will keep her safe. I love her.

If she doesn't come around soon, I will have no choice but to take matters into my own hands. I've started the process because I know in my gut she's going to continue to put me off. I really hope she understands what she means to me. I don't want to have to show her. I really don't. But I will if that's the only option she leaves me.

CHAPTER FORTY

NICK

My cubicle walls are plastered with notes, photos, and questions. The biggest question doesn't need to be on paper: Why? Why would someone want to kill people who have been through so much?

Two things tie the victims together. One, they're all survivors of long-term abduction, and two, they're members of Komo. Other than that, they're very different. There's no geographic connection. Their ages are different, their lifestyles and responses to their experiences are different.

Kait is—was—fifty-nine and lived in Connecticut. The man who abducted her was killed during her rescue, so he is not a suspect. Kait has—rather, had—sufficient financial resources, even without Komo's support. She was well prepared to live a good, long life. Her career in banking made her a saver before her abduction, and she inherited money from her father's estate when he passed a year after she was rescued. Kait was active in many things, both within and outside of Komo. She led an online book club for her local library. She wrote articles for the animal rescue league and monitored a missing pets Facebook page. She was a digital member of a women's club. She had a lot going on and was extremely well-liked. As the LEO told me on the phone, she was a local celebrity.

Tiffany was twenty-seven and lived in Wichita. The popular minister who kept her locked in a trailer on the edge of his property is rotting in prison. He will likely live out his life there since Tiffany wasn't his only victim—just his last. Of the three, Tiffany is the one that seems capable of deciding to end her life. She told Dr. Lisa she found her job boring but couldn't think of another that would interest her. She lived with two roommates who were strangers to her, hoping to get used to being around 'Norms' again. Unfortunately, the roommates found her odd and distant, especially since she would not speak. They stayed in the apartment they shared because of the location and the good deal on the rent.

Tiffany's only other interactions were on Reddit discussion boards. Those are a bit of a surprise. She had numerous sexual interactions. She created a setup in her bedroom to make and send videos without showing her face. The movies on her laptop are explicit, but she is genuinely enjoying herself. She did most of her engaging in a group that supports the minister who abused her. I wonder if any of the pillars of the community realize she is the same 'dirty whore' they claim seduced the innocent God-fearing man they continue to praise.

Karmen is the most brutal case to accept for me. The twenty-five-year-old mother of three did not seem the type who would take her life and leave her children without a mom. Everyone at Komo believed she was ready to fight her husband's legal efforts to the end, and if she lost, she would regroup and fight again. The fact there's evidence she was murdered is weirdly comforting. Her kids don't have to believe their mom made a choice to leave them. But is it better knowing your mother was killed, seemingly because of something terrible done to her? In either case, it's heartbreaking.

Starting with the common logistical denominators has me looking at everyone involved in Komo. In the last 48 hours, I've read the files of all 34 Hope members and the eighty-something people on the Promise side. I've also taken a deep dive into the staff files. I'm relatively confident there are no bad apples in the two dozen folks on the Foundation's payroll, but I've been surprised before.

Komorebi is not in the public eye. Participation is by invitation only, after candidates are vetted. It is not talked about in the media. It is only known to law enforcement personnel on a 'need to know' basis, mainly through my connections.

Promise and Hope are kept separate. Folks don't mingle unless they're connected outside the organization—for instance, the family of a survivor. But the very nature of Komo means someone involved in Promise would be able to deduce who might be involved on the Hope side. Could it be someone whose child did not return home? That's definitely a possibility.

Or could it be an actual Hope survivor? Maybe. Dr. Lisa said one member has a pessimistic outlook about life for survivors. Apparently, the same person makes some of the female Hope members uncomfortable. Jimmy Zamora's file is set aside on my desk.

Whoever it is, they must have resources, as the victims are literally spread across the country. If they have a job, they'd need to take time to travel to and from and pay for airfare, car rental, and hotels. That would require cash and flexibility. Maybe they drove. Maybe it's someone who can work anywhere.

The murders were committed on a Tuesday, a Friday, and a Sunday, so there's no detectable pattern. Plus, it's unlikely they did what they did without at least some reconnaissance first, which means they spent a few days watching their victims before acting.

And then, how did they get in? Kait and Karmen lived in single-family houses; Tiffany lived in a fifth-floor apartment. None of the victims were social butterflies, likely to open the door to just anyone, especially not a stranger. Kait recently told Dr. Lisa she hadn't seen another person 'in the flesh' since a year after returning in 2011. Ten years is a long time to not breathe the same air as another human.

Yet there are no signs of forced entry at any of the locations. In fact, they found two cups of tea at each site, suggesting some sort of social interaction before the killings. Always tea, so that must mean something. Unfortunately, Karmen's and Tiffany's cups were washed before the connection was identified. In fact, everything at Kait's home was packed up and donated, per her instructions. The delay before we realized these might be murders rather than suicides has negatively impacted our ability to get good evidence from any of the crime scenes; too much time has passed, and too many people have been in and out.

Is the killer persuading them to kill themselves? I suppose that's possible, but would someone really choose to slash their forearms if that's true? That is an excruciating way to die and a terrible way for your children to discover you. Karmen had no idea who would find her body. I must believe a mother who loved her kids as much as Karmen loved hers would choose a less gruesome way to end her life, especially if there was even a slight chance her kids would find her.

There's no indication of resistance from any of them. Kait was stretched out on her bed, prosthetics on her stomach, bag over her head. Tiffany was in the driver's seat of her roommate's car, head tilted back, music playing. And Karmen was naked in the tub, clothes folded neatly and set on the closed toilet lid.

If we are looking at murders, does the person think they're being merciful? Are they on some sort of angel of death kick?

Or is it possible these are, in fact, suicides? I'm having a hard time buying into it. But we've yet to find any physical evidence that confirms these are murders and not self-inflicted. Maybe after Kait's death, Tiffany and Karmen made some sort of suicide pact.

But why are there *two* cups of tea at each scene?

I unpin three photos: Tiffany in the car, Kait on the bed, Karmen in the tub. Something's tickling the back of my brain. What is it? I scan each photo, first looking at it normally, then looking at it 'abnormally.' I take a piece of paper and fold it in half, then cover Tiffany's photo, leaving a one-inch strip at the bottom. I start at the right corner and 'read' the image as if I were reading in Japanese:

my eyes shift left, then I slide the paper up and repeat. Even though there are no words here, it's similar to the way people sometimes proofread. When you force your brain to let go of what it expects to find, it can't fill in blanks as quickly. It makes things that don't belong or make sense stand out.

That's how I spot a small star sticker. Tiffany's roommate was not a neat freak, at least according to the car's condition. Apparently, the roommate didn't often drive since they were so close to campus. The old Volvo's interior reflects that lack of use. The dashboard and gauge areas are clearly dusty. But a single gold star, the kind a young kid would get in school, has been pressed onto the odometer. A tiny area around the star is dust-free.

I repeat the process with Kait's image. Nothing. Maybe I'm reaching for something.

I cover Karmen's photo with the folded paper and begin to scan. I'm near the top of the picture when I see something on the mirror above the bathroom sink. I can't make it out without assistance. I dig through my junk drawer and retrieve an ancient magnifying glass I found in the supplies area of one of our branch offices years ago. It might be something–a star or a smudge of toothpaste–but I can't be 100%. I pull down all of the photos from Karmen's scene and look for any that include the mirror.

There it is. A gold star sticker in the corner of the bathroom mirror.

We've got a killer.

CHAPTER FORTY-ONE

NICK

Lisa can't tell me much; she's bound by patient confidentiality laws and the Komorebi Agreement, but there's more wiggle room than there could have been, thanks to her foresight. When Peter started Komorebi, he knew it would be essential to protect patients' privacy. He also knew there could come a time when he would need to be able to bend, if not break, that wall of privacy. Working with Lisa and the greatest legal minds Peter could hire, the Komo agreement has clauses written around this very topic. Each member of Komo signs the agreement when they join and recommits every twenty-four months. The clauses allow certain information to be shared for the greater good: aka, life-saving.

I've spoken to Lisa, Peter, and Marnie about Jimmy Zamora to get what I can from them. There have been four complaints against Jimmy by two different female members within the group. In both situations, Jimmy attempted to start romantic relationships and was rebuked. There is no report from Angel, although Emily told Dr. Lisa about his behavior with her friend. Peter and Lisa retrieved the digital records of the incidents, wrote up a summary to protect others involved, and provided them to me.

I decided it was worth a quick trip to Jersey to poke around rather than relying on phone calls and email, so I'm here now. I meet with one of the officers involved in Jimmy's abduction case. He tells me more about the family dynamics and how the parents had one hell of a blame party while Jimmy was gone, and again upon his return at nine years of age. Per the police in Morristown, Jimmy spent more time in trouble than not between 13 and 20. Assault, burglary, car theft, B&E, and of course, drugs. When he was twenty, a court-appointed attorney knew about Komorebi and put them in touch. Jimmy went through rehab, joined the community, and has stayed clean... as far as we know.

Five years ago, he when his material grandmother passed, he inherited cash for a down payment and purchased a house in Morristown. He's paid the mortgage on time and had no trouble keeping up with taxes, insurance, and utilities. There have been no complaints about the exterior of the house or activities that required LEO intervention.

I'm headed there now. According to his Komo file, Jimmy is employed as a cook at an upscale retirement village. That will be my next stop.

When I arrive at the address of Jimmy's home, there are construction trucks and workers everywhere. Interesting. I get out of the car and approach one of the workers, who directs me to the boss. I introduce myself and ask, "Looks like Jimmy is doing some upgrading?"

He shrugs. "Don't know nobody named Jimmy. Frank is the owner. He buys houses and flips 'em. We've been working on this one for a month now."

Interesting. I thank him and walk down the drive, then take a left and cruise the sidewalk toward a sweet-looking little old lady watering her garden—code for snooping to see who the guy in the suit is. "Hi, there. My name is Nick. Do you know Jimmy Zamora?"

She doesn't smile. "Can't say I know him well. But he was a decent enough neighbor."

"Was?"

"He sold to one of those flippers."

"Did he say why?"

"I never once spoke with the man the whole time he lived here." She snaps. I get the impression she's not angry at me but still holds a grudge against Jimmy.

"Okay. Well, thanks."

My next stop is the retirement village. If I ever need to move into a group situation, I'm going for this kind of place. Beautiful gardens emphasize the classiness of the joint, and once you enter, it's like a cruise ship on land. Old folks are everywhere, chatting in groups in the library, having wheelchair races down the hall, playing bingo in the fancy dining room. I head toward the dining room and come across a young man in a starched server uniform setting out service on a sea of four-top tables. "I'm looking for Jimmy Zamora. Is he working?"

The kid shakes his head no. "Sorry, man, he quit like a month ago."

"Did he say why?"

"Nah. You should maybe talk to the manager if you want to know. I guess he might've pissed off one too many of the girls," the man says, smirking.

"Girls?" I would not call any of the women I've seen here today 'girls.'

"We sometimes rent out this area for networking and club events, you know? Society stuff. Jimmy would forget he wasn't part of their clubs and would be extra friendly with the female guests. Not physical, don't mean nothing like that, but he'd chat them up, even if they made it clear they didn't want to be chatted up. Then he'd go back and talk about how they were snotty stuck-up bitches." He looks apologetic about the swear word, and I wave it off with a smile. "Anyway, maybe he did that one too many times and got tossed. I'm not sure."

I thank him and head back to the car.

The timing is about right. And if he sold his house, he might have some cash to move around. Oh, Jimmy. What are you up to?

CHAPTER FORTY-TWO

OLIVIA

"Want to chat about anything?" Marnie stops by after gathering her things from the conference room table. She leans against the doorway into Nick's office, which I've commandeered. "Stay for dinner. I've been playing with a new spicy margarita recipe."

It's my fourth time at the Nest in two weeks. That's unusual, and clearly, it hasn't gone unnoticed. I smile. I'm good at projecting emotions I don't feel and hiding the ones I do. "Yum, margaritas!" I indicate my open laptop and the notebooks scattered around. "Let me finish up some things, and I'll come to the house."

"Kewlio, Julio!" She passes close enough to drop a kiss on my hair, then is gone, on to the next thing or person who needs her attention. Marnie was twenty-three when she and Dad met, and she's thirty-four now. Not much older than me. Some children might find the premise upsetting: a younger woman setting her sights on a wealthy older man. With Dad and Marnie, it was nothing like that. They were drawn together because they needed each other. If Mom can't be here, Marnie is a perfect Act 2 for Dad. Love flows from her like water over rocks. It's real. It's comforting. Plus, she's very astute and sees things others don't. She's good for all of us.

Dad and I are the only ones left in the offices. I hear his phone ring but don't pay attention until he puts the call on speaker. It's Nick. My ears perk up. Since he can see me through the glass walls, I pretend to focus on my computer screen. The cursor flashes at me impatiently.

"I'm flying into Canyonlands tomorrow. I'm sure you were wondering; there is no such thing as a direct flight from DC to Moab, Utah. It will take me almost seven hours from Dulles," Nick complains.

Dad laughs. "If you were in LA, it would only take–" I hear him clicking at his keyboard, and his sigh indicates this wasn't what he was hoping to see, "five and a half hours. She really does live in the middle of nowhere."

"I've about had it with her bullshit independence," Nick announces, and I silently cheer. "Her choices affect my stress level, and it's not acceptable." I want to nod in agreement.

"Tread lightly. We've both seen how Angel responds when she feels cornered. We need her to be cooperative, not defensive," Dad says in his most serious tone. "Whatever's happening feels like it's headed straight at us. I don't like it. Get her back here where she's safe."

"Will do," Nick says. "In other news... there was a star symbol at Tiffany's place, too. None of the team on site noticed because it was such a random detail, but it jumped out once I knew what I was looking for. There was a star on the bathroom mirror."

Dad is silent for a moment. "Damn it. Why? What is the killer trying to say?" He taps his fingers on the table, drum drum drum. "Were you able to spot anything at Kait's?"

"No. I've looked at every photo, and there's nothing star-related there."

No, there wasn't. I would've noticed.

"When the press really gets hold of this, they will come up with some stupid name related to star signs and horoscopes," Nick grunts.

"Let's keep the press away as long as possible. What are the chances they'd connect these dots?"

"Good, apparently, because at least one of the smaller foreign tabloids has already started. They did a piece on Kait's death. They ran breaking news alerts about Tiffany and Karmen as they happened, suggesting they're doing a bigger story. Can't remember the exact title, but it was a play on the stupid 'final girls' concept from movies," Nick says.

"Shit."

"Definitely shit."

"Okay. I've got to get to the house. Em is coming for dinner, and I believe my beloved daughter is also joining us." He smiles at me through the glass.

I give him a vague smile back, as though I'm deep in thought on whatever I'm working through. Don't want to make it obvious I was listening.

Emily Bright was part of Angel's last misadventure when she took on a crazed sheriff who abducted women, abused and tortured them, and hunted them for fun. Emily survived, but her best friend, Harper, did not, despite Angel's best efforts. Emily was severely traumatized and physically broken. She spent much of her recovery time under Marnie's loving wing at the Nest. Now she's basically a family member because Dad loves taking care of everyone.

The sun is starting to set as Dad, Marnie, Em, and I enjoy spicy margaritas on the patio. Grace and Rosie are at the stable. A whole salmon is roasting in the oven. Marnie and Emily are taking an online cooking course together, and this menu is from one of the lessons.

"While the girls are gone, I want to give you two a head's up," Dad says, looking from me to Emily. "It appears Tiffany and Karmen's deaths were not suicides."

Emily gasps, and I open my mouth in feigned shock.

"We're not sure about Kait, but at this point, it seems possible, likely even."

It's not.

"Why on earth would someone want to murder them? Haven't they been through enough?" Marnie demands.

161

Dad shakes his head. "Not clear yet. The one thing we have tying them together is a small symbol found at two of the sites."

"What kind of symbol?" Em asks, frowning.

"A star."

"A religious star? Or, like–a star?" Emily points up to the sky. The light pollution from the LA basin prevents us from seeing anything but satellites. Still, we all know what she means.

"A star." Dad points up.

Emily sucks in her breath. "Angel has a galaxy of stars on her arm."

Dad, Marnie, and I all stare at her. Because yes, yes, she does.

CHAPTER FORTY-THREE

Idaho

The others were easily persuaded to let me in, but this one refuses to even open the door, although I see her peeking at me through the small hole. I don't know whether her refusal is because of her agoraphobia or overall paranoia. Either way, a closed door won't stop me.

A few minutes ago, I saw the guardians load up with their two boys and head off to cheer on their future soccer star. Uniforms, folding chairs, and a cooler indicate they'll be gone for a while.

Unsurprisingly, Hannah stayed home.

Hannah struggles with agoraphobia, and she carries tremendous guilt over the deaths of her mother and brother. She's also Angel's pet. Everything I want from Angel, she gets. Am I 'helping' her purely from a place of compassion? Probably not. Do I feel bad about that? No.

It was easy enough to find her. The streets are named after trees, the cross streets numbered "lanes." The house is in one of those tracts where everything looks exactly like everything else on the block and the ten blocks around it. There are four paint schemes: blue and white, green and light green, beige and light beige, and a rebellious red. Houses in a similar paint scheme must be separated by two differently themed houses. The only way to tell one house from another is by the decor on the identical front stoops. Only sports team banners, school pride signs, and planters separate one from another.

The street lights have just come on. They're easy enough to dodge.

I'm a little surprised by the lack of security. There are no lights triggered by motion, no visible cameras, or even an actual fence. No dog, either. They almost deserve this.

I'm not heartless. *Almost.*

The property may not be secured, but the young lady herself isn't stupid. I watch her through a gap in a dining room curtain as she checks the front door and goes from window to window, ensuring everything is locked. I duck down as she enters the small dining room. The table is covered with homework and mail and abandoned jackets and sports equipment. I'd bet anything the family eats in the kitchen or in front of the TV. I'd guarantee the table is only usable from the end of November until January 2nd.

I can't see Hannah for a moment until the light in the next room goes on–kitchen, probably, since it's the back corner of the house. I move around the side of the house, occasionally popping up to look inside. My only concern is Hannah calling someone, the guardian, or the police. I didn't see her near the phone in the kitchen, but she has a cell phone like every other kid in America.

I'm counting on there being another door around the back. It will be locked, I'm sure, but I can get around that. I've picked up random skills over the past few years. No one will ever keep me against my will again. I've spent hours practicing picking locks, repelling down the sides of cliffs and buildings, holding my breath underwater. I can cut power and phone lines and circumvent alarm systems. I could be an excellent thief.

Hannah has made a mistake. She should have turned on every light in the house. Instead, she turns them off behind herself as she goes room to room, making it easy for me to follow her progress. Eventually, only the living room light and a single bedroom light upstairs glow. I'm sure that is her bedroom. Perfect.

I pull my toolkit from my pack and release the back door lock in less than thirty seconds.

In the kitchen, I pause and take a look around. As expected, good girl Hannah turned everything off and went upstairs, probably to lock herself in her bedroom, so she feels safe until Mr. and Mrs. Guardian get home with their boys. Unfortunately, she has a different destiny.

I slip off my shoes and leave them just inside the kitchen door. Houses can give you away with a squeak or creak if you're not careful. Going in bare feet is a better choice. I make a quick turn around the downstairs–from the kitchen to dining to living to the family room and back to the kitchen again–to be absolutely positive we're alone. Satisfied, I move carefully toward the stairs and climb slowly, listening to the second floor.

Since I wasn't invited in, the tea routine will not work. I will have to go with plan B. It's not as smooth, and there's a better chance of exposure, but at this point, it doesn't really matter. We're almost to the end.

I have a pre-drugged water bottle in my bag, which will get things started.

From the second-floor landing, I can see that the bathroom door is open and the light on; I couldn't see it clearly from the back of the house. There's a low-glow bulb that keeps the hallway from being pitch black. There are three closed doors. Hannah has left hers open, presumably so she can hear when the family returns. She's a thinker; she has music on because a silent house is a scary house, but she's kept the volume low so it won't cover the sounds of someone moving around.

Since the bathroom light is on, I bet she's polishing her nails, curling her hair, or playing with makeup. I decide to trust my gut and take a chance. The bathroom is good-sized, useful for the three teens that share it. There's a walk-in shower behind a curtain featuring a dinosaur wearing a shower cap. Excellent. I step behind the curtain and wait.

My gut did not fail me. It's only a few minutes until I hear the footsteps of a petite young woman in the hallway, the sound dulling as she moves from carpet to tile in the bathroom. Hannah thinks she's alone, so she isn't making any effort to be quiet. She inspects her complexion in the mirror above the sink, convenient for me. The vanity with double sinks is on the room's left side, and the toilet and linen cabinet are on the right. The shower takes up the room's width opposite the door and conveniently is not captured by the mirror.

Hannah doesn't hear me step out of the shower. She only reacts when my left arm wraps around her neck and squeezes. She's thrashing, her bare feet kicking at me. Once I have her in a solid hold, I use my free hand to pry her mouth open. It's not easy with the plastic water bottle in the same hand, and it takes a minute with both of us fighting to win. Finally, I get the bottle tipped above her opened mouth and drain its contents down her throat, ignoring the coughing and choking as she resists.

I see her look of surprise when she spots me in the mirror and struggles to put together who I am, but all that matters is I'm the last person she'll see.

The drug is not instant, but it takes effect quickly enough to incapacitate her because of her small stature. I half carry, half drag her to her bedroom and shove her onto the bed. Her body is still capable, but her mind is going through several new experiences. Her brain can't control her limbs. I have to roll her onto her back. I sit next to her, pressing her down into the mattress, giving the roofie enough time to work. It takes a while. Once she's mostly still, I open my bag and pull out another bottle of water and a container of pills. Vicodin seems like a good choice here. Easy enough to get, easy enough to take. I put a generous handful of pills on the nightstand next to the second water bottle, both within easy reach.

She's like a rag doll as I slip between her and the headboard and hold her up in a sitting position. I tip her head back against my shoulder and put the first pills in her mouth. I rub her throat like you would a cat to encourage the drugs to go down. I repeat this a couple more times. Her arm spasms involuntarily and knocks the water bottle over. I catch it before too much is spilled and slowly and carefully pour water into her open mouth to flush the pills down. Satisfied, I slide out from behind her and let her fall back on the pillows. She is relaxed, not moving. That is probably still from the original dose of Rohypnol. I don't think the Vicodin could work this quickly.

Once I'm confident she can't make a run for it, I take a moment and look around the room. There's a framed photograph of Angel on the dresser. She's squatting next to a dog. At least, I think it's a dog. It's one of the oddest creatures I've ever seen. Doesn't surprise me at all. Angel likes to collect the strays and the weirdos.

Hannah's laptop is open. The screen-saver has come on, and I jiggle the mouse, but I cannot move it away without a password. It would've been nice to know what she was up to right before I came in.

I put a few more pills on the nightstand to clarify what she took. I try hard to suppress the urge to leave a star but fail. I can't resist pressing the little gold foiled reward onto the photo of Angel and the dog. Appropriate.

I glance at my watch. It's only been about 40 minutes since I knocked on the door and was turned away, but I don't want to overstay my welcome.

My mission is complete. Now I can move on to the main show, the one that really matters. We are almost to the climax.

CHAPTER FORTY-FOUR

PRIVILEGED & CONFIDENTIAL

Komorebi file #140

Adams, Hannah

[Photos: First, smiling teenage girl with green eyes and strawberry blonde hair to her waist, no makeup, wearing high school track and country uniform. She's smiling and holding a medal. Second, hair chopped to chin length, eyes are downcast. Wearing a black oversized hoodie. Appear self-concious and uncomfortable.]

Location: Nampa, ID

DOB: 4/2/2003   **Abduction:** 6/12/2018

Recovery: 9/24/2018   **Current Age:** 18

Offender Status: Killed during recovery

Notes: Abductor was a friend of Hannah's older cousin. Hannah's brother and mother were killed during the abduction. Kept in a closet for three months. Friend of perp reported to authorities. Hannah lives with her mother's best friend and family. Becoming close to social phobic; doesn't like to leave the house. Taking college courses in graphic design online.

Tell me about the day you were taken. What do you remember about that time?

NOTE: Hannah will not discuss the events of that night. The following note is from the case file provided by the Nampa PD.

Hannah, high school sophomore, lived with mother (41) and brother (14). Father died in a car crash when Hannah was eight. Close family. Mom dated, but no one was serious. Met abductor at a church picnic. The boy was a friend of Hannah's older cousin. Cousin & abductor worked at a local fast-food restaurant. No one noticed the boy showing particular interest in Hannah, so no threat was perceived. A week after the picnic, the boy broke into the house in the middle of the night, stabbed Hannah's mother and brother in their sleep, and took Hannah to his house. His parents were out of town for the weekend and had no idea anything was going on.

Would you like to talk about your time in captivity? It can benefit short-term and long-term recovery, but it is totally understandable if you choose not to talk about it today. I will follow your lead!

There's not that much to tell. I was there for one hundred and four days. George kept me bound and gagged in his closet when his family was home. He brought me out to 'play with' when they went to work. He would show me his games, collectibles, comics, stuff like that. He didn't hurt me or try to have sex with me. I was his pet. He liked to brush my hair and stroke my arms.

I figured out quickly he had a really low IQ. He seemed to think I was a prize, like his comic books. He told me he kept the things he loved and valued the most in his closet to keep them safe when he was gone.

People asked me later why I didn't run away from him, since he wasn't very smart. For one, he was really big. I mean, really tall and heavyset, and strong. And he lived with his parents, who were—let's say not nice. I could hear them fighting, threatening to kill each other. I had no idea how they would react if they found out about me. Like, would they help him so he didn't get in trouble? It just seemed extra frightening.

What do you remember about being recovered?

One day he forgot to lock the closet door. I didn't hear the regular click. I waited a while and then tried turning the handle. I opened the door and looked out, and nobody was there. I had cuffs on my wrists and my ankles. I didn't want to stop to look for a key. Once I was outside, I realized his house was in a rural area. I had to hop barefoot more than a mile along dirt and gravel roads, hiding when a car came by because I was afraid it was him.

When I finally reached a real asphalt road, I hid until I saw a vehicle that felt safe—it was a little Meals on Wheels delivery car, one of those tiny cars. I recognized it because I volunteered for them the summer before. I jumped out in front of it, and the poor driver nearly hit me. He was so mad he got out and started yelling. I guess he recognized me, though. He put me in the car and drove straight to the police station. Nice guy.

What's your day like now?

I live with my mom's best friend Judy and her husband and sons. They're really nice. I finished high school online, and now I'm taking design courses. I want to be a graphic designer. I like making things pretty. And I can do that without leaving my house. I'm kind of scared to go outside. I'm working on it. Well, you know, because you're helping me. That's my big goal for the next year. To be comfortable going outside. You never know how much you'll miss the sun on your skin until it's not there.

Thank you for sharing your memories and experiences. I can imagine it is difficult to talk about.

It makes sense that recovering after something so traumatic can be emotionally messy sometimes. Would you consider yourself happy since your recovery?

Not yet. But I will be.

Notes were taken during her initial Komo session. LC

CHAPTER FORTY-FIVE

PETER

I'm dreaming. Someone is screaming, and someone is sobbing.
Who? Where? Why?

My eyes fly open. Not dreaming.

"Peter! The girls!" I see Marnie's back as she races from the room.
I roll out of bed and follow. We have had our children taken from
us in the past, and now there is no greater fear.

The girls' suite is on the other side of the living area. We navigate
couches and coffee tables and the piano thanks to a full moon cast-
ing bright light through the glass windows. I'm behind Marnie as
she charges through their shared sitting room into Grace's bedroom,
guided by the terrifying sounds.

Grace is huddled at the head of her bed, shrieking, blue eyes wide
with panic and fear. Rosie is next to her, thin arms roped around the
girl who is her sister in every way but blood. Between her own sobs,
Rosie soothes, "It's okay, it's okay, it's going to be okay."

Marnie crawls across the horse-themed bedspread and takes both
into her arms, creating a human tent of love. I perch on the edge of
the double bed because it's the only space left for me and reach for
Tank, the chihuahua, who is shaking even more than usual. Marnie
kisses her child's forehead, and the wailing stops, but tears continue
to stream down her face. "Did you have a bad dream? Did you both
have bad dreams?"

Rosie is crying so hard she begins to hiccup. Now that we're here,
she feels it's okay to be scared, too. She doesn't have to be the strong

one, and she collapses into Marnie, who squeezes tight.

"Girls, please, what's happening? What's going on? Please tell us!" I whisper, stroking Grace's arm. She's wearing horse-themed shorty pajamas that match the bed cover. Her blond hair is plastered to her forehead, sticky with sweat.

Grace squeezes her eyes closed and takes a deep breath, calming herself. We give her space, but it's hard. Her screams were heartbreaking, and I need to know what caused them. Finally, she says, "There's a kid at school. His dad owns one of those yucky tabloids." She sniffs, and her face scrunches as if she's going to cry again, but she holds it in. "Today, he was harassing me, saying I'm going to be next."

"Be next?" Marnie asks, smoothing her hair. "Be next for what? What does that mean?"

"Be the next survivor to die."

Marnie's eyes grow large, and I feel my heart drop.

"Because of Alfred." She adds.

Rosie clarifies. "He said someone is killing people who survived being abducted, and since Grace was abducted, she's going to be killed next!"

Because Grace was so young and rarely mentions that terrible time, I often forget she was there. I didn't realize Rosie knew about it at all. Someone is putting the pieces together. That's bad enough. To spew my girls with this garbage is unacceptable.

"He's wrong. Nothing is going to happen to you." I really want a word with the boy's father. What kind of asshole shares things like that with his kid, and what type of kid thinks it's fun to tell another kid they're going to be murdered?

Rosie looks at me with wounded eyes and drops another bombshell. "He also said you're not my dad. He said Olivia is my mom, not my sister, and Angel's dead brother is my real dad."

Marnie gasps. Time stops. The plan was always to tell Rosie the story of her birth. After talking with Lisa, we decided to wait until she was thirteen. For one thing, I needed time to get Olivia on board. She's reluctant to discuss her 'connection' to Rosie.

"We obviously have a lot to talk about. Grace, I promise you, no one is going to hurt you. Your mom won't let them. I won't let them. No one can access the house or any of us without passing guards, gates, and cameras. If it makes you feel safer, we can hire a security guard, just until this is solved. Would that help you feel safer?"

Grace's head is pressed into her mother's shoulder. She shakes her head, no. "You're right. I'm not really so afraid now. I had a bad dream about... him. That time. The woman. And Bud." She says his name with a sob and looks as though she will burst into tears again. I squeeze her hand and motion for Rosie to come closer to me.

Rosie shakes her head. She's mad. "Bud. That's my dad, right?"

I nod. "Yes. Bud, Angel's twin brother, is your biological father."

"Did he know about me?" Rosie asks, looking hopeful.

Grace answers. "He didn't. He died protecting me." And she falls apart again. She remembers a lot. Excellent timing.

"He didn't know about you. As Grace says, he died before anyone knew Olivia was pregnant." I reach over to Grace, raise her chin with my finger and look her in the eye. "He died because a terrible person killed him. It isn't your fault in any way, Grace. Not one single bit of it."

She gives me a forced smile. Her head knows, but her heart...

"And Olivia is–my mom?" Rosie frowns. "She doesn't even like me. Is that why? Because she didn't want me?"

Gut punch. "No, my love, no. When she had you, Olivia was just a young girl, not much older than Grace is now. She had been taken away from us and kept a prisoner for a very long time. She was traumatized. She wasn't ready to be a mother, but she knew she wanted you to be with us. That's how I came to adopt you. It's been one of the greatest blessings of my life." I realize I didn't protest her claim that Olivia doesn't like her. I'm not going to lie now.

Marnie meets my eyes over their heads, and her expression is full of compassion. We've had it easy. The time has come to pay the piper.

"I want to talk to Angel," Rosie says.

"We will make it happen."

Grace tips her head up to look at her mom. "Will you sleep in here? With Rosie and me?"

Marnie tries to lighten the mood. "What about you, big guy? You okay sleeping by yourself?"

"Yes, but I'm taking Tank with me," I respond, arranging the quaking Chihuahua in my arms. I'm ashamed to be relieved this part of the discussion is over. I need to talk to Lisa before round two. I need guidance. I'm pretty sure I won't get much sleep tonight.

CHAPTER FORTY-SIX

OLIVIA

Nick is scheduled to land just before 3 pm. I flew in yesterday. Otherwise, we would have been on the same connector from Denver to Moab because there's only one per day. That's okay. It left me plenty of time to rent a car and pick out a spot to watch from. Since the planes only have 50 seats, I don't imagine he'll be hard to spot.

There are wonderful hotels in and around Moab, but I don't want anyone to recognize me and wonder what I was doing there– or tattle. Yesterday I found a cute old-school motel and checked in using Christopher's surname, which I did not officially take when we married. I have been practicing grunging myself up. I got a great room decorated with local art and a perfect spot for my car right outside the door.

Last night I feasted on fast food while watching reruns of Keith Morrison episodes of *Dateline*. It was one of the most relaxing evenings I've had in ages. Maybe Angel has the right idea after all.

This morning I had breakfast at a local diner, then drove around town, trying to understand what draws Angel to this particular place... or maybe, if I get lucky, I'll spot her.

I don't know where Angel lives, exactly. Is she in town or an hour outside of it? Which direction? Sadly, she's never felt comfortable sharing that information with me. All I know is she has a PO Box in Moab, so it's one of the places I decide to check out first. Maybe it's mail day.

How will she react if I pop up in front of her? She'll probably be angry. Probably? Who am I kidding? She'll undoubtedly be angry. Furious, probably. She has definite thoughts about boundaries. First, she'll be pissed I'm spying on her and invading her personal space. Then she'll try to push me away. Eventually, she might agree to have a cup of coffee at some public space. One thing she won't do is invite me to her home. She calls it Stargazer. More Bud. I'll never see it, at least not at her invitation.

One of the few things I have on my side in this needle-in-a-haystack mission is that I know Angel drives a baby blue Bronco. It was Bud's dream car, and Angel bought it to honor him. She makes a lot of choices based on 'honoring' her brother. Nothing wrong with it, of course, as long as she doesn't lose herself in the process.

A baby blue Bronco will stand out in this land of yuppies and tree-huggers and van lifers. Unfortunately, there's not a blue Bronco in sight amidst the pack of Subarus, converted buses, custom Sprinter vans, and trucks.

At noon I go back to the motel, shower, and change. Usually, when I'm on "me time," I wear tailored trousers and light knit tops or sweaters. I learned a bit after New Jersey. For this mission, I'm wearing clothes I'd never wear in real life: hiking boots, camo-printed denim, a black waffle-knit shirt that snaps down the front, and a brown canvas jacket. I've pulled my expensively maintained pale blond hair into a tight bun and tucked it under a baseball cap. I'm makeup-free. I'm still an attractive female, so I'll get some notice. Still, I'm relatively confident no one will recognize me as Olivia Baden, especially not when I'm behind the wheel of a Ford sedan.

I need to be careful. While I wouldn't be upset if I ran into Angel, I have zero interest in coming face-to-face with our personal FBI agent. Nick would not appreciate my eavesdropping, especially since I'm using him for my own agenda. He'd tell Dad, and Dad would be disappointed, at the very least. And then Marnie would be sad, and Christopher would be confused...

No, I just need to stay out of sight and follow him wherever Angel is going to meet him. Then, I can follow her back to Stargazer. Once Nick leaves, I will finally share what I need her to understand.

CHAPTER FORTY-SEVEN

OLIVIA

Nick's plane lands on time. I watch him slip behind the wheel of a rented Jeep because, of course, he'd rent a Jeep rather than a practical sedan like mine. He's a guy you notice: tall and dark and strikingly handsome. Over the years, we've spent a lot of 'family' time together, so I'm used to seeing him in casual clothes. There's something different about him today. His jeans and French blue T-shirt highlight all his best qualities. Did he choose these clothes on purpose? I'm confident he knows what makes him look good. But did he intend to look especially good today?

It's 3:10, plenty of daylight left. Is he going to meet Angel somewhere? Does she know he's here? Or will he call her and ask her to meet him in town? Will she allow him to come to her home? The unknowing, combined with anticipation, is making me itchy. I hate not being in control.

Since this was the only inbound flight of the day, there's a bit of traffic, which I appreciate. My disguise is good, but I'm not 100% confident he wouldn't see through it if I was immediately behind him. When he turns toward Moab proper, I follow at a safe distance, keeping a car or two between us.

Nick doesn't go to a hotel or a diner. He acts like he knows exactly where he's going. Then it hits me. How did I not realize sooner? I'm an idiot! Since he set up and manages Angel's trust, Dad has the property address. He'd have no hesitation sharing with Nick if he was worried about Angel. He'd risk her wrath rather than let

179

her be put in danger.

I could have saved myself a lot of trouble if I'd realized this sooner. The one thing I've always been able to count on, my analytical brain, is slipping. I'm falling apart. Something's got to give.

CHAPTER FORTY-EIGHT

NICK

On the one hand, I'm excited to see Angel. On the other hand, I'm afraid to see Angel. I don't think she'll shoot me. At least I hope she won't shoot me.

Stargazer is near Spanish Valley, roughly 10 miles south of Moab along Highway 191. It's a beautiful drive. The Moab fault is to my right, its towering cliffs of red clay demanding my attention. As I pass through the town itself, I wish I was here for fun. Signs promote bike and ATV rentals, guided hikes and tours, and some restaurants look interesting. Maybe someday Angel will let me actually visit instead of forcing me to sneak up on her.

It's only 35 minutes to Angel's place. There aren't a lot of street signs. I pass a sign for Chicken Corners, and my curiosity is piqued. There's an RV park on the left. A sign announces another coming up on the same side. There are several pull-offs where cars have stopped, presumably so their drivers can explore a little bit. May is full-blown tourist season, and this is Disneyland for a particular variety of outdoors adventure folks.

I had to plug in the GPS coordinates as there's no address per se. But Google guides me easily. I stop on the west side of the highway fifty feet short of the driveway and get my bearings. A fence runs roughly a quarter-mile before the gate and a quarter-mile past it. There's a road of some sort at the southern end. The gate in the center is big and imposing and runs on an electric pulley system. I know I'm in the right spot because there's a tiny sign that announces

Stargazer, and there's a large mailbox. Angel orders books, videos, and stuff for the dogs she'd want to keep safe from the desert version of porch pirates.

It's just after 4:00 pm. There's a chance Angel isn't here. Still, I believe she'd respect Peter's request to let one of us know if she was heading anywhere, considering the circumstances. But she is Angel, and Angel has a mind of her own.

Should I use the call box I see by the gate or call her cell? There's a 50/50 shot of her responding either way. Put a pin in that. Do I try a charm offensive or attempt to use authority? That makes me snort. I can pretend she'd respect my authority, but why delude myself. My only hope is charm. All right. So charm it is.

I press her speed dial number on my phone, which is hooked to the Bluetooth in the Jeep. She picks up on the second ring and sounds like she's in a good mood. "Who is pestering me on my telephone device?"

"Howdy, Ms. Evanston. Whatcha doing?"

"Hi!" She's surprised to hear from me even though my name must have appeared on her caller ID. She's distracted. That's excellent. She won't have time to get herself riled up. "I'm having a very exciting day. I'm debating what to make for dinner and choosing a movie to watch."

"Have you seen *The Mist*? The ending about killed me," I volunteer. One of the interests we share is an interest in horror films.

"I haven't seen it, but I have it on DVD just waiting for the right night. Maybe tonight's the night." Angel chirps.

"What's for dinner?"

"I am trying my hand at lasagna using one of CB's favorite recipes. She and TJ are at some fancy investor dinner for their project, so she's not cooking with me this time. All by my lonesome." She sighs dramatically, no idea she has just set herself up.

"I'll help. I make a mean lasagna." I offer, pulling the Jeep up to the gate.

"Cool! Come on over!" She jokes.

"Already here. Let me in." Despite myself, tension creeps into my tone.

Silence. It kills me to keep my mouth shut and wait for her to speak, but I manage. She's good, though. I clock her at ninety-four seconds. That's a long damn time.

"You really are here." That's when I realize she's got a camera on the gate. I couldn't see it from the road, but it's clear now.

"I really am." I salute out the window in case the camera can't pick my face up through the windshield. And then I wait.

CHAPTER FORTY-NINE

ANGEL

"What the freaking hell." I'm trying to wrap my head around this. Why is Nick here? I mean, I'm pretty sure I know *why* he's here. But the very fact that he thinks it's okay to just show up pisses me off. Sort of. If I'm honest with myself, I'm excited to see him. Asshole. Damn it, he confuses me. I confuse me, rather. He's clueless. "Follow the drive up to the building. The residence is on the left side of the building. There will be chaos."

Chaos + Angel won't surprise him. Our relationship was born in chaos. The first time I saw him, I was half-dead in the basement of the burning Dollhouse. I thought he was welcoming me to Heaven. Then I ran away from a perfectly good–some might say great–home to be a teenage runaway. That still wasn't chaotic enough for me, so I jumped into a semi with a fiery Latina woman named CB and drove back and forth across the country for a while. A few years ago, I found a bloody girl in a truck stop bathroom and put everyone through all sorts of hell trying to rescue her friend from a crazy man.

Chaos + Angel? Not a surprise to anyone.

What will Nick think of my refuge? It's the place where my personality is most actively on display. No hiding here. Lots of color and loudness. No one would accuse me of concealing who I am after seeing my home.

The living room has an L-shaped sectional sofa upholstered in red dog-friendly microfiber. CB is the one who told me about the magic of microfiber and dog hair. It sounds like a bad combo, but you just put on a rubber glove and run your hand over the fabric to clean it. The fur comes right off! It's amazing. And the occasional oopsie has been hidden under colorful throw pillows, perfect for squishing for a nap, watching a movie, or reading a book.

Concert posters cover the walls, which are a deep yellow. There are plants everywhere. The living room and kitchen rugs are bright and busy, and washable.

The entertainment center with its giant monitor is the only thing in the building that might be considered expensive. But I really enjoy my movies. And music. And watching dog training and defense videos. It was worth the money, and I'm not embarrassed by it.

Even my office, the equivalent of a junk drawer, says a lot about who I am. Random mismatched furniture, an ancient couch, a recliner with a broken footrest have all come here to die. I bought them at garage sales in town when the building was first built. There aren't a lot of furniture stores in Moab. And back then, ordering furniture online wasn't the thing it is today. Neither was furniture in a box. I'm really good at putting things together.

Things, not people. People are harder to understand.

I tell myself I don't care what Nick thinks.

I grab a beer from the cooler and lower myself into one of my patio chairs. Out of spite, I will let the dogs have their way with him while I finish this beer and calm my nerves. Asa and Nope know him from the many times we've been together at The Nest, but the pups have unpredictable manners. And they haven't been one-on-one with a stranger since we left the rescue. He deserves whatever happens to him.

My stomach is making nervous noises as I wait for him to arrive. I watch the dogs investigate the land around us. Nick better be smart enough not to run them over. I know he is. But I'm letting my nerves get me wound up.

Of course, he's driving a Jeep. It's blue. He looks good in blue. Asshole. He spots the herd of animals charging toward him and puts the Jeep in park at the edge of the pad on the barn side of the building. Despite fifteen paws, four snouts, and four tails encasing him in a flurry of exploration, he doesn't hesitate to climb out. No part of him goes unsniffed. His dark jeans and tight blue T-shirt show off everything from his dark curly hair to his big brown eyes to his strong jaw to his broad shoulders, muscular chest, narrow hips, and fantastic legs.

Stop it, Angel.

It's not a secret I've kept from myself, but I've never actually acknowledged it. This is the man I want. Nick is the one I'm always waiting for. I think he may have some kind of feelings, too, but he's an FBI agent, and he has a damned code of conduct. Our relationship started when I was young, and he was a professional sworn to protect me. I'm now a fully-grown woman and no longer need him taking care of me. But he's got *morals*. I practically roll my eyes at the thought.

Screw that. I deserve to be happy. So does he. I think he'll be happy with me. I know I'll be happy with him. Maybe we can be happy together just for a night. That'd be a good starting place. I don't mind a good one-night stand. I've never actually been in a relationship. I've had my fun, I'm no saint, and see no reason to deny myself pleasure.

Besides, the idea of seeing the same person day after day, of having to take their wants and needs into consideration, is mostly repulsive. If it's the right person, it wouldn't be quite so terrible, maybe.

Maybe.

To his credit, Nick manages to cross the yard and make his way onto the patio despite the furry escort. He drops into the second chair and grins. "You weren't kidding. Damn cute chaos, though."

Nick looks at me. Cute chaos? Does he mean me? Or is he talking about the dogs?

No more beer for you, Angel. "You're an asshole. Hello." I finish the beer in my hand. There's a cooler between us that also serves as a coffee table. I flip the lid up, drop the empty inside and fish out another. "Help yourself."

He grabs a beer, opens it, and takes a long, deep drink. Then he sighs, leans back in the chair, and closes his eyes. Like this is a resort, and he's here on vacation. Asshole.

Asa flops down at my side, content to just hang out. Bored with the humans, Nope leads the puppies off for more hole digging and exploring. I run my hand over Asa's sleek fur. "What are you doing here?"

"Muhammad was a pain in the ass and wouldn't come to the mountain."

"Oh, you're a mountain now?" I raise my eyebrow. "You have the quote backward. You're supposed to be Muhammad. But I like it this way. What do you expect to happen, Mountain?" I ask and then blush because that's not what I meant.

He misses the blush. "I expect you to listen to me tell you what's going on in our world, and then I expect you to make smart decisions, for once in your life. That's all."

The blush embarrassed me, and that stokes my righteous indignation. "Tell me what harebrained idea motivated you to show up uninvited and unannounced at my gate. My gate that no one knows how to find other than one Peter Baden and his fleet of overpriced attorneys. What do you two think you're after?"

Nick gives me the FBI Special Agent look that's all intellect and no emotion. I've seen it for years now, although it's rarely used on me. I'm not intimidated. I'm just annoyed. He gives up with the look and shrugs, a wan smile playing on his lips. "Straight talk. People are being murdered. People like you. People you know."

I look at him, expressionless. This isn't news.

"If whatever is happening continues, you are going to be a target at some point. I know you're a badass self-sufficient woman. I am well aware," he's not even mocking, "of your many talents, skills, and things you've learned to keep yourself safe. I know. I really do."

I wave my hand in a 'go on' motion.

"Imagine it's five years from now. Grace and Rosie are in college. Of course, they're at the same school because they're Grace and Rosie."

My gut bubbles, and I narrow my eyes. I don't like where he's going with this at all.

"Someone is killing college girls who grew up in Palos Verdes. Very specific."

I give him a mean look and spin the empty beer bottle in my hand.

"Wouldn't you do everything you could to get them home to you until the danger passed?"

Asshole. I refuse to give him the satisfaction of a response. He knows I'd show up at their dorms in the night and haul their sweet little butts home. Well hell. I take a deep breath through my nose and look him straight in the face. "I hate you." Of course, we both know that's not at all true. But it feels good to say. "Fine. I'll go to the Nest."

"Good. I'll get a hotel room and get us tickets on tomorrow's flight—"

"I can't fly to LA, sir. Have you not noticed the four dogs? Cat will be fine on her own, but the dogs are not as self-sufficient as she is. I'll drive. I'll leave in the morning. You can ride with me or ride crammed into a can with one hundred cootie-carrying strangers. Whatever floats your boat." I give him a look, and my gut flutters. "As to a hotel, you might as well stay here. I'm sure the dogs will give up a bit of the couch. You promised lasagna."

CHAPTER FIFTY

OLIVIA

Because I've been sitting here for hours, my first reaction is that I'm hallucinating. I'm not. The sun is starting to sink behind the mountains, providing a beautiful backdrop to Angel's entrance. I don't need full light to recognize Jimmy freaking Zamora on the red dirt bike that's driven past Angel's gate twice in the last fifteen minutes. My heart races. There's absolutely no good reason for him to be here.

My phone rings, and I nearly jump out of my skin. It's Christopher. I debate letting it go to voice mail, but he's called three times since yesterday morning, and I haven't answered or even texted. He will freak out if I don't answer this time. "Hi, babe."

The endearment doesn't soften his mood. His tone is clipped. "Where are you?"

If I were on top of my game, I'd have spent some of the last 24 hours coming up with a story for just this moment. But I was too lost in my own thoughts. Now I scramble. "I'm sorry. I needed a little quiet. I'm in Arizona, at a spa. There's a strict no-tech rule, which is why I couldn't take your call before -"

"Cut the shit, O. You've found every possible excuse to disappear these last few weeks. I've about had it. I'm a grown man, so I can deal with heartache, but our daughter deserves better. Are you having an affair?" I've never heard him so angry. Part of me flares with delight, feeling desirable and wanting to fight. But the logical part of me realizes it will not serve me in my current situation.

"Don't be ridiculous! Christopher, I love you and only you!" That much is true. "I could never love anyone else the way I love you, and I would never cheat on you. Ever. It's nothing like that. I'm just going through some things right now, and I need a little space and breathing room to figure it out. If you could help, of course, I'd come to you, but this is something I need to deal with on my own. Please, baby, trust me. Give me a few more days."

My words are heartfelt, but my attention is drawn away when I see Jimmy drive by again. What the hell is he doing? What is he after? Why is he here?

If I end my conversation with Christopher now, the damage will be irreparable. I certainly can't tell him where I am. That will start a whole different chain reaction of bad things, things I'm not prepared for.

In LA, Christopher sighs. I can tell he's struggling to manage his emotions. One of the things that drew me to him in the first place is his ability to control himself in nearly any situation. That, and the fact that he's never been put off by me being me—which, honestly, has always included short periods of me being unpredictable and distant. Why is he so wound up this time?

Then I realize. The murders. He thinks I may be a target. He hasn't come out and said so because he doesn't want to put it in my head if it's not already there. But of course, it's already there. "Sweetheart, I promise you, I'm fine, I'm safe, I'm being careful. I know exactly what I'm doing."

"This spa, it has security?" he asks, and I'm pleased. I can hold this together.

"Top-notch security. It's not a location favored by celebrities. No one would ever look for me where I am." All true enough.

"Peter is freaking out. He wants you at the Nest until they figure out what's happening." Poor Christopher. He's using Dad to see if that's a carrot that will move me. It's not. I am not at all worried about being murdered.

"I will check in with Dad, and I'll be home in the next day or two. I promise."

Christopher sighs again, and his tone is less angry, more surfing attorney. "Cool. But hurry it up. I miss you. Susie misses you."

I ignore the resentment I feel and put a smile in my voice. "I'll be home, I promise! Everything will be all right if I get what I need here."

He hangs up. He's not happy, but he's not as concerned as he was. It'll have to do. God, I love him. When we're good, we're so good. There's a cabin we used to rent up in Big Bear, before Susie. We'd sneak up there during the week when it wasn't invaded by tourists. We'd stop at the store on the way in, load up on steaks and cheese and wine and breakfast goodness, and hide from the world. We'd make love, go skiing or take a hike or rent a boat and go out on the lake with our kayaks. In the cabin, we'd talk for hours about everything and anything and nothing at all. It's a cliché, but we were the only two people in the world, and our little world for two is where I always felt safest.

If I could feel that way again, even sometimes, I'd be okay. It's harder and harder.

CHAPTER FIFTY-ONE

ANGEL

I keep stealing glances at Nick. He hasn't changed much in the twelve years since we first met. I'll never forget waking up in the hospital and seeing him in the guest chair, this big, strange man I somehow understood I could trust. His dark eyes have a few more laugh lines at the corners. He's put on some weight but in a good way. It hits me that every man I've ever said 'yes' to has been a second-hand knockoff of Nick.

He wasn't lying about making a mean lasagna. He pooh-poohed the jar of premade sauce I was going to use and proceeded to create a glorious red gravy from scratch. I'm boiling noodles and grating nutmeg at his direction. I don't mind being a student. The whole point is to learn to be a good cook, and to do that, you watch and listen.

He claims he needs inspirational music on while he cooks. We're currently listening to one of his playlists. So far, we've heard American Italian from Frank Sinatra, jazz from Louis Armstrong, and a few Italian songs I've never heard but am enjoying. He bounces while he cooks. He's rarely still. I knew that, I suppose, but we've never been alone, just the two of us—okay, alone plus four dogs and a cat—and everything feels amplified by ten.

I fetch ricotta from the fridge, but he waves it away. "I didn't think either of us could wait five hours for food, so we're using a quick sauce, but we will not compromise on the bechamel!"

Apparently, that's the white sauce in the pan next to the meat sauce. CB and I made something similar for another recipe. "Isn't that just a white sauce?"

Nick gasps in mock horror. "*Just* a white sauce? My friend, no.

"All righty then," I laugh. It smells heavenly. I don't care what he calls it. I just want to eat soon.

"How're those noodles coming, chef?" Nick asks, taking a swig of a local IPA.

I check the pot and nod. "I believe we are just shy of al dente." I have already put the colander in the sink, so the pasta is drained and passed to him without delay. He instructs me on the proper order to build: sauce, pasta, sauce, bechamel. We repeat the stack four times, even though I'm afraid it will run over. When the tower of delight is terrifyingly high, he instructs me to drop globs of torn mozzarella on top. Finally, our work of edible art goes into the oven to bake for 45 minutes.

"Whatcha got for munchies? I haven't eaten since I left Dulles this morning." Nick drops happily onto the couch. It's six-thirty.

"Dig through the cabinets and fridge. Find something you like. I'm going to feed the canines." They follow me through the door that connects the residence to the barn. They know the routine. Four bowls, each with an appropriate serving, and a couple of supplements for Nope to help maintain her joint health. Having three stubby legs and a stout body that seems to be mostly butt requires extra maintenance. They sit without being instructed, each going to "their" spots. I place the proper bowl in front of its owner. Not one of them budges until I say, "Okay! Eat!" I'm so proud of the kiddos. They've learned this quickly. Older dogs teaching younger dogs is a great thing.

"That's impressive," Nick says from the doorway. I didn't realize he'd come to watch. He's got his hand wrist-deep in a salt and vinegar chips bag.

"They're good pups. Spence, the handsome black leopard, is

Charlie's dog, and Winnie," I try to think of a nice way to describe her, shrug, and give up, "is for Hannah. They're both thrilled. They're coming in two weeks so I can train humans and canines to work together. It's going to be good."

Nick gives me a look. "You're letting people invade your space? Human people?"

I make a face at him. "You're here. Not that you were asked."

"You realize that just makes my case." Nick grins. "I have to thank you for opening the gate. I'm honored."

"What would you have done if I didn't open the gate?" I'm interested.

"Peter ordered me to see you face-to-face, so if you hadn't made the wise choice you did, I would have had to call in your favorite—the cavalry. I'm sure the good officers of Moab would have loved to get some action." Nick smirks.

"Oh yeah? You don't have a warrant. Why would they care about some random woman living a quiet life out in the country?" I make a face at him.

"I can be persuasive when I want something."

A dozen unrelated thoughts cloud my brain. "Whatever. Give me a chip." The dogs are done and ready to get outside. I push past him through the doorway, catching the bag in my hand as I go. I try hard to ignore the feeling of his body brushing against mine.

I open the slider and step out into the fantastic evening. There are stars everywhere. "Did you know you can see more than two thousand stars here at night? This part of the country has very dark skies and little light pollution. It's one of the reasons the area is so popular."

Nick doesn't say anything.

I lean against one of the posts that hold the lean-to roof up and tip my head back. I find Bud star easily. I say a silent, "Hello."

Nick comes to stand beside me and tips his head back, too.

"Wow! Wow." That's all he says. For once, Nick Winston is speechless.

We stand looking up in companionable silence until my neck aches from the angle. I whistle the dogs back. The smell of garlic and cheese and fennel and tomato is mouth-watering. "Should be getting close now."

The dogs arrange themselves in their favorite sleeping spots, full from dinner and happy for company. Nick prepares a green salad while I pull the lasagna from the oven to settle. We will talk more about what he came to talk about at some point. I'm sure the conversation isn't over. Like a teenage girl, I want to hold off and pretend he's here under different circumstances.

I set the table, add wine glasses, place the salad in the middle and open a bottle of Chianti.

"We're going to be drunk," Nick laughs.

"As if that's a bad thing."

CHAPTER FIFTY-TWO

ANGEL

I'm not a clean freak, but I'm not messy. Between growing up in a home that was always kind of a shambles, to living in the Dollhouse where a mess was not tolerated, and then eventually spending most of my time in the cab of a semi, I've learned to be orderly, if not tidy. But, when you live with four dogs and a cat, there's hair on everything. Your furniture, your clothes, your counters. My one and only bumper sticker says, "Dog hair is a condiment, a fashion statement, and a decorating style."

While Nick is putting the finishing touches on the food, it might not be a bad idea to check the status of the bedroom. The king-sized bed is made, and the sheets are clean because I change them every Saturday morning, and it happens to be Saturday. The bed is made with a boho floral fitted sheet and a lightweight blue down-alternative comforter. It's light and fluffy and puts just enough material between me and sleeping dog bodies for everyone to be comfortable. I have a heavier one in the winter and cover it in a flannel duvet. A tree of life patterned quilt is on a chair by the bed if I get too hot. I move the laundry hamper into the closet, wipe a hand over the two nightstands to capture any dust–that's almost as bad as dog hair out here, and it's red–then call it good.

I slip into the bathroom through the adjoining door and dig through the cabinet until I find what I need. Maybe I'm overly confident about Nick's interest and abilities when I drop six condom packages into the nightstand drawer.

Every nerve ending in my body is on high alert.

CHAPTER FIFTY-THREE

NICK

Angel sends me to the couch, explaining, "You did most of the cooking, so I'll do the cleaning. "I'm never going to argue with that.

Surprisingly, neither of us is drunk, despite a few beers and sharing a bottle of wine. Happy, content, a little loose, sure. Sharing a fantastic meal with one of my favorite people in the world watching an incredible sunset over pink stone mountains has turned what I expected to be a difficult day into a perfect one. I've never had a dog of my own, but these four clowns make me wonder if I'm missing out. Watching Angel dance in the kitchen while she loads the dishwasher, I think I'm missing out on many things.

I wander to the bookshelves that take up the end of the room. It's filled with books, of course, but also vinyl records, DVDs, and even VHS tapes. I didn't realize you could still get those. The videos are mostly horror movies, but a few are related to dog training. The albums are varied—vintage classics, headbanger rock, modern everything from country to instrumentals. The woman likes her music as much as I like mine.

The books, though, that's where the gold lies. I start reading off titles. *Aggressive Defense: 100 Deadly Skills: The SEAL Operative's Guide to Eluding Pursuers, Evading Capture, and Surviving Any Dangerous Situation. Your Body Is Your Weapon: The Little Self-Defense Handbook. How to Survive Anything: From Animal Attacks to the End of the World (and everything in between).* "Okay, this one wins: *How to Survive a Human Attack: A Guide for Werewolves, Mummies,*

197

Cyborgs, Ghosts, Nuclear Mutants, and Other Movie Monsters."

Angel turns, confused, then laughs. "There are actually some useful tips in there. Don't mock!"

"Uh-huh." I flip through the pages of a few more. "I'm proud of you for taking your safety so seriously. Well, semi-seriously."

She doesn't respond, but I think I catch a smile.

"That's why I'm glad you'll come to LA with me. Until we figure this out, Peter and I would prefer to know exactly where you are at all times."

She turns, an exaggerated look of horror on her face. "Please reword. I have no intention of being anyone's prisoner, even in the nicest prison in the world."

"Dramatic much? You know what I mean." One of the dogs— Spence, I think?—decides he needs to investigate me. He clambers up onto the couch and plops his butt down on my lap, then inserts his nose into my face. He's probably hoping I'm a messy eater, and there's some lasagna lingering.

"I do know what you mean. But you also know that, dramatic or not, once I'm at the Nest, I won't be able to go anywhere without reporting to Peter and Marnie. I certainly won't be able to leave the property without someone with me. It's a country club, but it's a prison nonetheless." Angel sighs. "At least I'm fond of the other inmates. And we don't have to wear orange jumpsuits."

"I get it. I do." Spencer is now laying on the sofa, his head on my lap. I'm a little surprised to see my hand stroking his silky fur, seemingly of its own accord. It's relaxing. Kind of meditative. "Have I ever told you about my parents?" I know I haven't. I don't tell anyone because there's no need.

She sets a skillet on the island and watches me. "No."

"When I was six, and my sister Dru was seven, our parents were killed in a car accident. We had no relatives to take us in, so we were sent to foster care. A group home. It wasn't the worst, but it wasn't good, either. I spent a lot of time helping Dru defend herself against some older boys. I say 'helping' because my sister is a badass and can take care of herself, but when there are four of them, and one of you, and they're four years older and a lot bigger, having backup is good."

Angel nods and comes around the island, perches on a stool. Nope rubs against her leg and plops down on the floor.

"That place sucked pretty bad, but one good thing came from it," I smile, remembering the back of the hall closet and some of the other things I found there. "I found a stash of old comic books. Nothing rare or anything like that, but I'd never seen a comic book before, didn't know anything about superheroes. I fell hard. Especially for SHAZAM! Billy Batson was an orphan too. I could relate. I knew I would never get superpowers or anything like that, but becoming an FBI agent was a good second."

She smiles in a way that tells me she 'gets me' in a whole new way.

"My point wasn't actually to confess I'm a nerd who collects superhero stuff, by the way. Although I have a whole bedroom full, back in Virginia." Why am I telling her this? "The actual point was, I get what it feels like to be confined against your will. The group home was like that. A year later, Dru and I were moved into a foster home, a good one with this older couple, and we stayed all through high school. He was a retired cop and encouraged me to follow my dream to the FBI. She was a nurse, and she pushed Dru to a medical career, not as a nurse but as a doctor. They passed away years ago, but they were wonderful people, and I'm grateful for their love and kindness."

Angel nods. "So you're saying, sometimes the jailers have your best interest at heart and get you on the path to where you're supposed to be?"

I actually wasn't saying that only because I didn't realize until now, but I nod. "Exactly."

"Un-huh," she laughs. "I get it. I already said I'd go. But I don't want you to be too cocky about your powers of persuasion. Getting out of town is a good idea. I was going to tell you when we had our check-in call. There's this guy named Donovan."

CHAPTER FIFTY-FOUR

ANGEL

It's amusing to watch Nick get mad. He's yelled at me on the phone or Facetime, but I've never got to see it up close and personal. He's a pacer. And he uses his hands a lot. There's not really much yelling, more grumbling under his breath. Winnie is concerned for him. She has joined him in the pacing, back and forth, back and forth.

"Calm down. Like I said, I talked to the Moab police. They know about him. I haven't heard from him since the photos, so they must have talked to him. If I go to LA for a week or two, he'll find someone else to harass." I squat next to the bookshelves and flip through DVDs, searching for *The Mist*. It's in the King collection, of course. I remove the case, slip the disc into the player, and then drop onto the couch. "Come on, sit down, let's watch your movie."

Nick throws me a look. "Someday, you'll learn to tell me stuff sooner rather than later."

I shrug. "I tell you when you need to know. Are you going to be grumpy about this all night?"

That earns me another sharp look. "You realize people are dying, right?"

"I do. And I appreciate all the concern from you, Peter, and everyone. But I'm fine." I try to remember what possessed me to open the damned gate.

"I understand you think you can take care of yourself. But are these books really going to keep you safe?" He waves a dismissive hand at the shelves full of self-defense instruction.

"I think the information in those books taught me how to think. Hands-on practice taught me how to shoot, fight, plan." I snap. I'm amazed at how quickly things have gone wrong.

"I'm really proud of you for taking your safety into your own hands," he says, and it's not even condescending. "But you can't anticipate everything, ya know? Bad guys don't always announce their intentions ahead of time. They're sneaky bastards. You know that better than anyone. I'm asking you to give them less opportunity to put you to the test."

That's fair. I'm not ready to give in that quickly, but my fire has lessened. "Okay. How about this. If you can get free from zip-ties on your wrists and ankles within sixty seconds, I'll stop being a pain in your ass on this particular thing." I smile. "But if you can't, you stop being a pain in mine. I'll still go with you, but you have to chill out. Deal?"

Nick snorts, mood somewhat restored because he thinks he'll win. "Deal."

Oh, buddy. Let the fun begin.

CHAPTER FIFTY-FIVE

ANGEL

"You just keep those laying around?" Nick asks when I return from the barn with a large zip-close bag full of heavy-duty zip ties.

"You never know when you'll need to contain an FBI agent," I grin. "Where do you want to be? Standing? Sitting? Couch? Chair? Stool at the bar?"

Nick smirks and shrugs. "Wherever you'd like to put me, my friend."

"If you're comfortable, stay there, then," I call Spence and put him in a down. The other three dogs are already sprawled out on the cool tile floor. It's still warm outside, even though the sun has set.

Nick sits patiently on the couch, grinning like the fool he is. He is so confident he's going to win this one. I know he's not. His ego is going to get in the way. That'll be fun to watch. He offers up his hands, palms together, arms outstretched. Mistake. You want to make loose fists and put your hands side by side. This takes up more room in the circle around your wrists, and when you turn your hands sideways, you can possibly slide them out.

"I don't want to cut off your circulation," I say as I make the connection and tug on the tie. I leave a bit of room. My motives have nothing to do with his circulation. If you weren't able to leave enough room to slip your hands out, the next step is to go the opposite route and tighten the tie as much as possible. It makes it easier to break free because there's no give.

"That's fine," Nick says, and I swear his grin is even bigger.

I kneel and shove his sneakered feet together. "Damn, you have Shrek-sized boats." I can't help it, my mind wanders, and I look up at him with a smirk of my own. His expression changes as he tries to interpret the look.

"Okay, SHAZAM! Let's see you get out of this." I hold up a 'wait' finger and dash into the kitchen for my digital timer. "Ready?" He nods, and I set it to sixty seconds. "Let's see what you've got!"

Apparently, the FBI never trained Nick in how to escape this situation. He's working strictly on instinct. No logic, no strategy, definitely no finesse. I laugh as he twists his hands this way and that, trying to loosen the circle around his wrists.

"Forty seconds." I yawn.

He tries twisting his hands in different directions. It doesn't do much except loosen the ties–the exact opposite of what he should be aiming for.

"Thirty. Damn, dude, I think you're in trouble."

He shoots me a look, stops moving entirely, and takes a couple of precious seconds to think. Finally, he has a plan. He raises his hands in front of him, above his head, like he's holding Simba, the lion cub. Then he pulls his arms down, hard, using his body as a wedge to force the zip tie open. It doesn't work on the first try, but it does on the second.

He looks cocky until I say, "You just spent eighteen seconds. You have twelve seconds left."

He's bent over his feet, figuring out how to apply the same effort. That won't work. He looks around for something to cut the tie with, and I don't object. Mainly because it's fun to watch him hop like a bunny around the living room and kitchen.

"Five. Four. Three. Two. Done." I grin and shoot my hand up in a winning salute. "You're toast, pal."

"I'm not going to lie. That was harder than I anticipated. You gonna give the old man some tips?" He's leaning against the kitchen island. He couldn't get to the knife block because of the carpet of dogs in the way.

I tilt my head. "I dunno. I can see how holding you captive might be a handy trick to keep up my sleeve." And before I have time to think about it, I am in front of him, standing on my toes, and I catch his lower lip between my teeth.

Nick is stunned. He doesn't stop me, doesn't object.

I suck his lip into my mouth and taste it with my tongue. My hands are sliding up his sides, going slowly, oh so slowly. I've thought about his body for so long, imagined what it would feel like under me, over me, inside me. I've dreamed about it. The smooth muscles under my fingers twitch as I tug at his shirt. I don't want anything between me and his flesh.

"Angel–" he says, but it's not an "Angel, stop in the name of the FBI!" tone; it's a more desperate "I want what I can't have" sound. That's easy enough to ignore.

"Shut up, Nick," I mumble. I've got his shirt raised, a broad expanse of smooth, bronzed skin begging for my attention. My brain–*oh, wait, no, that's not my brain*–demands a taste, and I run my tongue from the top of his belt to his collar bone. His hands are free. He can stop me anytime. He doesn't.

My fingers are on the button of his jeans, then I slide my hands under the denim and run them around his hips to cup his ass. He has an incredible ass. For ten years, I've been thinking about this. If I am allowed to go much farther, there will be no stopping. I tilt my head up and stare him in the eye, challenging him to stop me now or accept his fate.

I step away and peel my shirt over my head. I didn't know when I got dressed this morning I should wear a good bra. A boring beige sports bra will have to do. He doesn't seem offended. I pull it off. I'm kind of proud of my breasts. I unzip my jeans and let them fall to the floor, kicking them away. Thank God all my underwear pass muster. I can tell these are approved because his eyes are wide and dark. I smile and lick my lips.

"This will be much more fun if your feet are free." The music from dinner is still playing, and I take advantage, swaying my hips. I've been told I have great hips, so I'm going to use them. I bend at the waist, shoving my ass against him, then pulling away just enough to give him a good look as I slide a fingernail into the square locking mechanism of the tie at his ankles, and release the ratchet.

"Jesus, Angel," is all he says before he grabs me around the waist and pulls me up against him so he can ravage–that's the best word for it–my neck. I don't think I've ever felt so wanted in my life.

"About freaking time, you big chicken," I whisper. I grab his hand and drag him toward the bedroom, stepping over the dogs. This is a party they're not invited to. "I get to be on top."

"At least the first time."

I can live with that.

CHAPTER FIFTY-SIX

I can't sleep. I can't stop thinking about the man lying next to me, one of his long legs covering mine. After our first time, which was as intense as years of denied desire would demand, we collapsed on the bed to recover.

"So many scars," he said softly, running a gentle finger along my spine. "What are all these circles?"

"Paint guns. One hundred paint gun pellets." I sigh. I want to purr like Cat, who is sitting on the headboard, glaring down at Nick. To be fair, he's in her spot.

"And this one?" Nick touches the finger-shaped mark on my right hip.

"Sheriff Jonny Law."

His lips graze the pink scar. "Oh, right. I'm glad he's dead, or I'd have to kill him again."

"Too late. I took care of it."

Nick slaps me on my bare butt. "Yes! You did!" He says it in a "you go, girl!" tone, and I can't decide whether to laugh or hit him.

I roll onto my side and give him a look. "Be careful, son."

He snorts. "That sounds like a challenge. What are you going to do to me?" We both know exactly what I'm going to do to him.

Life with Nick is fun. Food. Music. Arguing. Sex. I could make this a habit.

My brain won't stop replaying our activities, and my body is amped. Still, I don't want to wake him—yet—and open another

207

condom package. He's not exactly old, but he's no spring chicken.

Unpleasant kitchen smells are growing more intense by the minute. I slip out of bed and grab Nick's T-shirt from the floor. Not because I'm that girl, but because it's the closest thing to me, and I don't want to wake him. Okay, maybe I'm a little bit that girl.

After I haul out the stinky stuff, I'll throw together a frittata so it's ready in the morning and set up the coffee maker. Then I'll get back in bed and enjoy the view of the absolutely gorgeous man lying naked on top of the sheets.

Nick is naked in my bed. I can't stop smiling.

"I put a spell on you," is repeating in my head. I can sing, but I can't sing like Nina Simone. Still, I whisper the words onto the wind of the canyon. I don't care if Nick hears me. I'm not worried. When last we saw our hero, he was snoring like a chainsaw. Gonna have to fix that if this becomes a habit.

Wow. Twice now, I've thought of Nick as a habit.

One night at a time, Ang. One night at a time. Bud says.

I never thought of this before, and that's probably because, Ewwww, but I'm glad you got to experience sex before you died.

Me too! Bud Star agrees with a chuckle.

It was 90 plus degrees today. Now it's a comfortable 60 or so, and the breeze is soothing. It feels good on my skin. I round the corner of the house and use my bare foot to pull the gate open. I'm about to heave the garbage bag up into the bin when two hands grab me around the waist.

"Don't sneak up on me like that!" I snap, my good mood completely gone, shocked Nick would do something so stupid.

Of course, *Nick* wouldn't do something so stupid, but apparently, Donovan would. He spins me around, so I'm facing him, one hand clenching my shirt, and presses his other hand against my mouth. He's slim but taller than me and strong. I remember his muscular build from the City Mart. My assumption is now confirmed as he presses himself against me. Nick's T-shirt offers no protection from anything. I feel every inch of him.

"You made this a lot easier than I was expecting!" He is delighted.

I bite the fingers pushing against my lips. He yips in surprise and pulls his hand away, just long enough for me to holler. He's got a death grip on my lips, pinching them between his fingers, twisting so hard it feels as if they might be torn off.

Did I shut the slider? Will the dogs hear and come? *Shit!* The dogs are in my office! *Shit shit shit*

For a minute, I'm defeated. What's the point in training so hard, learning so much, if some asshole can grab me anyway? Then I remind myself, you can be prepared as all hell, but if somehow you don't see it coming, you will have to use your brain rather than muscles. That's why you train both your body and your mind.

Fucker.

"This doesn't need to be difficult. But if I'm honest, I don't mind that much." Donovan leers down at me, and I swear his eyes are so black they seem to have no irises. He's still pinching my lips, and it hurts so bad my eyes are watering. He pulls a roll of duct tape from somewhere and tears off a chunk. He replaces his hand with the tape. Then he uses more tape to wrap my wrists together–once, twice, three times. After I'm secured, he lifts me as quickly as if I were a doll and throws me over his shoulder. His hand runs across my bare butt and goes exploring. I jerk and try to kick away from him, but it doesn't work. He digs his fingernails into my calves and slaps me hard on the ass. "This can be hard, or it can be very hard. Your choice, my darling!"

I let my body go limp. I'll be heavier that way. I take a calming breath and think. He doesn't seem to know someone else is in the house. When Nick wakes up and realizes I'm gone, he'll come looking for me. If he's smart–and Nick is crazy smart–he'll let the dogs out. They'll find me fast. But will I survive that long? Will I even be on the property? If Donovan is fanboying over Alfred, he'll want to take photos, which will require preparation. I'm relatively sure he's not going to kill me right away.

Where the hell are we going? There's no path on this side, just narrow runs where dogs' feet have pounded dust for years. There are lots of trip hazards and even a couple of rocky outcroppings that will make the going tough, especially while carrying another human on a dark night. He seems to have confidence. He has a plan. Is he taking me to the river? Or the cliffs? Did he use a boat to get on the property? That makes sense. I was an idiot for thinking blocking the opening in the fencing would make any difference. Being ever-hopeful, I assumed once the bad person was told no, they'd hang their head in shame and move on to something else.

If I get out of this alive, I'm putting security on all the fences. That doesn't make me happy, not one bit. I've had my fill of fences and cameras. But this fence and these cameras will be keeping people out, not in.

Donovan's hand has loosened just a bit on my feet, so I try a wild kick, hoping he's tired from the effort of moving through the night desert, and it might make him lose his hold on me or at least his balance, but no go. He simply clamps his hand tighter and presses his nails deep into the skin of my bare foot.

A coyote howls to remind us we're in the wild, but they're no threat. The only danger here is humans.

Damn it. What did I do to make myself a magnet for crazy men? Alfred. Jimmy. Donovan. Maybe Jimmy was right; there's something about me that's off, that's wrong, that makes me okay to abuse.

Fuck that bullshit.

And then I realize where we're going. We're headed up the hill and south toward the dead-end road boaters use to access the river.

CHAPTER FIFTY-SEVEN

OLIVIA

It's after 2 am, and it's dead quiet. I haven't seen Jimmy since before Nick pulled up at the gate. I should head back to my motel, but it's so peaceful. The cloudless sky and lack of traffic or city lights fill the night with stars.

Bud Star. That's what Angel calls her dead twin. He was my first–something. We weren't in love. We were simply clawing out a minute of kindness in a terribly painful situation. I was fifteen. I didn't feel anything other than a need for comfort. It wasn't like Christopher.

This is the perfect place to have a relationship with a star. It's starting to make sense. Emily reminded us of the tattoo Angel carries on her left forearm. It's the Gemini constellation, with Castor and Pollux's stars drawn prominently. After Bud's death, Angel was obsessed with the story of the twin sons of Zeus. One survived, one did not, but their bond remained close even in the afterlife. Now the name of her property makes sense: "Stargazer."

Just more proof Angel has one foot in the land of the living and one in the land of the dead.

Nick has been in there with Angel for nearly ten hours. Maybe she shot him. That makes me smile. But no, the last person Angel would ever harm is Nick. Not intentionally, at least. I'm afraid what's happened is the exact opposite of shooting. She has finally acted on the attraction she's carried for years.

On that note, I decide I might as well go catch some shut-eye so

I can be back here early in the morning. I hit the button to move the seat into an upright position. I spot a beat-up RV pull onto the road in the side mirror out of sheer luck. The camper heads south, away from Angel's, away from town. I hadn't realized there was vehicle access at that end of the property. It makes sense, I guess. That's where the fence stops.

Maybe Bud Star is with me because the angle is just right to give a glimpse of dark hair in the driver's seat of the camper when it turns. Is that Jimmy? What the hell is happening? Is that why he was riding the dirt bike? It was less noticeable than a really ugly RV?

Something tells me to follow Jimmy. At this point, it is clear Nick is spending the night. They're not going anywhere. Keeping an eye on Jimmy seems more urgent.

I wait thirty seconds, then pull onto the road, keeping an easy hundred yards behind.

This is not right. This isn't part of the plan. What the fuck.

CHAPTER FIFTY-EIGHT

ANGEL

I'm groggy as hell. I don't remember how I got here. I would slide right out of it if I wasn't tied to an ancient wooden chair. My head is swimming and feels disconnected from my body. Am I drunk? I don't remember what I was doing before I was here.

I seem to be in an RV. There's a kitchenette. A booth with two seats and a table. Beaded curtains separate the front from what is maybe a bedroom. Everything is orange. It smells musty. Rotten. The chair I'm strapped to is behind the passenger's seat, turned at an angle so I can see the rest of the camper. A door is to my left, past a tall coat closet-type cabinet. I think. None of it is clear or well-defined, just vague concepts that feel fundamentally familiar.

A shape comes through the beaded curtain. "Oh, good, you're back." My vision is fuzzy, but I think it's the Donovan guy from the meat counter. Now, close up, he looks familiar even without the hair net.

Back? Where am I back from? Why do I know him? My brain is so muffled, like every thought is encased in cotton. I try to say words. "Whu" is all that comes out. In a way, it's accurate. Why am I tied to a chair? Who is the man? Where are we? Where's Nick?

"Don't worry, I didn't give you much. I need you to be lucid when we chat. You'll feel better soon." He's digging for something in a cabinet. He's unconcerned. Detached. Shouldn't he be more–something? He's kidnapped me. Why is he so calm?

I blink my eyes rapidly as if that will help clear the fog. It doesn't move the fog, but it does help clear my vision. I try shaking my head back and forth, quickly, short little bursts to dislodge whatever rot has taken over my skull. That only gives me a headache.

There's a cheap plastic clock on the wall above the small stove. It says it's 3:12. It's still dark outside. I can see cracks of black around the ancient shades that cover the windows. The RV itself is ancient, probably from the 70s. Anything that might have been cool has been stripped out, and now it looks like someplace squatters would take over for drug parties. Nothing is dirty, exactly, but it's so run down and scarred and cheap it's depressing.

He finds whatever he was looking for and slides into the booth, facing me. He opens what looks like an atlas–I'm particularly fond of my Rand McNally, so I recognize it–and seems to be working out a plan. There's a small box of gold stars on the table next to the atlas. He moistens a finger and pokes a star out of the box, then applies it to a spot on the map.

I'm not going with him. He can't think I'm going with him. The alternative would be that he will kill me and leave me here.

I try speaking again. "Who uh ou?"

That was a tiny bit better. It's been 19 minutes since I last looked at the clock.

"Who uh ou?" he mocks. "I'm the one who isn't good enough for you."

I don't understand that. What does that even mean? "Uh?"

"Uh?" he repeats in a mocking tone.

I sigh deeply. I know what I need to do. "Peas?"

"Please? Now you say please. Better late than never, I suppose." He turns the atlas over so that it's face down on the table, pages spread open. "Don't you recognize me?"

I nod. "Ci-e mar."

He makes a face. "I suppose I should be flattered that you remembered that after just one meeting. But that's not what I'm talking about."

I think and think. "I do no."

"I do no." He mocks again. Angry. Bitter.

And then I get it. "Immy?"

"By Jove, she's got it! Nice to meet in person, even after you tried so hard to keep me away."

I'm too surprised to speak. Jimmy. He doesn't look like his Komo photo. He's thinner, much better looking without the baby fat. Without glasses. With longer, trendy hair that's pulled into a man bun. He has a beard and mustache, emphasizing his strong jaw and prominent nose. He's definitely good-looking, yet something about him suggests he's wearing a costume. Just under the handsome surface is a whole different creature. A scary creature. A mad creature.

"Wa-er?" I ask. That might help clear things up. I'm not concerned he'll drug me again. His goal is to have a conversation, and he needs me somewhat coherent for that.

He shrugs, opens the small fridge, and pulls out a filtered jug. He doesn't get a glass. Instead, he approaches me and dribbles it into my mouth, unconcerned when excess runs down my chin and onto my shirt. Nick's shirt. For a few seconds, I wonder if he's trying to drown me. He doesn't stop, doesn't give me time to catch my breath. I start to choke. He laughs and finally takes the bottle away.

This guy recently professed to be the only one who could ever really love me. He's doing a damn fine job showing me what his love is like. Jimmy Zamora may have been a victim, but I genuinely believe if Fate had taken a slightly different path, he would have been a perpetrator all on his own.

I swallow and feel like my tongue is normal-sized and less hair-covered. "Than you." Better. Much better. "What you doin here?"

"I came for you, obviously," Jimmy says, sitting back down on the bench at the table.

I mutter, "Pictures?"

He looks pleased with himself. "The doll photos? Yes, those were me! Great touch, right?"

Apparently, my face is asking, "Why?" since my mouth isn't doing a great job.

"It was an easy way to misdirect. You thought I was a basic Alfred fan. The photos kept you off balance. I saw you go to the police. They spoke to me, by the way. Made my job at City Mart uncomfortable, but I played my part well, and they never guessed." His energy changes, from bragging to intense. "I'm tired of waiting. My work is done, no more reason to stick around here."

"Work?" He can't mean the meat counter.

He doesn't. "Yes. Work. Tiffany. Karmen." He pauses and smiles. "Hannah."

My eyes grow large, and I suck in a breath. "What mean?"

"I helped end their pain. I released their spirits to peace so that they can come again and find a new, more welcoming home." He sounds like he actually believes that bullshit.

I'm trying to remember exactly what he said, but my brain is still not functioning 100%. "Killed?"

He looks amused. "I released them. They wanted to die. I simply offered an assist."

"Karmen didn't want." I shake my head. "Don't believe."

Suddenly he's angry like a switch was flipped. "You think you know everything. You're so smart. But you're deluded. A liar. You lie to yourself and everyone else."

I shake my head, no. *Calm down, calm down. Tiffany. Karmen. Who was the third–* "Kait?"

"I can't take credit for that one." He adds, "If I'd thought of it, I would have. She was in love with me, you know. As if I could be with someone with claws for hands. That ugly old bitch would do anything I asked. She even sent me a love letter. I suppose it was a suicide letter, but it was all flowery and mushy."

I'm desperate to have complete control of my words, but my tongue still feels big, and my mouth is so dry. *Don't react. Don't respond. Later.* "What you do now?"

"My part is done. The remainders will be handled by someone else." He looks smug. Remainders? What does that mean? "As for me, I've told you my plan. I will take you away and show you what it's like to be loved by someone who knows how to love you the way you deserve. I'm going to teach you everything you need to know. Truthfully, it may be rough at first. You think you know everything, so I'll need to break you. Tame your spirit. Then I can train you. Then we'll be happy."

I'd take a run at sweet-talking if I thought he'd believe me buying into his ridiculous plan, but he's not stupid. He'd know I was bluffing. We've spent years sharing details from the darkest times of our lives. We know each other's secrets, know each other's buttons, and know each other's tells.

"Here's how it's going to go. I need some sleep. The last couple of days has been stressful. You're going to let me rest. Then tomorrow, we're heading south, somewhere in South America. I haven't decided where yet. Under these circumstances, you probably will lose access to your trust. That's unfortunate. But we'll make do. Cost of living is cheap."

Jimmy comes toward me. He pulls a folding knife from his pocket. "I will untie you so you can walk like a big girl to the bed. Tonight's not our night, so don't think about that. I want all of you present when we take that step. And I want to be fully present, as well. So, just behave, cooperate, and everything will be okay."

I hear a noise, a squeak. What's that?

He hears it too and turns back toward the bedroom. "What are you doing here?"

Someone has opened the outer door.

I start to yell for help, but he backhands me hard across the face, and I'm dizzy.

I hear a woman's voice, low and angry. "Come out here."

My head is pounding thanks to the slap combined with the drugs. I watch him disappear out the door. I fight through the pain and the dizziness and look for something to free myself. My ankles are duct-taped to the chair, but my hands are tied together behind me with zip ties at my wrist. Nick made fun of me for all those self-defense books, but it will come in handy. I hope I get out of here to tell him so. I push my hands away from each other with as much force as possible, then jerk up against the chair to create a wedge. It takes a few tries, but it works.

Hands free, I bend down to get the tape off my ankles and nearly fall out of the chair. A wave of dizziness crashes over me, and I have to pause and take deep breaths until it passes.

I have no idea where he went with the woman or how long they'll be gone. They may be standing just outside the door. *Shit.*

Tape off, ties off, I stand and give myself a second to catch my breath and test my balance. I listen. I don't hear anything just near the door. I move toward the back of the RV, thankful for the ugly shades. A window in the bedroom area must be cracked. I hear low voices on the right side of the RV. The opposite side of the camper.

Things are looking up.

I open the door slowly, carefully, just a crack, and listen. There's no one in sight. I think we're at the edge of a campground, but possibly not within the actual boundaries because there are no other campers. Unfortunate, but I'll make do. I've had to run across uncomfortable terrain before, and I'll do it again.

CHAPTER FIFTY-NINE

OLIVIA

"What the hell are you doing here?" Jimmy demands as he follows me away from the RV, which is even older and uglier up close. I lead him toward an overgrown area to the side of a simple concrete restroom structure. I don't want to stand in whole light, but we benefit from the relatively dim glow from a bulb on the front of the building.

His skin is splotchy, and his eyes are red. Is he high?

"What am *I* doing here? What the fuck are you doing here? Is Angel alive? She better be alive, Jimmy!" I hiss-yell. There are no other vehicles parked at the primitive rest stop. Everyone with any sense has continued to the modern one a few miles ahead.

"Calm down. She's alive. There's been a slight change in plan," Jimmy snaps. He's using the tone he uses to lecture people in Group. Holier-than-thou, Dr. Lisa called it once. Accurate.

"What do you mean? What kind of change?" I keep my hands in the pockets of my hoodie. It's a little colder than I expected, but it's not why they're tucked away. In my left hand are the keys. In my right, something else. I don't trust Jimmy, and I'm sure he doesn't trust me. A girl has to protect herself.

"I did everything as we agreed. I helped Tiffany, Karmen, and Hannah. I'll leave Grace to you, but I want Angel. She's my reward," Jimmy says, and his face is hard.

"Jimmy, no," I shake my head. "You can't 'have' her. That's not the point. That was never the point. We're giving them salvation. If you hurt Angel, that's the exact opposite–"

"I'm not going to hurt her! I love her! I can give her a life worth living!" Jimmy nearly yells, the splotches redder.

Calm him down, Olivia. You need to get him relaxed. I adjust my tone, making it soothing. "Okay, sure. It makes sense to give it one last try. Perhaps she just needs the right person to help her realize what she's hiding from. If anyone can help her, it's you."

He's not buying it. His eyes narrow. "Don't talk to me like one of your chat show guests. I'm not an idiot." His hands are clenched at his sides. "I'm going to take Angel on a road trip. Maybe east, maybe south, maybe we'll go to Mexico. Don't know yet. I'm going to take my time with her. And if she doesn't come around in the end, then... well."

"Don't you hurt her," I growl. "Don't you do it!"

"Or what, you'll tell Daddy what I did?" Jimmy smirks. "How can you without implicating yourself?"

I'll be dead. I don't care if I'm implicated. I straighten and shake my head. "Okay, Jimmy. Do it your way. But please. Don't hurt her. She's been through enough."

Jimmy makes a disgusted sound, all pretenses gone, and heads in the direction of the RV. Before he's taken more than a couple of steps, I slide up behind him, and my right hand comes out of my pocket. I've already loosened the cap, so it's simple to plunge the syringe into his shoulder. I'm not careful, much less gentle, and the prick and burn come as a shock. He tries to turn toward me, eyes wide, fury and fear in his eyes. "What did you -" He collapses, his body splayed in an awkward, graceless mass, half on the grass, half on the sidewalk.

It doesn't take long. The heroin has been laced with fentanyl. The dealer I bought from thought I was nuts, but I've known him since college, so he did what I asked. Even if someone should come along with a carload of Narcan, it's too late.

I've got to get to Angel. But how am I going to explain my being here? If I tell her the truth–well, a modified version of the truth–will she believe me and willingly take me back to her home? Doubtful. It's a weird story, even I realize. Besides, Nick is there. No. Even though it breaks my heart, Jimmy has forced me to change the plan. Bastard.

I'm sure there are cameras. I tug my hat farther down over my face and trot back toward the RV. I want to spend as little time on their video as possible.

I stop by the rental and retrieve the second syringe from the glove box. I go to the RV and open the door with a deep sigh.

Damn it.

Angel's gone.

CHAPTER SIXTY

ANGEL

I don't have the luxury of stopping to think. I need to get back to
Nick and tell him what happened. My brain is spinning. Donovan
is Jimmy, Jimmy is Donovan. There's something he said, something
he told me, that my brain is holding hostage. What was it? What
was it?

Except for Nick's t-shirt, I'm naked. I have no shoes on. I'm sore.
I'm still a little foggy from whatever drug he used on me. Thank
god the campground where he parked is on a decent road. Running
barefoot through the desert would be dangerous.

I thought my days of running through untamed places were done
after the Oklahoma ranch. That's a flashback I can live without.

Another bit of luck: this campground is only a mile from 191,
and as soon as I reach the highway, I know exactly where I am,
maybe three miles to my place. I'm still feeling loopy, but I have
faith in myself. I have no other choice.

What the hell is it that he said that I can't remember?

It's dry and dusty, but the smell of pine is amplified by what
might be a storm. A desert storm in June would make things
infinitely worse.

Because it's the middle of the night, the highway is not busy,
which is great, considering my lack of apparel. The few times a
car approaches, I move to the road's edge and act like everything
is normal. If I was dumb enough to accept a ride from a stranger,
things would probably go from bad to worse.

Holy hell. Jimmy. You're bonkers, man. And who was the woman that came to the RV and got him outside? Why did she do that? I wasn't about to stick around long enough to find out and say 'thank you'—too many red flags about the whole damn thing.

Besides, that's another thing my brain is jibber-jabbering about, but not in a way I can understand. Something is very wrong. Many things are very wrong. What am I missing? What am I forgetting?

I see my gate 100 feet ahead and feel a massive sense of relief, although this is far from over. I put on a little more speed, ignoring my sore feet, ignoring my tired legs. They have quite the workout tonight.

I pound the numbers into the keypad and slip through the gate when it's wide enough. Then I hit the "close" button to stop the gate from continuing its motion. I don't want someone following me in.

I can't see the building until I'm a quarter mile up the hill and around the curve. Then I do. Lights are on everywhere. Nick knows I went missing. What's he doing?

I push myself into a faster jog, although my lungs are bursting and my legs are screaming. I'll breathe when I get inside.

The dogs sense me because they begin barking, and I hear the sliding door against the frame just as I'm coming around the corner. The pups crash into me first, and then there's Nick, wearing undone jeans and no shirt because I'm wearing his shirt.

"What the fuck happened? Where have you—" before he can finish the question, I fling myself at him and hold on tight. For just a minute, I need the solid feeling of my own personal FBI agent reassuring me it's all okay.

Except it's not. My brain has decided it's safe to let loose its secrets.

"He said he killed Hannah!" I shriek. "Call right now! She can't be dead! She can't!" I pound on his chest. Then I remember the second thing. "We have to get to California—I think Olivia and Grace are in danger!"

CHAPTER SIXTY-ONE

NICK

I'm being forced to make a choice I don't like. Maybe I misunderstood something. "Slow down. Start again."

Angel drops onto one of the Adirondack chairs on the patio and hugs the dogs as they crowd around her, offering comfort. She's wearing my t-shirt and nothing else. She's tall, so the shirt didn't protect much. Her legs are covered with scratches and the beginnings of bruises. The bottoms of her feet are bloody and raw. The long blonde hair that was tickling my chest earlier is now tangled and spiked with twigs and burs. Her eyes look off somehow. Does she have a concussion?

"I couldn't sleep, so I decided to take the garbage out. Someone grabbed me. The guy from the grocery store. He knocked me out, and I was in a camper when I came to. I recognized him from the store but didn't recognize–didn't realize–it was Jimmy. Jimmy Zamora."

Why did I not think of this? How did I not put two and two together when she mentioned the photos? I'm angry with myself but don't have the luxury for that. Later.

Angel rocks back and forth, and Asa pushes himself into her lap. "I didn't know. I've only ever seen the photo he uses in the group, which is old. He's lost weight, muscled up. He looks more like he should be a model for GQ or a rock star. That's not entirely accurate, but I can't quite express how different he looks now. I was bound to a chair in this RV, and he's bragging to me that he killed

Tiffany, Karmen," her voice hitches, and I can see panic rising up again, "and Hannah. Then he said the remainders are being handled by someone else."

"Remainders? What does that mean? That's a strange word." I'm scrolling through numbers in my phone, looking for my contact in Idaho.

"Yes. Very strange. Then he's telling me he's taking me to Mexico yadda yadda so I can be his happy slave wife. He needs some sleep, so we're going to go tomorrow. He's about to take me to the bedroom area–and all of a sudden, there's a voice telling him to come outside. He asks what she's doing there–it was definitely a woman's voice–and he goes out the door. I got myself free and crept to the windows to figure out where they were, and I took off and came back here." Angel's crying and rocking and hugging Asa.

I call our office in Idaho and follow up with the Nampa, Idaho police. They've got cars on the way. Now I need to contact the cops in Moab and get to the campground. Jimmy has likely fled by now since his captive escaped. We don't have much time. But there's something more than Hannah that's got Angel worked up. Something more than running nearly naked for miles.

"Ang, tell me why you think Olivia and Grace are in trouble." I lean through the wall of dogs and lift her chin, forcing her to look at me.

She cries harder, nearly choking on her tears. "Because–because I think the woman who came was his partner. I think she's the one who's going to 'help' the 'remainders.' I don't think the fake suicides are done yet. I think there are three more. Me, Grace, and Olivia."

Unfortunately, I agree with her assessment. I need to warn Peter to get Olivia and Grace and keep them safe at the Nest until I can support them. "I'll call Peter -"

"No!" she screams.

"What do you -"

"You can't call Peter. He won't believe you!"

"Won't believe what? What are you–" I stare at her.

"It's going to kill him," she whispers, and I watch every ounce of blood drain from her face.

"What's going to kill him?" She's been through a lot tonight, and she's clearly traumatized. I get it. But I'm confused and need her to get me caught up.

"The voice. I know who the woman is. Jimmy's partner. It's Olivia."

CHAPTER SIXTY-TWO

ANGEL

This is insane. I've got to be asleep. This is just a nightmare. Hannah isn't dead. Olivia would never hurt anyone. Definitely not Grace or me.

I can't think about that now. I must focus on things that can be changed. I must have misremembered the voice. I don't believe Olivia would do something like this. Except if what Jimmy said is true, she might. She would.

Nick agrees we can't tell Peter yet. Nick doesn't fully believe Olivia is involved, but he's willing to consider it. All I care about is that he isn't insisting we call Peter. That man has given so much for his children, those he's related to by blood and those he's related to by love, and this is going to crush him. I can't begin to imagine the pain he will be in if I'm right. And if I'm wrong, I will be the happiest wrong person that ever lived.

It took some negotiating, but we've got a plan. I'm loading up the pups and driving to the Nest, 11 hours if I don't stop. I'm too amped to sleep. Nick is meeting the local PD at the campgrounds. If I go, they'll keep me in Moab, and I can't stay, but Nick is a good LEO and can't walk away from the scene of a crime. Once he's told them the story, he'll drive the rental Jeep to Salt Lake City and catch a flight to LAX. We should get to the Nest at about the same time.

Before he takes off with my directions to the campgrounds, Nick gives me a look that suggests he'd rather be kissing me and says, "We will talk about what happened. Later. After all of this."

I roll my eyes and wink, desperate for anything to make me feel less awful. He doesn't even smile. Did I lose everything tonight?

Asa and Nope are pacing. They know something's up because I'm packing the go-bag. Winnie and Spence have no idea what's happening, and my nervous energy is winding them up. I'm trying hard not to snap at them. Deep breaths, deep breaths.

After what feels like hours but has only been 15 minutes, I've got the Bronco loaded: go-bag, dog food, water jugs, bowls, harnesses, leads, and leashes. My phone, iPad, charger, laptop. I debate bringing my gun, decide against it. If I get into a position where I need a gun... I don't know that a gun will help. I don't know if I could use a gun on someone I love.

I'd planned to get an oil change and have the fluids checked before my next trip to the Nest. Someday, I'll learn to work on cars, but I haven't yet. I'll rely on crossed fingers and prayers to the car gods this time. I bought my restored 1992 Bronco finished and ready to go. I had a couple of custom details added, including three steel animal transport cages in the back. If we're ever in an accident, the kennels will keep them safe from most anything. I only use them for Nope and Asa when I leave them unattended for more than a few minutes, which is rare. Nope likes to stretch out on the back seat, and Asa is the copilot. They're creatures of habit. I suppose we all are.

The Bronco has enough gas to get us to Vegas. I know from past trips I'll need to fill up twice. Vintage Broncos aren't known for great gas mileage. That's time I don't want to waste, but I don't have a choice.

"Load up!" I smack the tailgate of the Bronco, and Asa and Nope are up and inside, finding their spots. I have to help Spence and Winnie. I debate letting them ride free but decide against it. They need the kennel training for their people–I can't think too hard about those people right now–and I can't deal with puppy shenanigans as I'm coming off drugs, stress, and running on fear.

As we head down the hill toward the gate, I feel a surge of nervous energy. Jimmy has to have left the campgrounds by now. What if he's waiting for me at the bottom of the hill? And where is Olivia? My gut clenches, and I stab at my phone to turn the screen on, hoping to see a text from Nick saying they've got him. Nick sent a text, but Jimmy is definitely not at the bottom of my hill.

"Jimmy is dead. PD coming to talk to you. Go."

It's all too much, and my foot slips off the gas, and the Bronco jerks and falls into a groove in the dirt. I slam the brakes to stop us from ending up off-road. "Sorry!" The apology is half-sob, half-yell.

This can't be happening. Because if Jimmy is dead, Olivia is the one who killed him.

CHAPTER SIXTY-THREE

NICK

The evening started so damn well. Then it did a one-eighty and turned into a shit show in less than twelve hours. I did not expect to end up in Angel's bed. I also did not expect her to be kidnapped from under my nose. I did not expect the kidnapper to be Jimmy Zamora. I did not expect him to end up dead. And I sure as hell did not expect Olivia to be connected.

Another camper discovered Jimmy's crumpled body near a cold fire pit. Sufficient light and a close look presented an empty syringe inches from his right hand. From Angel's recounting, he would not have realized she was gone immediately because he was outside the camper. If he was going to shoot up, for pleasure or to end his life, wouldn't he do it inside the RV? Not next to an unlit fire pit twenty-five feet from the camper and fifty feet from the public restroom. It doesn't make any sense.

Someone helped him to his death, like the others. Except he confessed to being the helper in the other deaths. It appears someone else took that role. If Angel's right... can Angel possibly be right? Her mind could have been muddled. She was still coming down from the drugs Jimmy used to take her. Maybe she thought it was Olivia's voice, but it was some other woman.

At least three of his Komo peers have died in recent weeks. I'm still waiting to hear about Hannah. If he had been killed in New Jersey, I wouldn't think twice that this was part of it. But he's not in New Jersey. He's a couple of miles from Angel's home–the home no one would find unless they're given the exact address.

It wouldn't have been difficult to follow her after he spotted her at the market. What is harder to understand is how he knew she was near Moab. That is not public information or even information available to other members of Komo. I pull up the Komo app on my phone and look at Angel's bio. The Residence field is blank. The mailing address is a PO Box in Palos Verdes, near the Nest. Angel is very cautious—rightly so—about her space. A couple of days ago, all I knew was that she lived in a desert. I didn't know what desert or even what state. I assumed the southwest.

I only knew the specific location today because Peter shared it with me.

Peter shared it. Recently he mentioned Olivia has been around more than usual. Could she have found the information in his office? She's a resourceful woman. And Peter has little reason to be overly cautious about the information in his office. Literally, no one goes into the Foundation's space except Marnie, Lisa, Peter... and family.

I'm starting to fear Angel might be right. What does that mean if she is? Angel said, according to Jimmy, there were 'remainders' still to be taken care of. Angel thought that meant Grace and Olivia. Jimmy suggested Angel was supposed to be one of those, but he changed the plan by taking her away. Jimmy Zamora was a psychopath on so many levels.

Is Olivia planning to kill Grace and Angel and then herself? Holy Jesus. That can't be it. She's a champion for people like them. She would never presume to determine the value of their lives for them, to make a decision like that, final and unchangeable.

Would she?

"Well, Special Agent Winston, I'm sure you'll be surprised," the chief of police approaches, annoyance clear on his face as dawn begins to rise to the east, "Angel Evanston is not at the property."

She is gone, her vehicle is gone, her dogs are gone. I don't suppose you'd know where she might have headed?"

Am I ready? Do I have a choice? "No idea, officer."

Decision made.

CHAPTER SIXTY-FOUR

ANGEL

My brain won't stop spinning. Jimmy is dead. Jimmy is Donovan. Jimmy is a murderer. Hannah. My poor sweet Hannah. I can't think about Hannah. If I let myself think about her, I will become paralyzed. I don't have time for that. I will fall apart later. There are thirty other survivors in Hope. Was Jimmy planning to kill everyone? Would he have stopped once he had me? I have a vague memory of him saying Grace was in danger. Did he mention Em? Charlie? What put someone in the 'ignore' column versus the 'kill' column? What about Kait, Tiffany, and Karmen made Jimmy and his co-conspirator decide their lives weren't good enough to continue?

I don't want to think about Olivia. How she seems to be not only part of this, but possibly the mastermind. Olivia is persuasive. It wouldn't be difficult for her to manipulate Jimmy to do her bidding, especially since it seems to be a task he relished. What I can't get around is the idea that she would want someone to be killed. Unless…she considered this a merciful event. They're being helpful. Kind. Doing what 'we' can't do for ourselves. At least that's the way it looks from here.

Except Jimmy clearly had a very different plan for me. Bastard. He's no better than the perpetrators who abused us in the past. I think Jimmy Zamora was destined for darkness regardless of which path took him. Fortunately for him, he had a good number of years being seen as a good guy before his true villainous colors showed.

Try as I might to resist, my mind circles back. Olivia has been strange for the last six months, maybe longer. She's always been bossy and controlling. She took the big sister role very seriously even though that's not something I wanted or needed from her. Of course, I love her. We've been through so much together, and her family has become my family. But she's not my sister, not the way she wants to be.

I've been in the orbit of men who held different personalities inside their physical bodies twice now. It was a shared space with Alfred, with each version appearing when needed. With Sheriff Jonny Johnson, I believe he absorbed his father's cancerous soul when he killed him. Jonny thought he'd defeated the devil; he simply replaced him.

Is Olivia fighting to contain two versions of herself? I suppose we all are. The good, the bad. Each event, each day, allows us to decide which way we're going to go. The trouble seems to come when we let too many bad decisions sneak through. The bad begins to knit together, becoming one solid thing instead of loose bits of flotsam.

My thoughts are bouncing, popcorn in a microwave. Does Christopher know about Olivia? And what about Susie? She's only two, but young children pick up on things. Olivia has never been particularly affectionate toward her daughter. Blood rushes to my face. She's never been close to either of the children she gave birth to. Olivia wouldn't hurt Rosie, would she?

I press my foot harder to the gas pedal but have to be mindful that the Moab PD may have put out some sort of alert for me. Hopefully, Nick handled that, but I need to not be stupid.

Nick. Nick. Nick. A massive bit of goodness in the last day. Has it really only been a day? If I push everything out of my mind, I remember the feel of his hands on my body, his lips on my skin, his mouth against my ear promising all sorts of wonderfully dirty things. I hear him singing badly; I see him preaching about

Bechamel. I feel the warm length of his leg against mine as we watched *The Mist*, and how sad he was at the end, even though he knew it was coming. I remember his laugh when Winnie clambered onto the couch between us, pushing her butt into my face. The aftermath of our first frenzied coming together. A tangle of limbs. Out of breath, dazed but happy. If the first was vintage rock, the second was instrumental. More intense, less giddy. Answering all the unspoken questions that lived in my mind all these years. Finally. Why couldn't we have stayed there?

Peter.

Poor Peter. He's so strong and so kind. This will be a blow no man could easily withstand. I don't know how he'll bear it if he even believes. Will he? I don't know that I could or would if it were my child. Marnie will be there for him. Ben. Rosie. And Grace. And me... if he'll still have anything to do with me.

Why do I think that? I didn't do this. I am not responsible. But I will always be a reminder of his little girl, who was taken away and returned to him broken.

I've got six more hours to go. I can't fall apart. I need help. I call CB.

CHAPTER SIXTY-FIVE

NICK

It's 9 am, and I'm finally on the road to Salt Lake City, three hours later than I anticipated. Angel will get to LA before I do, and I don't trust her to do the smart thing. She's an intelligent woman, but her heart often overrules her brain, and I think her sense of self-preservation was so worn down by the events around the Dollhouse it's barely there at all.

Angel doesn't make stupid, thoughtless decisions. The problem is that her need to protect others is more intense than her instinct to protect herself. I know she blames herself for Bud's death. If she had been successful in their plan sooner, she believes he would still be alive. No amount of therapy has been able to change that belief.

If what she says now is true–that Olivia is involved in this, as a bad actor–Angel will need support. If it's true, Peter will be in no position to help anyone, and Marnie's focus will rightly be on him and Grace and Rosie.

Two people I care very much about are on a roller coaster towards hell, and I can't stop it. The best I can do is call in the emotional cavalry.

I instruct Siri to call "Crazy lady." That's my nickname for Concetta Bonaventura, aka CB, Angel's surrogate mother. It's 11 am in Chicago. TJ, CB's partner, answers CB's phone on the second ring. Before I can say a word, he says, "Conch is packing. Hold on." Aww, he calls her Conch. That's sweet. I like TJ. He's good people.

CB's voice blasts through the Jeep's speakers, and I quickly tap

236

the volume down. "I'm packing now, booked on the next direct flight to LA."

"Angel called you and told you what's happening. Good." My fingers are playing scales on the steering wheel. Is there anything worse than being stuck in a car when you're desperate to be somewhere else? Every minute feels like an hour. Torture. "She's going to need you."

"She also told me about you," CB says. I can't tell if she's happy, angry, or some other complex Concetta Bonaventura emotion. I decide to keep my mouth shut and see what happens.

Unfortunately, she knows my tricks, and she says nothing to me. I hear her ask TJ to grab her travel bathroom kit. The silence drags on. She is good, better than Angel.

"Fine. I hope she told you she instigated it. I tried to resist." I feel defensive, but I'm trying to keep that from my voice. The thirteen-year age gap is nothing now that we're adults, but I will never forget that Angel was barely into her teens when we met.

"You're an idiot." CB declares. She thanks TJ for bringing her something, then continues, "She's had feelings for you as long as I've known her. I'm not talking about 'you rescued me from a bad man' feelings grounded in some stupid hero fantasy. You're the kind of man she needs: confident, kind, easy-going but also solid. You're smart enough to keep up with her, strong enough to keep her from running you over. A relationship won't be simple, but you already know that. She'll push you. She'll test you. She'll get into a funk, feel insecure, and do everything to prove she's right about not deserving love. Right now, she is convinced the two of you are a sex thing, and that's fine by her. She won't let herself accept that it could be more than that. That's a tremendous risk because you're a keystone in her life. If she does something wrong—and that's what she thinks will happen, she will do something wrong—you'll leave, and a foundation she's come to expect over the last ten-plus years will disappear."

I'm nodding because I know all of this. "I -"

"I'm not finished," CB announces. "Let's talk about you. I realize that being involved with someone you previously helped rescue is complicated and potentially against the Bureau's precious code of conduct. I also realize that you're a good man despite how often I mock you. You wouldn't have let her succeed in her instigation, as you call it, without being aware of the potential consequences. I don't believe you would have let things go where they did if you weren't going to do whatever you needed to do to keep things right for her. You don't need to convince me."

"Now may I—"

"Almost. One last thing. Okay, two. First, you have my blessing."

My eyebrows arch up, and I almost say something snarky, but think better of it. Whether I want to admit it or not, having her blessing is important. Damn it. I'm stuck with the Crazy Lady.

"And two. You hurt Angel by being careless, thoughtless, or stupid, I will kill you. I don't mean figuratively. I'm old. I've lived a good life. I will take the jail time." I hear TJ protest, and then CB says to him, "Don't worry doll. He's afraid of me. It'll never happen."

I laugh at that, shocked and a little bit charmed. She's right. I'll never hurt Angel intentionally. Humans hurt each other, but I'll do my best to be mindful and aware and keep my asshole moves to a minimum. "Are you done yelling at me now?"

"I believe so, yes. I have a plane to catch. I'll see you in LA." And the phone goes dead.

Well, hell. I haven't really had time to think about Angel and me, what last night—death aside—means for us, what a relationship would look like, all that grown-up stuff. My sister Dru will be delighted.

But right now, I need to call Alex, FBI geologist. I need him to find Ben, convince him to get on a plane, bring him home, and give him whatever he needs once he gets here. Alex is about to be indoctrinated headfirst into the family. We'll see whether he meets expectations. I really hope he does.

CHAPTER SIXTY-SIX

OLIVIA

Dad won't know I wasted money on a private jet to get me home until it doesn't matter anymore. I've got plenty of quiet time to finalize my plans since Jimmy destroyed the original plan when he took Angel. I don't believe Angel knows I was at the camper, but I can't be sure, and I must proceed as if she does. I can't risk losing control again.

I'm grieving the original plan. It was beautiful. Ceremonial, even. Worthy of the three spirits it will honor.

Now everything has gone to hell. Damn Jimmy. No control. No finesse. No beauty. Things will be messy.

I'd hoped to go home first, see Christopher, and spend some time with him. He has been a joy and a blessing to me. I hate the hurt I'm about to cause him, but I'll be giving him permission to find the kind of love he deserves.

I can't risk taking the time to see him. If Angel has even an inkling of what's happening, she will head straight to the Nest to try to 'save' Grace.

If only she understood this! This is the best, the only, possible outcome for us. We could do this together, the three of us, with love. They don't understand yet, but eventually, when we arrive in Heaven and are finally released from the pain we've carried all these years, they'll get it. They'll be grateful.

I wonder if Angel knows Jimmy is dead. I'll admit that killing Jimmy was extremely satisfying. He wasn't the man he showed me in New Jersey. That was all an act. The real Jimmy was a murderous, cruel bastard who would have taken Angel and made the Dollhouse seem like a preview. I'm glad I was able to stop that.

It has only just occurred to me, and it's too late to do anything about it. Might the Moab police somehow tie Angel to Jimmy's death? Could she end up in police custody? That would make things difficult. I can't keep chasing people down. Once I have Grace, I need Angel so we can get this over with. I can't help Grace and then tried to persuade Angel. I'm too tired. So tired. Grace is the key.

CHAPTER SIXTY-SEVEN

ANGEL

"Um, this is weird, you never use the telephone portion of your–" Emily's laughing voice should be a relief, but I don't have time.

"That's because this is an emergency," I have just hit the 605 near the Santa Fe Dam recreation area. I have at least another hour to go, and I'm worried I will be too late. Rain is pelting us, and LA drivers aren't the best in the rain. "I need you to go to the Nest immediately. I don't care if you're recording with Beyonce; she'll have to wait. Find Grace and Rosie. Would they be in school? Is it a school day? I don't even know what damned day it is. Get them from school. Take them away. Don't talk to Peter or Marnie, and especially don't talk to Olivia. Just grab the girls and take them somewhere. The mall. See a movie. Something. Don't bring them back until you hear from me!"

Em is rightly shocked. "What the hell are you talking about? What's going on? Are you okay?"

"I'll tell you, but you need to go right now. Get in the car and call me and then I'll explain. And bring White." As if she wouldn't.

"All right, all right. Give me a second. I'm not dressed for a movie date with teenagers." She sounds exasperated. I don't blame her.

"Call me once you're in the car. Hurry!" I slam my fist on the steering wheel in frustration as I see brake lights in front of me. Fucking LA! I'd get off and take surface streets, but they're not better. It would take just 20 minutes to get the same distance in Utah.

My phone rings, and I stab the speaker button. I catch Emily up on events in Utah–not all events, I'll tell her about Nick later–and then pause to take a breath and give her a moment to digest.

"I can't believe this. I really can't. I want to think you've lost your mind, my friend," Emily says what I've been thinking. I wish I'd lost my mind, too.

"I hope to God I'm wrong. I really do. I'll happily take a six-month vacation to recover my senses in that case. Em, you have to get the girls before Olivia does. And I have to point out that you're a potential victim too. You fit the criteria. Jimmy didn't mention you, but..."

She's silent as she ponders this. Emily Bright is a badass in her own way. "Screw that. I can take Olivia in a fight. She's not getting the girls once they're in my care. I promise."

"Thank you. This is insane. My heart is breaking on so many levels." I wipe tears from my eyes and flip off a truck that cuts me off.

"I'm glad you're okay. Jesus, girl, you're a magnet for trouble. We need to work on that." Em is trying to joke, but there's facts buried in them there words, and we both know it.

"I know it. I'm going to work on it. Promise. I want a boring life after this. Maybe I'll take up some soothing hobbies. Rug weaving. That could be fun." I'm trying to relax my body. I'm stiff from driving ten hours straight, running four miles barefoot and naked, and being drugged by a crazy man. And maybe a couple other activities. Talking to Em is helping, but I'm still strung as tight as a guitar string.

"Should we call the police?" Em asks.

"I thought about that. I'm worried that if Olivia feels trapped, she'll do something unpredictable. Or that Peter will get hurt trying to intervene. I left the final decision to Nick."

Emily reports, "According to GPS, I'll be there in 30. How far out are you?" She's coming from Playa Del Rey, a suburb between

Santa Monica and the South Bay cities.

"I'm guessing I'll be there twenty minutes after you, barring traffic issues." I hit my horn when an idiot without brake lights slows unexpectedly and nearly has my Bronco up its ass.

"What do you think about warning Marnie? She'll understand why we don't want to tell Peter."

I think about that, long and hard.

So long, Emily asks, "Ang?"

"Sorry. What's your gut say?"

"I think we should."

"Do it. She's closest to the girls and has the best chance to get them out without drawing attention."

"Hold on. I'll see if I can loop her in, and we can talk to her together." Em puts me on hold, then comes back to me. "Went right to voicemail."

"Shit." I slap the steering wheel again.

"They had a meeting with an advocacy organization. I don't remember if that was today."

Shit, shit, shit. "Okay. Will you message me when you get there? Please?"

"Absolutely. Love you."

"Love you."

CHAPTER SIXTY-EIGHT

OLIVIA

Los Angeles International Airport is only 35 minutes from the Nest. I took a car service to the Burbank airport when I left town, and now I need to rent a car. The line is long. The delay is annoying. If Angel beats me to the Nest and alerts Dad, Plan B is over. I have a plan C, but I don't want to use it.

Finally, I get to my assigned car. Instead of an innocuous sedan, I intentionally chose something showy but not too flashy. I need it to fit into the Palos Verdes environment and not call attention, but I want to blend in. I choose a BMW SUV and head south toward the Hill, as it's known locally.

My nerves are shot. I decide to take Sepulveda rather than getting on the 405, although that would save me a couple of minutes. This will be my last drive along the coast. My last glimpse of the beach cities of Hermosa, Manhattan, Redondo. The last time I'll navigate the beautiful and windy Palos Verdes Drive West. The last of so many things. Even in a storm, it's beautiful. Perhaps more beautiful.

The dark sky and torrential rains match my mood. Instead of sorrow, I feel relief.

There's only one thing that makes my heart ache, and that's Christopher. I need to say goodbye. I connect my phone to the car's Bluetooth and dial.

He picks up on the second ring. I hear him tell others he needs to take this call, then it sounds as though he's moving. "Are you home?"

"Not yet. Almost." Of course, I mean something different by

'home.' I debate pulling over, but I don't want to risk giving Angel any time to get ahead of me. I must get there first to succeed. "Sweetheart, I love you more than I could ever express. I need you to know that."

"Olivia, don't say shit like that. It sounds like you're saying goodbye." Christopher sounds panicked.

"I have loved every minute of our time together. You're my best friend. Being your wife has made my life worth living. Thank you so much for being the man you are. For loving me despite everything. For being so patient." I'm crying, but he can't tell. I have had a lot of practice shedding silent tears. "This isn't going to be easy, and I apologize for that. I wish there were another way." And there would have been, if not for Jimmy. "You'll have some things to deal with. I wish I could prevent that, but I can't. Susie is young enough she won't remember. You can start over. LouLou is a great person, a great woman. Don't push her away if she wants to help. Sweetheart, I would have done anything for this to end differently."

"Baby, no, I don't know what's happening. Where are you? I'll come right now. Stop whatever you're thinking, go to a police station or hospital or just stop. Just stop! Don't do anything you can't undo. Wait for me. I'll come get you. We'll fix this. It's okay it is I promise please baby don't leave me Olivia -" the river of words and the anguish in Christopher's voice is too much. I can't bear it. I end the call, roll down the passenger window and fling the phone out.

I don't need it anymore.

CHAPTER SIXTY-NINE

OLIVIA

The guard doesn't question that I'm in a different car. Why would he? He just smiles and waves me through. Thank you, guard #2. A few minutes later, I realize I should have stopped to ask if he'd let Angel through. Damn it. Just another sign it's time. I've lost my edge.

I navigate the curving road to the Nest. It's really coming down now, and the sky is dark. There aren't streetlights because that would disrupt the million-dollar views. That forces me to slow down, but not too much. If I happen to slide off a cliff, that's the way it's supposed to go. God will send a sign.

I arrive at the Nest without issue. Marnie's and Dr. Lisa's cars are parked in front of the Foundation. No sign of Dad. Good. Facing Dad through this will be the hardest of all. I can't even let myself think about him, or I won't be able to do this. I move quietly into the house. No one here. Good. I only need a minute.

Grace's Mazda is parked near the stables. Perfect. I drive the SUV toward the main stable doors. A covered walkway connects the stable and gym to the main house. The walkway is eight feet wide, roofed in terracotta, and bordered by enough Bougainvillea vines to keep it mostly dry underneath. As I get close, the door opens, and Rosie bursts out, happily bouncing on the balls of her feet. The girl is always in motion. She reminds me of Bud. Sweet, protective Bud. Grace is right behind her, jabbering a mile a minute.

I flash my lights to get their attention, lower the passenger window, and wave. "Grace! Hey!" They both pause and look my way but make no move to come out from under the protection of the walkway. Rosie starts to wave, then abruptly drops her hand. What's with that?

Did Angel alert them? No. If that were the case, Dad would be here, and the girls would be hidden away somewhere. I still have time. I can still save them.

I try again. "Grace, I need your help!" I motion for her to come to the car. She shakes her head and points up, indicating she doesn't want to get wet. Her energy is off. Something has changed. I don't know what. I don't like it. "Come on, please, I need to talk to you for just a sec. It's important!"

They're only fifteen feet away. I guess I'll have to go to them. I slip out of the car and put a hand up to keep rain from my eyes. I hurry toward them, making a show of protecting myself from the rain. I smile as I get close and under the safety of the roof. "Hi! Sorry, that was rude, wasn't it? Hey, Rosie, could you go find Marnie real quick?"

"Why?" Rosie asks, suspicious.

"I need to talk to you all about something. I'd like to do it together," I explain.

Rosie gives me side-eye and starts to move reluctantly toward the house. Then she stops. "Why don't we all go inside? Get out of the rain?"

"I need to show Grace something in the SUV. It's a surprise for Dad."

Rosie still looks dubious, but she heads toward the door.

My anxiety pushes me, and I move too fast. "Come on, Grace, come see."

When she doesn't move, I wrap my hand around her wrist. She pulls back. I pull harder. Her eyes grow wide. I drop all pretense and drag her toward the car. Neither of us is very big, but I work out. I'm stronger than I look.

I am about to push her into the passenger seat when Rosie comes flying at us. Now I'm angry. I shove Grace into the SUV and turn to Rosie. "Stop right now, or I'll shoot her. I promise you I will." And to prove I'm not bluffing, I pull a small revolver from the pocket of my leather jacket.

Grace is crying. Rosie gasps in shock.

"Don't do anything stupid. I will use it," I warn and move around to the driver's seat. The engine is still running. I start to back out. The back passenger door flies open. Rosie dives inside before I can hit the child locks. "Fine! Have it your way."

CHAPTER SEVENTY

OLIVIA

"Rosie, you should have stayed at the house. You were never part of this. You're just like your aunt and your father, action first, thought later," I say, glaring at her in the rearview mirror.

She's leaning forward, pushing between the front seats, demanding acknowledgment. "I texted Dad! He's going to come to find us!"

It had to happen, but I wish it hadn't.

"What are you doing, Olivia? What's happening? Where are we going?" Grace whimpers. She's pressed herself into the far corner of the seat. She'd jump from the moving vehicle if the doors weren't locked.

"You were too little to remember the Dollhouse. Jennifer. Alfred. Bud. You weren't there long before we were found, thank goodness. But you were there long enough. You saw Jennifer–Alfred–murder Bud. She did that because of you." That's cruel and untrue, and right now, I don't care. I want to lash out. Anger and resentment are growing in me like a cancer. Being this close to what I want seems to have opened an emotional floodgate. I'm feeling things I have never allowed myself to feel before. The Olivia who is so proud of being in control all the time doesn't like it, but for the true Olivia, the deep down Olivia, the release of pressure feels damn good.

"Stop it. That's not true. You're horrible, and you're a liar!" Rosie yells. Then she says, "I know you're my mother."

That catches me by surprise.

"It's okay. I know you don't like me. I kind of understand why.

But don't be mean to Grace," Rosie pleads.

"It's not that I don't like you." This is not a conversation I was expecting to have, ever. I'm not sure what to say. For once, I decide to not overthink. "You're a permanent reminder of everything that happened. A living scar. I had the choice. I could have decided carrying a child wasn't something I could do. Or I could have given you away. But Angel and Dad were desperate for you. Dad needed something hopeful. Angel needed a piece of her brother. If I'd only known how far she'd take that. Everything she does is for him. Not for herself."

"Are you feeling bad because the other Komo people killed themselves?" Rosie asks. Always Rosie with the questions. Grace is still pressed into the seat, wordless.

"I don't feel bad, no. They weren't happy people. They were just pretending to be happy." We're at Hawthorne Boulevard. I turn left and head west toward the ocean.

"But to commit suicide..." Grace whispers. "How much pain must a person be in?"

"They didn't commit suicide. If you must know. Well, Kait did. But not Tiffany. Or Karmen. Or Hannah."

Grace gasps in horror. "Hannah! What's wrong with Hannah? What do you mean? "

I've made another mistake. I ignore the specific question and give a broader answer. "Someone cared enough to give them the help they needed since they weren't strong enough to do it themselves." Even as the words leave my mouth, I realize I should shut up. These two aren't stupid. They may figure it out before I want them to. I'm not worried about them telling someone else, they won't have that option, and it wouldn't matter anyway. I'm concerned that understanding will encourage them to resist. Rosie in particular.

"They were killed?" Grace whispers.

"No! They were helped. They needed help. Someone cared enough to help."

I see a baby blue Bronco headed up the hill. Does she see me? Angel does. I wave and point back toward the coastline.

Follow me.

CHAPTER SEVENTY-ONE

ANGEL

Emily called to let me know she's at the Nest. The girls aren't there. She and Marnie found an envelope addressed to Peter in Olivia's suite. Since Peter's not home, Marnie opened it. It's not good.

I'm headed up Hawthorne toward Crest Road when I see a BMW SUV going the opposite way. The storm is pummeling the road, forcing me to go slower than I want to. But if not for that, I would not have seen the hand come out of the driver's window, wave, and point back toward the coast.

Olivia. Someone petite and blonde is in the passenger seat. *Shit.*

Where is she going? Oh, I know. They're going to Abalone Cove and Sacred Beach. The girls love it there. The whole family does. Somehow that seems appropriate for this entire insane situation.

"Hold on, kids!" I say and make a sharp U-turn, praying a tech bro in a Tesla doesn't T-bone us. We make the change without incident. I yell at Siri, "Call Nick!"

"Calling Rick." Siri announces, and I scream, "Cancel!" Who the eff is Rick? Do I even know a Rick?

"Siri, call Nick. NICK!" I yell again.

"Calling Nick's Gas Station–" Siri says. Where the hell is Nick's Gas Station?

"Screw you, Siri." I breathe.

"I won't respond to that." The AI voice informs me.

"Call Nick Winston. Please." I try once more, using as sweet a voice as I can muster.

This time she gets it right, but I go right into voicemail. "Nick! I saw Olivia headed west–or is it south?–on Hawthorne. Toward the coast, whatever that is. I'm pretty sure we're going to Abalone Cove. Ask Marnie or Peter where that is. Or the police. Send the police. She's got Grace in the passenger seat. Hurry, please hurry."

Shit shit shit shit.

My phone rings. I stab at the accept button. It's Emily and Marnie, not Nick. I tell them, "We're headed to Abalone Cove. I left Nick a message, but he won't know where that is. We need cops. All of the cops."

I hear Marnie speaking to someone. Emily says, "Marnie is talking to them now."

"Good. Is Peter with you?" I feel like I should whisper, but what's the point?

"He's not. Marnie has left him a couple of messages. She called Dr. Lisa, too, but she's not going to be able to get here quickly at this time of day. Holy hell, Ang. This is terrible." Emily whispers the last bit. Not just me feeling that way. "I'm scared."

"Me too," I admit. "I think she has Grace."

"And Rosie," Marnie says, apparently done with the cops. "They're both gone. I just watched the security cameras. Olivia dragged Grace to her car, and Rosie jumped into the back seat." Her phone rings, and she says, "Peter."

Em and I are quiet as we wonder how Marnie will tell her partner that his daughter has lost her mind. She doesn't say it like that. "Sweetheart, where are you? Oh, good. You're not far. I need you to listen to me, and I really need you to stay calm. Meet me at Abalone Cove. Go right now. No stops, no detours. Olivia is having a mental break. Angel, Em, and I are headed there right now. Nick is on his way." There's a pause as she listens to his responses. She's still maintaining her cool. Marnie is amazing. "I know, sweetie, I understand. Like I said, Nick is on his way. I've called the police. We are all here for her. But we need to get there fast. It's raining hard up here, so be careful. But hurry. Okay? I'm going to hang up now. I'll see you in a few. I love you."

I want to throw up.

CHAPTER SEVENTY-TWO

ANGEL

The parking lot has one of those gates where you have to wait and take a ticket. The arm is so slow I consider jumping out of the Bronco and making a run for it. Finally, it raises enough I can slip through.

I pull the Bronco into the spot next to the BMW. I fish out a baseball cap to keep the rain out of my eyes and lock the dogs in. I put the keys on the driver's side running board. If something happens to me someone will take the dogs, keep them safe.

At first, I don't see Olivia through the downpour, but then the rain slows for a minute, and I do. Olivia has her arm around Grace's waist and is half-dragging her toward the cliffs. The cliffs that are blocked off by "do not cross" barriers. Rosie is behind them. Why is Rosie following like a puppy? Why isn't Grace resisting? And then I see it... a flash of metal. I think Olivia has a gun. If Olivia points a weapon at Grace, Rosie will not leave her best friend's side. She'll follow and try to find a way to save her.

Olivia would never shoot them. That's murder. No pretending there's mercy in that, and Jimmy made it clear their stupid demented plan was all about 'mercy killing.' I don't believe Olivia could murder Grace or Rosie. I think she's bluffing. I have to believe it because I'm going to bet everything on it. And then I remember she killed Jimmy. But that's different. That has to be different.

It's raining so hard that it's tough to see anything clearly, but they've crossed the barrier and are now walking on the old path. I move quickly. No point in delaying. I need to catch up and try to talk Olivia down. Literally and figuratively.

Bud, Bud, what the hell do I do? I bend and dip under the barrier.

This is one hell of a pickle, Sis.

Yeah. I guess I may see you sooner than I expected.

Fuck that. Nobody is dying. You'll figure it out. You always do.

Not always. You're dead, jerk. I'm getting closer. I'm not going to run. That seems pointless. And it might trigger Olivia to do something stupid sooner rather than later.

For the ten-thousandth time, you couldn't have stopped that. You're the horror movie fan. Remember Final Destination?

Of course, I do. I've watched it. But you haven't. We were like six when it came out.

If you've watched it, I've watched it. Duh.

Okay, so what's your point, exactly? I step over an area of crumbling rock. Probably the reason this section is blocked off.

My point is nothing you did or didn't do could have changed that outcome. Alfred was determined to kill me. Nothing to do with you.

You're not helping. Olivia is determined to kill me, Grace, herself, and maybe Rosie.

Bud's voice goes silent in my head. I guess I backed my weird brain into a corner there.

"Angel!" Rosie screams as I get closer. Olivia is standing at the top of the cliff, back to the ocean. She has a firm grip on Grace, but Rosie is free. I don't think Olivia included Rosie in the plan. That's just for Olivia, Grace, and me—the survivors of the Dollhouse.

Down in the lot behind me, a horn is honking, over and over and over. For a minute I think it's one of my dogs. Then I realize it's Emily's Prius, letting me know she's here. Marnie is out of the car before it's entirely stopped. Peter's Jeep is seconds behind; he must have broken every speed law to get here. Where is Nick? If I'm going to die, I want to see him one more time before I go.

The rain has slowed, but the sky is a menacing backdrop.

I know there's a steep drop off to the ocean below from being here dozens of times. If we fall, we will surely die, our bodies broken on the rocks below, the churning sea finishing the job.

CHAPTER SEVENTY-THREE

PETER

Marnie's face is grief-stricken as she joins me on the trail. She's trying to hold it together, and I love her all the more for it. We're moving quickly but not running. I'm wearing slick-bottomed loafers, and she's wearing sandals. We won't be good to anyone if we fall and hurt ourselves.

"She left a note in her room at the Nest," Marnie says, her voice soft. She grabs my hand. I don't resist. "She's ill. She hasn't been feeling herself for a long time."

"I will kill him." I grind out. "After we get her safe, I will kill him."

"Who?" Marnie asks. "What do you mean?"

"The person who started this. Who faked these suicides for his own evil purposes! Who put this idea into her head!"

Marnie tugs on my hand and forces me to stop. I pull my hand from hers and continue on the path. Her voice is loud and determined when she yells over the rain, "Peter! You don't understand. Olivia was involved in the killings. She's not copying anyone. She started this. You can read her letter later. But right now, you absolutely must understand that Olivia is determined to end her own life and Grace's and Angel's. And Rosie is at risk, too."

I jerk to a stop. I couldn't have heard her correctly. The look on her face tells me I did. No matter how much I wish it were true, I didn't misunderstand. I suck in a deep breath and continue toward the edge of the cliff. Marnie is beside me again. I don't grab her hand. She doesn't reach for mine.

Olivia sees me. Her eyes widen, and she screams in anger. Her grip tightens on Grace. Rosie sobs and yells. Angel is ten feet from her.

Time stands still.

CHAPTER SEVENTY-FOUR

OLIVIA

Well, the gang's all here. I didn't intend to make it a big party, but here we are. Rosie. Angel. Marnie and Dad. I have a feeling there's more company on the way.

"Dad, I love you. I'm sorry I'm not the person you thought I was." Now that the internal censor is gone, apparently, I have no filters at all. "I understand and appreciate everything you've done for me, and for Angel, and for Grace. But you can't really fix it. You can't take away the scars. Do you know how hard I've fought every day to seem normal? Healthy? Okay? I'm living behind a mask, inside a costume. Showing the world what it wants to see. There are two paths for people like us: go insane or fall apart. Pretend to keep your back straight, put it all behind you. But you can't really do that. Angel knows I'm right, don't you, Angel?"

Angel looks at me but doesn't say anything. Sirens are approaching, and Angel's ears twitch like a dog's.

"You know why I crave the spotlight? Because that means I'm never alone! When I'm alone, the darkness tries to take over. It's exhausting fighting it back. Exhausting. Sometimes I think I want to hurt people, the ones who think I should *get over it*, or it wasn't *that bad*. I want them to feel just a tiny bit of what I'd feel if I didn't lock everything up. Locking everything up is rotting my insides." I tighten my grip on Grace's shirt and pull her back a step toward me. She is a mess. This is the right choice for her. She'll never survive the real world.

Rosie is no longer crying. She's locked on me as if she's trying to solve a puzzle. "Olivia, please don't hurt yourself. Please don't hurt Grace. Please don't leave me like Bud did. Don't let that terrible man take both of my parents from me."

I want to scream, *Shut up, shut up, I'm not yours, you're not from me, don't say those words, stop, stop.* I can't think. The air is pressing in, squeezing me. I hear the voices around me, and I hear the waves as if they're coming from two different speakers in the same space.

Dad is thinking about coming closer. I see it in his eyes.

"Daddy, you need to let me go. You have to let me do what's right for us." I turn to Angel and hold her gaze. Her blue eyes, so like mine, are full of sorrow.

"Please don't do this, O. Please don't. I love you so much. I know I've been shitty to you. I'm sorry. It was never about you. I'm just scared of relying on anyone, and you want so much to be relied on. I don't want to be a baby anymore. I needed to stand on my own."

Angel is trying to convince me, and I believe her. Her eyes are filled with tears. But it doesn't matter.

The rain has slowed to a drizzle.

A dozen uniformed police are rushing up the hill toward us, guns drawn. They don't know who to yell at. Nick Winston, ever the hero, bursts ahead and runs toward Peter and Marnie.

"Angel, get back," he shouts. She turns her head toward him but doesn't move. The look he gives her breaks me. Christopher used to look at me like that. My Christopher. What would our lives have been like if I'd met him as a different version of me? We'll never know.

I'm only a few feet from the edge. I glance over my shoulder and see waves crashing onto the rocks below. This isn't a sun tanning beach. This is a tidepool beach with all sorts of wonderful creatures. If we step off the cliff, we won't see death coming. It's not as good as my original plan, but it's not bad.

It's time. I look at Angel. "If you love me, you'll help me like we helped Tiffany and Karmen and Hannah." I hold out my free hand to her. "Please, come. Please. Let's go find Bud. The real Bud, not Bud Star."

Grace sobs and struggles to pull away from me, but I pull her tight against my chest and wrap my arm around her waist. I shuffle back a step. The sound of falling rock is unmistakable.

Rosie screams, "No!" and leaps forward. If she reaches us, we'll all three go over.

God damn it.

God fucking damn it.

"Angel, you're the strongest person I know." I shove Grace toward Rosie to counter her momentum, and I step backward. "I love you."

The last thing I hear is my father and Angel screaming my name.

CHAPTER SEVENTY-FIVE

ANGEL

There won't be any bullshit accusations about Olivia's death because there were too many witnesses. The police, the helicopter pilot who somehow captured video of Peter scrambling down the trail to get to Olivia, the medical examiner, and all of us, the family.

Grace and Rosie have not let me go in the last hour. I'm not about to tell them to go away. I need their touch as much as they seem to need mine.

I can't stop stealing glances at Peter. He's sitting on the bumper of an ambulance while paramedics clean up some scrapes and cuts he got on the way down the hill. There's a reason that part of the trail is closed. His face is covered in dirt. His brown trousers and black V-neck sweater are wet and covered with sand. Marnie is with him but not too close to him. I think she's giving him some space.

My heart literally aches. I didn't know that was possible. What are we going to say to each other? My brain can't even begin to understand what he's feeling.

"Dad!" I hear a shout, and there's Ben, running toward Peter, not bothering to hide his tears. He throws himself into his father's arms, and Peter holds on so tight I'm worried one of them might break. I thought I was cried out, but apparently not. Fresh tears pour down my face.

A tall man, dark-haired and handsome, is standing off to the side. That must be Alex.

"Come on," I whisper to the girls, and we greet the newcomer.

"Terrible conditions to meet someone, but I'm Angel. This is Grace," I tip my head toward her, and she forces a half-smile, "and this is Rosie." Rosie squeaks out a "Hello" and then goes back to crying. "You must be Alex. Thank you for bringing him."

Alex nods. "I'm so very sorry. We–" he looks like he doesn't want to say what he's going to say and mouths the words, hoping the girls won't notice, "heard about it on the news headed here from the airport."

Jesus, the buzzards are fast. Damn helicopters. Damn tabloid snitches.

"Come with us. You don't want to stay here. Someone from the press will try to grab you." I lead us back to the family cluster. Nick is talking with the police, but he keeps looking my way to be sure I'm okay, or maybe just to confirm I haven't run off. I don't know.

There's so much to process. *Olivia killed herself. Olivia was a murderer.* Marnie told me she left a letter for Peter at the Nest. I hope to read it, but I'll understand if Peter declines. God. I just–I don't know how we'll recover from this. Is there enough therapy in the world?

I'm worried about Rosie. She knows Olivia was her mother. How does she feel about that? Confused, I'm sure. On a good day, she's a walking collection of emotion, my Rosie. This will inform the woman she grows into, hopefully in a positive way. I'm not worried so much about Grace. Grace has her mother's calm. She's in great pain, but she'll find her footing and move on, stronger.

Again, I come back to Peter. He has given everything to protect his children. To go through so much to save her and discover she was beyond saving. That's not fair. No. She wasn't beyond saving. She was in pain. She was hurting. She tried to fix herself. She thought she was doing a good thing, the right thing. Her intentions were not malicious. Her head was messed up, that's clear.

For a brief moment, I wonder if I have some sort of secret

hiding from me that will eventually burst out and eat me alive. Please, God, I hope not.

Marnie comes to us, and the girls release me and move into her arms. She smiles a thanks at me, and I nod, then take advantage of the aloneness. I want to go to the Nest. I want to go home.

CHAPTER SEVENTY-SIX

ANGEL

Charlie and Hannah are coming to Stargazer in a few weeks, as soon as Hannah is recovered enough to travel. Before all the craziness, I was a titch nervous, if I'm honest. Now I can't wait. I want all the people I care about around me. I'm tired of this lone Rangerette stuff, as Nick calls it. *Nick. Nick. Nick.* After lying to the Moab PD, he feels it's probably time to hang up the official FBI gear and join Komo full time. I'm all for that. Especially since he can live anywhere he wants. I'm hoping, at least for a little while, 'anywhere' might be with me.

I didn't have to ask Marnie to bring the letter. She came to the pool house as soon as she got back to the Nest.

"Emily, Ben, and Alex—I really really like him—are entertaining the girls with pizza. Nick is still with the police, but he wants you to know he'll be back soon. He told me about you two," she smiles, and it's a genuine smile, even though she must be exhausted and in pain. "About damn time is all I have to say. Don't you go messing this up with him!"

"Damn straight!" CB adds, appearing suddenly behind Marnie. Even with her five-inch heels, she has to stand on her toes to kiss Marnie's cheek. Marnie wraps an arm around CB's shoulder and pulls her in for a hug. My two moms. I am a very fortunate woman.

"Where's Peter?" I didn't intend to whisper, but that's how it comes out.

"He's in Olivia's suite."

Olivia's suite. I think of hours we spent there, wrapping Christmas gifts or watching TV together. I know I wasn't the sister Olivia dreamed of, but we made good memories. "What about Christopher and Susie? Have you talked to them?"

Marnie nods. "Apparently, Olivia called him on the way to the Nest. He's a mess."

"I feel so helpless." I sigh. CB sits on the bed next to me and squeezes my hand.

"We're all in pain, and we're all going to feel lost and confused for a while. But we have each other, and we're a good group," Marnie says. She's getting teary. She's probably tired of being the strong one. "Anyway. Here's the letter Olivia left for Peter. He said it was okay to show you. I think she'd have been okay with that too."

She bends and kisses my hair, smiles at CB, and says, "I'm going to go grab a piece or two of pizza before they eat it all. Come on over when you're ready."

CB bumps me with her shoulder. "This is the first time I've seen you without a pack of dogs."

"They're in the house with White and Tank." I sniff. Tank shakes like a leaf around people but put him in a pack with dogs five times his size, and he's the boss.

"I'd ask how you doin', but I know," CB says. "I'm not going to lecture you. Don't you dare say, 'for once.'"

We both laugh.

"You read the letter. Take your time. Feel bad. Then let that shit go. We each have our own journeys. Olivia had hers. She was eaten up by sickness, and in the end, the sickness won. It's not her fault, and she's not a bad person. But the sickness isn't contagious. You aren't going to catch it, and you didn't give it to her." CB stands up. "I'm going into the house too. I'm there if you need me, and so are all those other people who love you so very much. Nick is worried sick." She pauses and gives me 'the look.' "You break that boy's heart,

I will kick your ass. He's waited a long time for this, and he's had to wrestle with his own shit to let him get here. You need each other. Don't fuck it up."

I can't help it. I snort-laugh. "Go away."

I take a deep breath and read the letter.

CHAPTER SEVENTY-SEVEN

OLIVIA

Peter John Baden, the greatest man the world has ever known:
Your kindness, your courage, and your smarts are uniquely yours. I
love you so much, and equally important, I respect you. I am the luckiest
girl alive to have been born to you. No matter the challenge, you were
always there for me: loving me, protecting me, cheering me on. You have
given me everything.

First, to clarify a few things. Kait's death was a suicide. I helped
because she asked me to, but she had everything ready. When I met
with Jimmy, we made a plan to help those too weak to help themselves.
I thought Jimmy was like-minded. Now I realize he was a psychopath,
and I gave him the perfect vehicle to satisfy his needs. I had no idea he
was stalking Angel in Utah until the day I killed him. He was going to
take her to Mexico, and I have no doubt life would have been terrible
for her there. I couldn't let that happen. I did what I had to do.

Please, I beg, don't let my actions take any of the "you" from you.
More than anything, I want you to be happy. I want you to be loved. I
want you to share yourself with Marnie, Ben, Rosie, and all the little
birds you collect.

I hate that my illness has won. I hate that I couldn't find the thing
that would solve it, solve ME, make me feel good, and at least partially
whole. I hate that I cannot love my girls because they deserve to be loved
by their parents as I was loved by you. And my dear Christopher deserves
a wife who is a true partner, not a burden.

If success were enough to keep me right, I'd be stronger than the demons. But I can't live like this. I can't live with this. I've made choices and done things that can't be undone. I couldn't bear to live in prison or a psych ward, and I couldn't possibly go free. This is the only choice. I'm okay with it. I truly am.

If I can help Angel and Grace as I intend, please know that it comes from love. I want to save them from what I've felt these last few years. I couldn't bear knowing they were being tortured from the inside the way I have been. My Plan A, if you will, was beautiful. Ceremonial. Calm. Unfortunately, events took that opportunity away, so things might not be going quite as gently as I had hoped. I'm sorry for that. Above all, I don't wish to cause them pain.

I am finally going to be at peace. I cannot wait. Anticipation of sweet nothing has kept me going for the last weeks and months.

I'm not going to dwell. There's nothing to be gained by going on and on. Just know that I love you so very much.

Yours always, Olivia

CHAPTER SEVENTY-EIGHT

PETER

Outside the door, life is happening. People are talking, telling stories, probably crying a bit. In here, the silence amplifies my other senses. I can smell the Chanel perfume she wore for as long as I can remember. Her conditioner. Some of her clothes are hanging in the dressing room. Sundresses and slacks and a couple of professional outfits, just in case. Her shoes are in a heap, one big pile. You'd think a woman who loved fashion as much as she did would take better care of her things, but keeping her shoes organized was one of her flaws.

I can't come to grips with the idea she's gone. I'll never hear her laugh again. Make faces at her across a room. Play tennis. Talk about a business strategy. See her name in Komo.

My body aches. Not from the cuts and scrapes and bruises I earned sliding down the hill. This ache is soul deep. It reminds me of how I felt when she was taken all those years ago. The longing, the emptiness I couldn't satisfy. It's so familiar it's comfortable in a twisted way. I'd hoped to never feel it again.

What could I have done to prevent this? I thought Komo was the solution. Did it fail her? Did we fail her? Did I? It would be great to have someone to blame. But I honestly don't think I can. As she said, she had an illness, and it couldn't be cured. It took her life. Not without innocent casualties. Those I am struggling with. My daughter was responsible for other lives being lost. That is going to be harder to live with.

Thank God Hannah survived. According to her aunt, she somehow managed to vomit up a good portion of the pills and her family found her in time to get her help.

The door opens, making me jump. It closes quietly. I don't think Angel sees me sitting here in the dark. She runs a hand across the dresser top, picks up a frame, touches the photo. I hear her sniff. Big, bad Angel. Always fighting so hard to be tough.

"Hey." I try not to scare her, but she startles anyway.

She finally sees me sitting on the bed, and her voice catches as she says, "I'm sorry. I'll go."

"No. Please don't," I hear the catch in my voice. I hold my hand out for her. She takes hesitant steps toward me. I gently pull her down next to me and wrap my arm around her, pulling her close. "You didn't do this. You're in no way responsible."

"I should have recognized how much pain she was in," Angel starts to say.

"No." I shake my head and squeeze her, kiss her forehead. "No. She loved you. She knew you loved her. Neither of us could have prevented this. I promise you. Did you read the letter?"

Angel nods against my shoulder.

"She knew herself. She understood the consequences of what she'd done. She was right. The only possible outcomes were prison or a lifetime in a mental facility. Neither of those was acceptable."

Angel nods again.

We sit, bonded in our grief.

CHAPTER SEVENTY-NINE

ANGEL

There are actual stars in the Los Angeles sky tonight. How is that possible? I'm not going to question. I'm grateful. I need to talk.

Hey.

Hey. I hear Bud Star's voice, clear and bright.

This fucking sucks. I clasp the rail of the fence and squeeze.

Yeah, it really does. He agrees.

You'll take care of her, right? My lower jaw is quivering.

Already am. He's smiling.

Don't miss any of the titles in the Duality Series, in order:

Two Lies & a Truth (free short story prequel to The Dollhouse)
The Dollhouse
The Hunted: Sins of the Father
Veronique (free short story epilogue to The Hunted)
The Mercy: Angel of Death

You can get *Two Lies & a Truth* and *Veronique* by emailing charlie@saraennis.com and asking for the links to the free stories.

Visit saraennis.com and be the first to know when the next book is coming out. You can also sign up for Charlie's newsletter, and enter to win a free books and goodies.

One of the best compliments an author is if you like a book, tell people about it. If you enjoyed *The Mercy: Angel of Death*, please leave a review wherever you bought the book—and thank you!

I'm on Goodreads, Facebook, and Instagram and would love to connect.

ACKNOWLEDGEMENTS

Writing this book was bittersweet. I knew from the end of the first draft of *The Dollhouse* how things would end. I knew Olivia wasn't going to be okay. I also knew Angel and Nick would end up together.

Because I always try to be as accurate as possible, I worked with a great source—the real Dr. Lisa!—to be sure I wasn't taking too much fictional license. Dr. Lisa will likely appear in future books because she's a really smart chick and we have a really good time brainstorming together. It's fun letting someone who is known for being 'the nice one' show their dark side.

Most people know about service dogs, but many people are unaware there are psychiatric service dogs. Some people think that's just a fancy name for an emotional support animal, but there is a significant difference: A service dog must be trained to recognize and respond to certain medical (mental or physical) situations. Emotional support animals provide great comfort to humans, but are not trained in specific behaviors.

This book really went to the dogs! The information about animal rescues on reservations is real. You can show your support with dollars, by volunteering, or by adopting! Just search the internet for "reservation rescue dogs" and you'll find a number of options. One of my favorites is Underdog Rescue Moab.

Special thanks to my bestie Tracy, who has to suffer through multiple "what if" and "read this" and "can I...?" conversations with each book I write. She's a painter, not a writer, but she gets my brain.

And of course, I must thank the beta gang—Adrienne, Diane, Kim, Kristin, Mary, Mercedes, Michelle and Mike, the brother I never had but always wanted. Or something like that.

ABOUT THE AUTHOR

Sara Ennis has been telling stories since before she could hold a pencil. First she used flash cards, then a typewriter her grandfather gave her for her sixth birthday. When she was seven, she'd write book reports about books that only existed in her mind. In third grade, her class produced a play she'd written. People who know her well think some of the details from her real life would make a fascinating story, but Sara says the stuff she writes is much more believable and a lot less traumatic. She is a fan of good tequila, travel, cooking, and animals, not in that order. Sara was born in Santa Monica, California, but moved on purpose and with intent to Des Moines, Iowa. She lives with her canine personal assistant Charlie, who edits her newsletter, and Charlie's seeing-eye cat Eartha Kitta who spent one of her nine lives on the Kitten Killer disease and lived to tell the tale. (If your cat has FIP, look for FIP Warriors 5.0 on Facebook. There's hope.)